THE SKIN
THAT FITS

David Massengill

MONTAG

First Montag Press E-Book and Paperback Original Edition June 2018

Montag Press
ISBN: 978-1-940233-56-7
Editor - Kate Sargeant
Original cover photos © Johannes Plenio; Kat Jayne; Jason Briscoe
Jacket and book design © 2018 Niall Gray
Managing Director – Charlie Franco

A Montag Press Book
www.montagpress.com
Montag Press
1066 47th Ave. Unit #9
Oakland CA 94601 USA

Montag Press, the burning book with the hatchet cover, the skewed word mark and the portrayal of the long-suffering fireman mascot are trademarks of Montag Press.

Printed & Digitally Originated in the United States of America
10 9 8 7 6 5 4 3 2 1

Praise for *The Skin That Fits*

The Skin That Fits is an absolute page-turner! This pulse-pounding horror story that takes place in the southern United States, from Savannah to New Orleans, is filled with memorable characters, searing scenes, and a pace that rarely gives you time to catch your breath. In this story, you are transported into the supernatural swamps where so much of the terror takes place. You can hear the insects, smell the water, and see the Spanish moss. Just don't be surprised if you feel a presence and look behind you as you read, only to see nothing there.

— Jonathan Rose, author of *Carrion*

The Skin That Fits will give you chills. Massengill's Southern gothic horror plunges you into an eerie underworld of supernatural terror. Told in taut, aggressive prose and gory detail, it's a literary knife to the guts that will leave you breathless.

— Michael G. Keller, author of *Toy Soldiers*

Praise for David Massengill's debut novel, *Red Swarm*

Riveting, intense, and unpredictable, *Red Swarm* takes the reader on a deliciously creepy, wild ride. With his masterfully macabre prose, Massengill does for bugs what Hitchcock did for our feathered friends in *The Birds*. You'll never be able to look at an insect the same way again. This is a must-read for horror fans!

— Kevin O'Brien, author of *They Won't Be Hurt*

Never have I read a novel that creeps me out so bad that I want to get it as far away from me as possible, like by tossing it onto a freighter headed overseas or something, and yet at the same time I find so compelling and insidious and engrossing and inevitable that I am forced to continue reading against my will, all the while feeling the phantom tingle of redbugs burrowing in my neck...

— Garth Stein, author of *A Sudden Light*

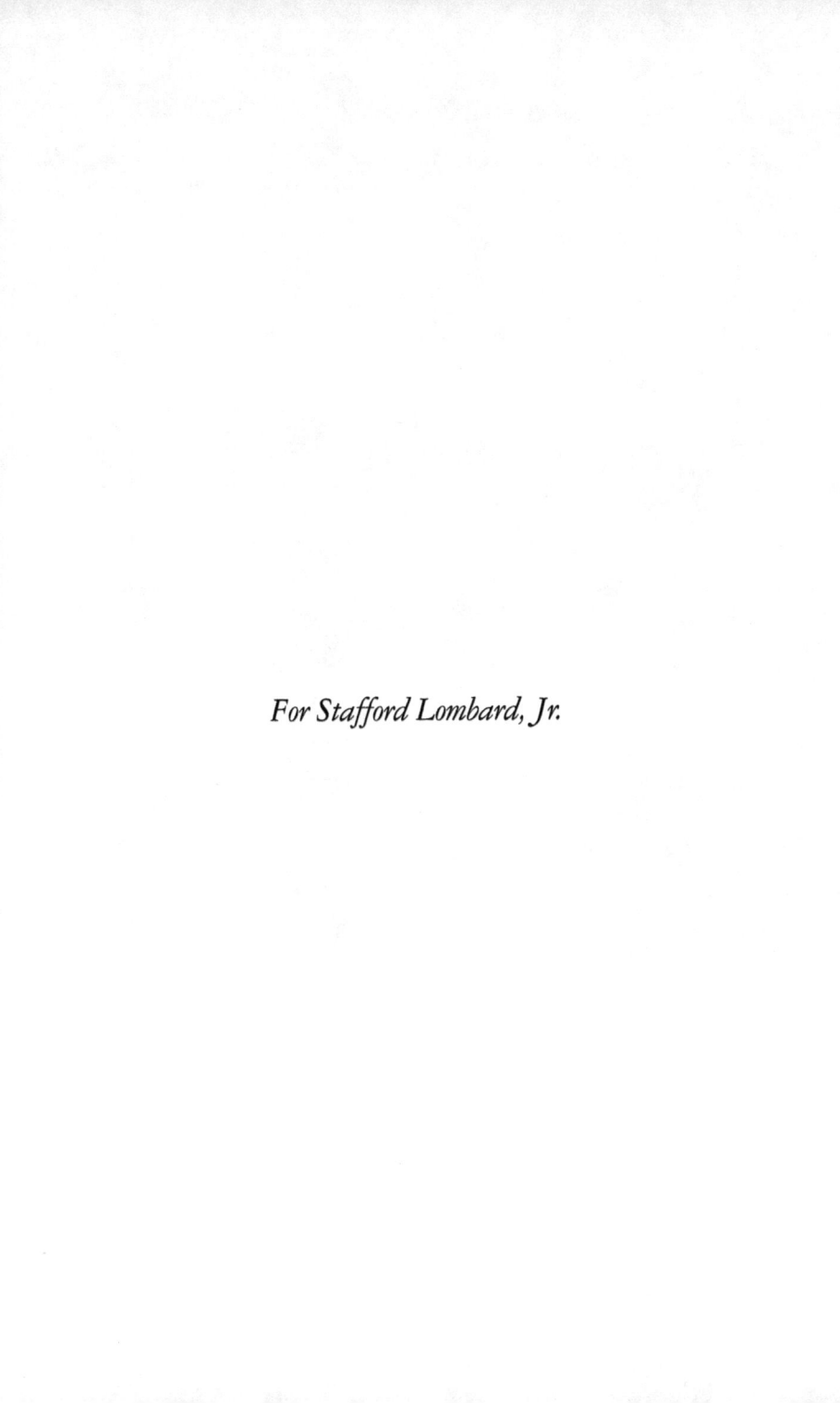

For Stafford Lombard, Jr.

Thirteen Years Ago

Mack looked out the kitchen window and thought he spotted an old woman standing by the banana tree in the backyard. He only saw the small, bent figure's silhouette, but she seemed to be staring at him. He also had the idea her face was somehow deformed.

"Honey, did you hear what I asked?" Rosalie said.

"I'll have a deviled crab sandwich and the waffle fries." Mack turned to his wife and saw tears in her eyes.

Rosalie immediately glanced down at the notepad on the kitchen counter and scribbled something. "So you and Hoyt are getting the same thing." She was clearly trying not to sound upset.

"What is it?" Mack asked. He looked out the window again before approaching Rosalie, but he no longer saw anyone. The sky was pink from the mid-October sunset, and all the trees bordering the beach were black and still. He figured the old woman must have been strolling along the sand and ventured up to the edge of their yard to admire the charming, yellow historic house.

He hugged his wife of 18 years and breathed in the sweet scent of her coconut lotion. At 44, Rosalie was still a beauty. She'd tied her dyed blond hair into a messy bun on top of her head, and she wore a sleeveless aquamarine blouse that clung to her breasts and revealed her bronzed arms. Mack momentarily wished he and Rosalie could be alone in their Tybee Island home this weekend, but they'd come here to be with the boys.

"It's Sander, isn't it?" Mack asked. He pulled away from Rosalie and peered into her eyes.

She nodded. "I don't understand why he has to be so damn...venomous." She seemed ashamed of using that adjective when speaking about their son. "I know he's 17, but that's no excuse for him snapping at me like that when I ask what he wants for dinner."

"No," Mack said. "No excuse. Sander!"

"Don't," Rosalie pleaded. "We're here to bring the family together, not keep fighting."

"Sander!" Mack shouted anyway. He folded his arms over his polo shirt as he waited for his eldest son to enter the kitchen. Mack's hands formed fists, and he wondered if he'd made a mistake by never so much as swatting Sander as he'd grown up.

Sander shuffled in from the living room. As always, he wore his charcoal-gray hooded sweatshirt and the jeans with all the holes in them. He had his father's thick black hair, but his locks were long and greasy and nearly covered his blue eyes. He was surprisingly pale for someone who lived in Savannah and had been on the beach all day. Then again, Sander had spent most of today moping around beneath the pier.

"Get in here," Mack said, his arms still crossed.

Hoyt appeared in the doorway behind his older brother. Even though he was 15, he was taller and stockier than Sander. His hair was military short and an even blend of blond and brown. His easy smile and dimples made him a favorite of the girls in his grade. A position as fullback on the football team also helped. He held a football in one hand now, ready to play catch with Mack while Rosalie picked up dinner at The Crab Leg.

"Head on outside, Hoyt," Mack said. "I need to talk with Sander. I'll be there soon."

"Busted," Hoyt whispered as he passed his brother.

"Tool," Sander muttered, glaring.

"That's enough!" Mack gripped Sander by the shoulder. He waited until he heard Hoyt's footsteps on the veranda, and then he said, "I think it's time you apologize to your mom."

Sander glared at Rosalie, and his cold gaze gave Mack a chill. Mack remembered watching a TV news story about one of those loner kids who'd shown up at school with a semi-automatic and thinking, *This could be Sander one day.*

"I'm sorry." Sander spoke as if he were reading the words off a piece of paper.

"It's okay," Rosalie said, sounding unsure. She remained some feet away from her son. "We just want to understand what's going on with you. You're always so...irritated by us."

"And the poor grades," Mack said. "I mean you used to be an A student in junior high."

"You had friends back then," Rosalie said. "Justin, and Danny, and-"

"Stop," Sander said. He looked in the general direction of his parents, but he didn't look at them. His lips curved into a creepy smirk. "You don't understand me," he said. "And I don't understand you."

Mack was well aware of what Sander didn't understand. His son made many a comment about his parents' needing to have so many material things. "You're in this ridiculous race with all your phony, wealthy friends," Sander had remarked after they bought their sailboat. The comment resulted in his being grounded for a weekend. Not that he ever left the house anyway. He was usually in his bedroom reading weird books about alien sightings, Aztec civilization, and black magic.

"One day when you're an adult and we're old folks, you're going to realize we did a hell of a job raising you," Mack said, "and you're going to understand you were privileged to have all that you had growing up."

Rosalie nodded, but she still seemed uncertain. She told Sander, "Maybe you'll find yourself becoming just like those dear old parents you used to think you despised."

Sander finally looked Mack in the eyes and said, "It's not going to be like that at all because we'll never have anything in common. When I was born, my spirit came into the wrong body and the wrong family. I realize that now. And I also know my spirit is on a journey away from you and this empty life. I've received messages."

Mack was too stunned by his son's words to respond. He looked at Rosalie, who stared back at him with tearing eyes. Her expression communicated, *What now?*

Mack searched for words, and then he remembered his and Rosalie's repeated discussions about medications possibly improving Sander's moods. "Son, there's a doctor in Ardsley Park the Burrems told us about," he said. "He helped their youngest girl when she was going through her hard time."

Sander's smirk returned, and he stared straight ahead of him at the wall above the stove.

"Maybe you could have a session with him," Mack continued. "It's normal these days for a teenager to see a therapist."

Sander still didn't look at his father. Mack glanced at where his son was staring. That was the patch of wall where Rosalie hung her protection doll, and Mack noticed there was something wrong with the object.

Rosalie had received the doll as a gift from the round, kind-faced Haitian woman who sold them chicory coffee at the farmers market every Saturday. The doll somewhat resembled a ginger-bread man, except it had white feathers for hair and a bright red dress. Neither Rosalie nor Mack had any interest or belief in voo-doo, but they both thought it sweet that the woman would give Rosalie a doll to keep her safe.

Now the doll hung upside down with thumbtacks studding its body. The doll's head dangled from its neck by a single piece of brown yarn.

"Did you do that?" Mack asked Sander with an accusing tone. He pointed at the wall.

But before Sander could answer, Hoyt cried from outside.

"What the hell?" Mack asked. He walked to one of the windows looking out on the veranda and part of the yard. His heartbeat quickened when he saw Hoyt on his hands and knees on the lawn. Surrounding him were two men and one woman wearing fish head masks. The men held knives and the woman carried a machete.

"Get upstairs!" Mack told Rosalie.

"What is it?" she asked.

"Take Sander. Lock yourselves in our bedroom and call the police. Tell them we're under attack." He ran to the side door and grabbed Hoyt's metal baseball bat from the basket of sports equipment that was beside the door.

"Get away from him!" he hollered. He rushed down the steps that led from the veranda to the lawn. Hoyt had collapsed with his face in the grass. His football was beside him and looked deflated. Despite the evening dim, Mack could tell his son's attackers were young—maybe in their late teens or early twenties. They had lanky limbs and wore faded T-shirts and black jeans. The rubber fish head masks were green with bulging red eyes and fins protruding from their tops.

"You hear me?" Mack said, raising the bat over his shoulder.

The trio backed away. They slowly retreated along the driveway with their weapons pointed at Mack. Mack noticed one of the knives was wet with blood.

"Please, no," he said and hurried to Hoyt.

"He's not worth anything," the girl said. She and the others were now in the street and appeared to be leaving. "Your son inside is the special one."

Mack ignored her words and gently rolled Hoyt over onto his back.

His youngest son's throat was slit and soaked with blood.

"Hoyt!" Mack sobbed. He dropped the bat and cupped his hands over the slash mark.

Hoyt wasn't breathing, and his eyes were shut. Blood spilled out of the corner of his mouth.

Tears burned Mack's eyes. "Someone help!" he screamed. But he knew the neighboring homes were empty. They were vacation homes, just like his and Rosalie's, and October was the off-season.

And besides, there was nothing anyone could do to help Hoyt now.

Mack glared in the direction of the three figures, which ambled down the road as if they'd just finished TP-ing a house rather than murdering his son. All he wanted to do was sprint after them and crush their skulls with the bat, but the sound of a window opening made him turn toward the house.

"It's time for you to come inside."

Mack looked up at the second floor and saw a fish head staring blankly down at him from the window of his and Rosalie's bedroom.

"See you upstairs." The voice could have been that of a college-age kid.

Not Rosalie, Mack repeated inside his head. *Please, not Rosalie.* He wiped his bloody hands on his polo shirt and picked up the baseball bat. He reluctantly left Hoyt's body on the lawn.

Inside, the house was dark. Mack quickly passed through the kitchen and dining room. He remembered that he, his wife, and their sons were supposed to be sitting around the table eating their meal from The Crab Leg right now. They'd done that for many a year in this house, and Mack never guessed the tradition would end. He gripped the bat with both hands as he climbed the stairs. He was prepared to swing if anyone appeared.

He saw light coming from the hallway that led to his and Rosalie's bedroom. When he reached that hallway, he had a clear view into the room.

Rosalie's bedside lamp was on. She lay across the foot of the mattress with her face planted in the comforter. Sander sat next to her on the side of the bed, staring down at the striped carpet. He looked as if he were in shock, and as Mack hurried toward his family members, he saw his son's body was trembling.

Mack also spotted a large red stain on the back of Rosalie's blouse. He ran to his wife and shook her with one hand while he gripped the bat with his other. There were knife wounds between her shoulder blades. Tears rolled down his cheeks. "No, Rosalie," he whimpered.

She was dead.

He heard someone clear his throat. He looked up and saw a wiry man standing behind the plush chair where Rosalie read her magazines. His fish head mask came down to his jawline. He, too, wore a T-shirt—one with the Southern Comfort label on its front—and black jeans. On the right side of his neck was a large, circular tattoo depicting an alligator chasing its tail. He wiped the knife on the back of the chair, leaving a bloody streak.

Mack stood and raised his bat.

"Batter up," the stranger said. "But what happens if the ball comes from behind you?"

Mack glanced over his shoulder and saw another masked intruder. This one was a woman, and the limp brown and gray hair protruding from under her mask revealed that she was older than the others. In her hair was a string of blood-red beads. She pointed a shotgun at Mack.

Feeling defeated, Mack glanced down at his wife's body. Then he stared at Sander. "You let them in the bedroom, didn't you?" he asked with obvious disappointment. He suddenly felt more anger toward Sander than he did toward the people who'd broken into his house and done this to Rosalie.

"No, Dad," Sander said, finally looking up from the floor. He, too, was crying. "I sensed they were coming, but I didn't know every-"

"You *sensed*?" Mack said, scowling.

"He sensed because he's the successor," the woman said in a calm voice. "Maman's successor. We know this all seems quite terrible to you, but it's necessary for your son to realize his greatness. Terrible things precede great things."

"His greatness?" Mack asked, giving Sander a scornful look. His son hadn't had a single friend in years, and now these people were revering him?

"Hush," the woman said, holding up a finger to her fish lips. "She's coming."

Mack heard the stairs creak, and a person's slow footsteps.

"Minister," the young man asked, "should I-?"

"Silence," the woman said. "Use your instinct, as we've taught you. Sander, come here. Maman is ready to meet you. She shows herself to so few."

Mack was astounded when his son rose from the bed and walked across the bedroom to the woman. He gave his father a brief apologetic look.

The footsteps were just around the corner from the hallway. Mack looked in their direction.

"Turn away," the woman told him. "You can't see her. Only the privileged can see her." Sander stared down the length of the hallway. Mack was disgusted to see the eager expression on his face. Sander hadn't looked like that since many Christmases ago.

Mack's fingers tightened around the baseball bat. He thought if he sprang at the woman now, he'd possibly reach her before she could fire the shotgun.

His body grew tense when the woman told Sander, "Maman has heard your unhappy thoughts. She knows how much you'd enjoy being part of the Family. And one day you're going to be the head of the Family."

"That's enough," Mack said, but he wasn't able to continue speaking as a knife sliced through his throat. He saw his life spew onto the floor.

While pressing his hands against his gushing neck, he could see an old woman's shape limping toward him through the hallway. Though the shape was hazy, there was something strange—something terrifying—about it. The woman didn't seem to be quite human. The arms were a dark green color, and the fingers were too large, too sharp.

Mack saw his son go to the old woman and hug her tightly, and then all went black.

Last Spring

1

Kim turned her head to avoid a kiss on the lips.

Malia pecked her cheek and said, "Well, that's not what I was expecting." She scooted away from Kim in their semicircular booth in a rear corner of Phuket Sunset.

"I do want to kiss you." Kim couldn't believe how much she wanted to. Her entire body was tingling, and she felt a pleasant burning sensation inside her. If they weren't in a restaurant, she would have pulled off her V-neck sweater to cool down. Instead, she sipped her Thai iced tea and glanced around the dim, mostly empty dining room. She saw pale paintings of turquoise seascapes and Buddhist temples on the walls. She'd suggested this place for their date because it was in Lake City—far enough away from her fiancé's condo in downtown Seattle. It was also an acceptable distance from the University of Washington Medical Center, where Kim worked as a coordinator for various oncology research studies and Malia managed Oasis, a flower and gift shop on the first floor of the hospital.

"So you don't want me to kiss you in public," Malia said with a grin. She jokingly shook a finger at Kim. "I know how you're squeamish about that. But you did kiss me in the store the other day."

"It's not that," Kim said. It's just that you and I have been moving so quickly, and I haven't broken it off with Eustace yet."

"You'll talk to him when you're ready. You're not regretting what's happened between us, are you?"

Kim reached over to place her hand on top of Malia's. "I don't regret any of our moments together." She remembered the first time she'd seen Malia in Oasis, when she bought a bottle of aloe vera lotion for her dry hands and forearms. The hospital's air conditioning always made Kim's skin feel brittle. As Malia rang up the bottle, she chattered how she and her sisters had used real aloe for all kinds of skin ailments when they were growing up on Kauai.

"You just tear off a leaf," Malia said, "and the goodness oozes right out." Her brown eyes were so big, and they looked as if they held no secrets, only compassion.

Now those eyes stared pensively at the fresh rolls Kim and Malia were supposed to be sharing.

"I'm going to kiss you again," Kim assured her. "I just need to deal with my situation first." She lifted her left hand from Malia's and stuck out her ring finger. The stone of her emerald engagement ring almost appeared gray in the dark of the restaurant. Kim withdrew her hand when she realized it looked like she was flicking off Malia.

"I don't like being a cheater," she added. "Eustace has been so kind to me. He deserves honesty."

Malia nodded, but she didn't seem to agree. "I think something special is happening between us," she said, "and we should go with it. I think we're both hoping to grow this relationship."

Kim knew how much she cared for Malia and how much she was attracted to her. The three times they'd slept together had been electric. A pleasurable throbbing continued inside her body for hours afterwards. But they'd met only a couple months ago. And Kim had never been with a woman before Malia. She'd had same-sex crushes, but nothing as intense as this. She'd only dated men in the past, and, even though she was nearly 30, not many. Eustace was her longest, and if she ended their relationship this month, like she'd planned, they wouldn't even reach their two-year anniversary.

"Can you please just give me a little more time?" Kim asked. "I promise to talk to Eustace soon, and then I'll be in this with you 100%."

"Here's the Green Curry Chicken," the waitress said, setting the dish before Kim. "And the Pad See Ew." She asked the women, "You don't like the fresh rolls?"

"We're still working on those," Malia said with that smile that always put Kim at ease.

When the waitress started back toward the kitchen, Malia spooned food onto both of their plates and offered Kim one of those smiles. "Hey," she said, "why don't we lighten up? We can still have fun even if it's PG-rated." She lifted a cube of tofu with her chopsticks. "Give me some gossip from work. Have you or the nurses caught that girl stripping in her boyfriend's hospital room again?"

Kim grinned as she finished chewing a spicy chunk of chicken. "He dropped out of the study after his surgery. Fortunately, the tumor in his testicle turned out to be benign."

"Life can be sweet," Malia said, "can't it?"

The words caused a fluttering in Kim's chest. She loved that this woman constantly saw the brightness in things. There was an icy drizzle outside, Malia was in a slightly depressing restaurant with a conflicted love interest who was still engaged to a man, and yet she relished life.

Kim set her fork on the table and scooted toward Malia. Malia gave her a surprised look, and then Kim kissed her on the mouth, wetly and deeply.

"Do you want to get boxes for this and take it back to your apartment?" Kim asked. "We can eat it later. I want to be in bed with you right now."

The two women held hands as they crossed the parking lot in the direction of their cars. The rain had stopped, and the air had lost its winter chill. Kim noticed tulips inside the flowerpots lining one wall of the restaurant.

"I love April in Seattle," she said. "Soon there'll be flowers everywhere."

Malia squeezed her hand. "Follow my car closely, okay?" she said before heading toward her Prius. "You've never been to my place, and there are a lot of winding streets in my neighborhood."

"I'll be right behind you." Kim unlocked the driver's side door of her Jetta. She felt a pang of guilt because Eustace had bought her this car—just like he'd bought her so many things during the 14 months she was without work. The gas, the groceries, the train ticket to Vancouver, where he gave her that retro black velvet dress and matching high heels. Eustace had gazed at her with his "wow" eyes when she put on that outfit, and she momentarily stopped feeling like a loser for getting laid off from her last coordinator position. She would give up the gifts she'd received from him.

But you'll have Malia, she told herself when she sat behind the steering wheel. Looking in the rear view mirror, she saw happiness in her green eyes. She fixed the bangs of her long, dirty blond hair and started the ignition. She suddenly felt sure she'd end her relationship with Eustace tomorrow. She wouldn't delay it any longer.

Her cell started ringing when she was tailing Malia on I-5. She didn't recognize the digits lighting up the screen, but she gave her number to all her study participants in case they had any questions.

She tapped the speaker icon on her phone. "This is Kim."

"Hello," an older woman spoke. Her voice sounded strained. "My name's Betty. I live in the same building as Eustace."

"Yes?" Kim asked with concern. Eustace had said he was going to be working at his law firm late tonight. He often worked late. "Is anything the matter?"

"I'm sorry," the woman said. She paused. "Eustace is dead. I heard a gunshot, and I called the police. His door was unlocked. I'm with him—with his body—right now. He wrote your name and number on an envelope."

Kim gripped the steering wheel with both hands. She tried to speak, but she couldn't.

"I think he did it to himself," Betty said in a hushed voice. "I'm so sorry. Can you come over? The police are on their way upstairs right now."

Kim pressed her foot against the gas pedal and swerved around Malia's Prius. She didn't look in the rear view mirror as she sped toward downtown.

Kim left her car in a loading zone and hurried across the street toward Eustace's condo tower. There were two police cars and an ambulance parked outside the building's entrance. Kim wiped the tears from her eyes and cheeks and glanced up at the tower. She couldn't tell Eustace's balcony from any of the others. She'd tried to convince him to put some plants on the balcony—maybe a rosebush or some succulents—but he told her he liked to keep his space simple. "And besides," he said," I'll be leaving this place soon enough. We'll be looking for a home together."

Kim entered the building with her key card. Alone in the rising elevator, she told herself Eustace couldn't be dead. What reason did he have to kill himself? At 30, he seemed to possess more self-awareness than people much older than him. He was a successful attorney at the well-known firm Mentson-Keeler. He owned a condo in one of the most beautiful cities in America. He'd proposed to her just a few months ago.

Kim remembered slipping her tongue between Malia's lips tonight, and she blushed. Was it possible Eustace knew about them? She doubted it. He'd been away at conferences the few times she'd had Malia sleep over at her apartment. And, other than being a little less available on weeknights, Kim hadn't given any signs of wanting to end her engagement with Eustace. He'd told her more than once, "I don't have faith in many people, but I believe in you."

DING. The elevator doors opened on the 19th floor.

Yellow police tape blocked off Eustace's doorway at the end of the corridor. A policeman holding a clipboard stood outside the apartment.

Kim felt nauseous as she approached the officer. She recalled walking down this hall when she used to attend a yoga class at the building's gym. Eustace would always open his door before she reached it, as if he psychically sensed she was coming. She'd experience a little burst of pride when she saw her handsome boy-friend waiting for her, his blue eyes smiling and his black hair parted to the right. Sometimes he reminded her of one of those debonair movie stars from the 1930s, like Cary Grant or Gary Cooper. She'd always thought her mom would eagerly approve of this man if she were still alive. After all, he was the one who'd helped Kim believe in herself again after so many months of failing to find a job. He'd provided constant financial and emotional support when a lot of guys would have tired of her middle-of-the-night anxiety attacks and mid-afternoon depression. He made her feel strong when she was at her weakest.

And now he was dead.

The policeman asked Kim for her "relation to the deceased," and she replied in a distant voice, "We're engaged." After Kim gave him her contact information, he removed the tape and opened the door.

Two policemen stood in the living room with a woman who must have been in her sixties. A couple medics packed up a kit that lay on Eustace's couch. The woman turned to Kim. She had short, dyed red hair and wore multiple pearl necklaces and an expensive-looking green pantsuit.

"Kim? I'm Betty."

Kim didn't respond. She entered Eustace's home and glanced around the sparsely decorated space as if she were seeing it for the first time. She noticed the empty, asymmetrical Japanese vases and the few framed depictions of animals by a local Native American artist. And then she looked in the direction of the dining room.

"Oh!" Kim pressed one hand against her mouth in horror.

A man sat slumped over Eustace's dining room table, a gun near one of his pale hands. A light blue bath towel was draped over his head. Blood had soaked the towel and pooled on the table. The man wore a white T-shirt and white briefs.

Behind him, a middle-aged police officer was taking photographs of the grisly splatter on the wall. The man offered Kim a sympathetic look and then continued his task. One of the policemen from the living room asked Kim, "Are you the fiancée?"

"Yes," she sighed. She felt like she was lying.

She flinched when someone touched her arm. She saw Betty standing beside her.

"I'm so sorry," the woman said. "I put the towel over his head so you wouldn't have to see his face."

Kim looked back at the body. She felt nauseous when she recognized the tattoo peeking out of the right sleeve of Eustace's T-shirt: an alligator trying to bite its own tail.

"It represents the mortal coil," Eustace had once explained. "The troubles of daily life we won't escape until we die. I got it when I lived in New Orleans. It gives me perspective."

Kim ran to the bathroom and dropped her purse on the floor. She vomited into the toilet. "Oh, god," she choked. "He's really dead."

While rinsing her mouth out, she heard her cell phone vibrating in her purse. She thought of Malia waiting and worrying at her apartment. Kim wasn't ready to speak to her yet. Once the vibrating stopped, Kim stared at her face in the bathroom mirror. Her eyes were pink and tearing. Her lips quivered.

She glared at her reflection. *Eustace did it while you were on a date with Malia*, she told herself.

Kim felt foggy-headed as she responded to the policeman's various questions. She and Eustace hadn't fought in the recent past. No, he didn't have a history of depression. He hadn't given any clues about wanting to commit suicide.... All her responses were true, and yet they seemed false in the shadows of the greater, unspoken truths looming over them. She had fallen for a woman. She'd been planning on leaving Eustace because she'd felt disconnected from him for some months after they got engaged. He was amazingly kind to her, but he was also often vague or secretive about his past, and what he said to her sometimes sounded scripted. Eustace William Laplante—an attorney who hailed from Savannah, Georgia, and studied law at Tulane University in New Orleans—had a life that looked good on paper. But who was he deep inside?

Kim wasn't sure. Maybe she should have tried harder to learn. She began crying again.

"Officer, do you mind if I take her next door to my place?" Betty asked. "I think it'd be good for her to get out of here for a bit."

Betty soon ushered Kim into her own living room. While Eustace's home had minimal decorations, Betty's living room was filled with photographs of family, floral paintings, and crystal figurines.

"Please have a seat," Betty said, motioning toward a pink couch. She went into the kitchen.

Kim sat on the edge of the couch. She looked down at her shaking hands.

"Can I make you some tea? Maybe chamomile to soothe your nerves?"

"No," Kim said. "But thank you." She heard another vibration coming from her purse, which was beside her. She set the purse on the floor by her feet.

Betty approached her with an envelope in one hand. "I wanted to show you this before I gave it to the police. It was outside my door. He must have put it there just before he...."

Kim took the envelope. On its front were the words *For my fiancée, Kim Lansing* as well as Kim's phone number. Kim unsealed the envelope and unfolded the piece of paper that was inside. Eustace had written:

I'm sorry. Don't blame yourself. I'm responsible for this. Death is not an end. We will see each other again.

I've mailed you instructions on where to take my ashes. Please respect my wishes.

I'm grateful for your commitment.

Love,

Eustace

Kim winced when she read the word *commitment*. She felt a spark of irritation inside her. Even in his suicide note, Eustace revealed so little. Kim saw a pair of crystal figurines—one male and one female—standing on the coffee table before her. She wanted to fling them against a wall.

Instead, she hung her head and wept.

"Oh, sweetie," Betty said, sitting beside her. She handed Kim tissue and patted her back. "I can't imagine what you're going through. My husband passed, but he was in his seventies. I didn't realize Eustace was going to be married. It seemed like he was home alone so often."

"Did you know him?" Kim wiped her eyes and stared at Betty.

The woman's face darkened with a look of guilt. "I had to talk to him about the noise a couple times."

"The noise?"

Betty pointed at her kitchen wall. "It came from his living room. It sounded like some kind of a rattle. Maybe it was a recording. Both times there was also this foul smell, like burning meat." She shrugged. "I knocked on his door and asked him to keep it down."

Kim had never seen a rattle or any other musical instrument in Eustace's condo. "And did he?"

Betty nodded. "He seemed out of it both times. His face was all sweaty. I figured he was drinking or something. It's not for the old to figure out the ways of the young."

Kim was confused. Eustace didn't drink.

"I'm glad I never called Patricia," Betty continued. "It really wasn't a big deal."

"Who's Patricia?"

"My cousin. She owns his place. She's been renting it out to him."

Kim frowned and shook her head. "That's Eustace's condo."

"No, sweetie," Betty said. "Patricia bought it in 2006. Did Eustace tell you he was the owner?"

Kim's nausea was returning. She didn't want to soil Betty's bathroom. She picked up her purse and stood. "I should go back to Eustace's. Thank you for bringing me over here."

Betty accompanied her to the door. "I'll be here if you need anything."

Kim wandered out into the hallway, feeling confused by the information she'd just received. Why had Eustace told her he owned when he rented? She guessed he'd probably just wanted to impress her.

Her nausea passed, and she suddenly needed to hear Malia's voice. She dialed Malia's number.

"Kim, what happened? Where are you?"

"Eustace is dead," Kim said, her voice cracking. "I got a call about it after we left the restaurant. He took his own life...with a gun."

"Oh, Kim. I'm so sorry. Where are you? I'll come right away."

"No," Kim said. She realized how quickly she responded. She added, "Thank you. I'm at Eustace's place. I need to take care of things."

"You shouldn't be alone."

"I'll call you soon. I'm sorry. I just can't talk about this now."

"I'm here for you, Kim."

Kim thanked her and hung up. She knew she needed to be here for Eustace. She would answer any of the policemen's remaining questions and clean up Eustace's condo—his apartment—after his body was gone. She'd failed him when he was alive, but she wouldn't fail him after his death.

Ten days later, Kim leaned against the railing of Eustace's balcony, exhausted. She'd just finished boxing up the last of her fiancé's belongings, which didn't include a rattle or anything that would even make a rattling sound. Staring at the nearly full moon hovering over Seattle's skyscrapers, she felt like she was partly at fault for Eustace's death. Rather than work on her relationship with a man who'd treated her so kindly—so lovingly—she distracted herself with Malia. Of course, she knew why: Malia's warmth and beauty touched a place so deep inside her core, a place Eustace had never been able to reach. But then Kim should have told him the truth about how she was feeling, shouldn't she?

While the chasm widened between her and her fiancé, something must have changed inside Eustace. Something broke.

She knew if her mother was still alive she'd disapprove of how Kim had let her relationship disintegrate. When Kim had been a teenager, her mother told her, "I'd like you to find a normal, stable man who loves you. Marry him and love him back. Don't make the same mistakes as me."

Kim sat on the cushioned bench she'd shared with Eustace on many an evening and rested one hand on the steel urn beside her. Strangely, Eustace had left that urn for her on his kitchen counter, next to the coffee maker they'd used when Kim spent the night. With her other hand, Kim scrolled through the list of contacts on her cell until she reached Malia's name. She tapped Malia's phone number and listened to the ringing.

"Kim!" Malia immediately answered. "I'm so happy to hear from you."

Kim had only called Malia a couple times since the night of Eustace's death, and when she did call she kept their conversations brief. She felt guilty while they spoke, and she would imagine Eustace's soul or spirit or whatever listening to their words. Something melted inside Kim when she heard Malia's voice tonight, but she tried to harden her heart. "I've been really busy."

"I popped by your wing at the hospital to see if you'd come back to work. Dr. Tranh told me you were on leave. I know this must be awful for you."

"I guess I deserve some awfulness. I was awful to Eustace in my own way."

Malia was silent on the other end of the line. Finally, she said, "You've only been following your heart, Kim. We've both been doing that."

Kim felt a tightening in her throat. She told herself not to cry, not to surrender to Malia's sweetness. It would be so easy for Kim to get in her car and drive to Malia's apartment right now. Kim cleared her throat and stood. "I'm going to Charleston tomorrow." She walked from the balcony into Eustace's now empty living room. She once again glanced in the direction of the dining room to make sure the bloodstain hadn't somehow reappeared on the wall.

The wall was still a cream color.

"South Carolina?" Malia asked. "Why?"

"Eustace wanted me to divide his ashes between family members who live in different cities: Charleston, Savannah, Pensacola, New Orleans."

"That's odd."

Kim had never heard Malia voice judgment before. She didn't like hearing it. She walked to the one small table that remained in the living room and glanced at the names of family members listed on a piece of paper that lay on the table. "He wrote this request for me. I need to honor it."

"Of course you do," Malia said. "Are you going alone?"

"Yes," Kim said, trying not to reveal her nervousness about the journey.

"Have you ever been to the South?"

"Once. My mom's from Tennessee. A small town outside Memphis. I went with her and my stepfather to visit my grandmother when I was a teenager." She suddenly pictured her tiny and adorable grandmother, who'd passed in her sleep about a decade ago. Always dressed in an apron, Nana would smile so widely and listen so closely when her granddaughter spoke. Kim wished she could confide in her now. But she also remembered what Nana had said when they were alone together one night of that trip to Tennessee: "Don't become like your mama and make foolish decisions about men. But don't become one of those unnatural types who scorn men either."

Malia said, "I could meet you on the road if you want company. I've got some vacation days I need to use."

"Thank you for offering. I've got to do this alone. I feel like I didn't get to know Eustace as much as I should have when he was with me. I think this trip will help me know him better." She wandered from the living room into the bedroom.

"Tomorrow's so soon," Malia said. "I'm assuming you already had a memorial?"

"Eustace didn't want one." Kim was partially lying. There'd been no memorial because Eustace didn't have any friends in Seattle. Or at least any friends Kim knew of. She'd called the firm where he worked and left several voicemails about his passing, but nobody called her back.

"Well, when you're on the road," Malia said, "know that I'm just a phone call away. And...."

Kim held her breath as she waited for Malia to finish her sentence.

"And I'm here tonight. If you want to...."

Kim wanted to, but she knew she couldn't. If she woke up in Malia's bed, how would she ever make it to the airport? "I can't. Not tonight. I'm sorry."

"I look forward to hearing from you," Malia said, sounding deflated.

"Good night," Kim said.

She hung up the phone and stood staring into the bedroom closet. She felt as empty as Eustace's apartment, and so alone. She'd seen few people during the last 10 days. All her conversations with friends had been over the phone. She worried that if she saw them in person, she'd crack and spill the truth about falling for Malia. And then maybe they'd wonder if her affair had something to do with Eustace's death.

She stepped forward when she noticed the small cardboard box on the shelf that spanned the top part of the closet. When she'd first found the empty container, she saw that Eustace had written the words *HELPING HANDS* on its side. She'd left the box on the shelf because she guessed there were hand-shaped sculptures or other art pieces that belonged inside, but she'd never seen any while clearing out Eustace's possessions.

She pulled the box off its perch, and while she carried it to the pile of trash by the front door, she spotted a piece of paper tucked under one of the internal flaps.

She unfolded the paper, which was yellowed and thin. It looked as if someone had torn it out of a book. Some of the words were so faded they were barely decipherable. The page read:

In the ancien days, the swamps reached all corners of the lan
*   And their g ds walked among the tre s*

Killing, feed , radiating
Though the sw mps are fewer, some of the old gods remain
Invisible y t colossal
Steadfast in hurricane , destroyers of slave and master
Watch for their green lights

1855

Kim shivered when she finished reading the words. She wondered why Eustace would keep such a creepy piece of writing. Maybe it was some folk legend from Georgia, and Eustace had saved it for nostalgia's sake.

Kim crumpled up the piece of paper and dropped it in the plastic bag she was going to take to the recycling bin. While she reached inside the bag, she heard her phone ringing. She couldn't help hoping that Malia was calling her back.

She pulled her cell out of her pants pocket. She didn't recognize the number on her phone's screen. "Hello?" she asked.

"Hello, is this Kim Lansing?" a man spoke.

"Yes?" She went out on the balcony to pick up the urn. She was going to take the container home and pack it in a box for her trip.

"My name's Henry Favelli. I'm the lead paralegal at Mentson-Keeler. I apologize for calling so late, but I just received the messages you left for us last week. We've been having some issues with our voicemail system."

"Oh, that's all right." Kim nestled the phone between her shoulder and her ear so she could lift Eustace's remains from the bench. She brought the container inside.

"I'm sorry about your loss, Ms. Lansing. But I also wanted to say that Eustace Laplante didn't work here."

Kim paused in the living room. "What do you mean? Of course he worked there. He was an attorney at your firm."

"I'm sorry, Ms. Lansing. We've never had an attorney by that name."

Kim set the container on the carpet and looked at it as if it held an alien. She concocted a lie: "You know, I realized I called the wrong number. My fiancé worked for a different firm."

As she locked the door to her apartment the next morning, Kim wondered about what other lies Eustace might have told her. He didn't own a condo, and he didn't work for a law firm. Was he embarrassed about where he really worked? Or perhaps he was ashamed of being unemployed?

Also bewildering was the fact that Eustace didn't have any financial records in his apartment. Kim had found no bank, credit card, or tax statements in any of his drawers. She couldn't locate any information about him on the Internet. Eustace had never been on Facebook or any other social media sites. "I find my friends," he told her. "I don't need them finding me."

She questioned whether he was really from the South and had gone to the schools where he'd said he studied. She assumed he'd told the truth, because she'd spoken to his sister, Teressa, to tell her she was coming to Charleston with Eustace's ashes.

"I'm so happy you're doing this for him," Teressa had said. Kim was surprised Teressa didn't sound more upset after hearing about her brother shooting himself.

"I don't think I could live with myself if I didn't do it," Kim said.

"He knew you were the right person to be with."

"Did he tell you about me?" Kim asked. Eustace had never spoken about any family other than his parents, and he only brought them up a couple times. Once, after Kim had talked about wishing she could still have Sunday lunches with her mom, he told her, "I often feel lucky that my parents are dead." When Kim asked about them, he said, "They didn't care for me much," and then he changed the topic.

Teressa chirped, "Course he told me about you."

Kim mentioned there were other relatives who were to re-
ceive Eustace's ashes—his brother, Harlon, in Savannah; an Aunt
Lizanna, who lived in Pensacola; and his grandmother, Vess, of
New Orleans.

"Eustace only gave me your phone number and address," she
said. "I have no way of reaching the others."

"I'll give you all that when you get here," Teressa said. "You
should come here first. I'm afraid I don't have room for you to stay
with me."

"That's okay. I booked a room in a B&B."

Kim checked the door handle to her apartment to make sure
it was locked. She then picked up her suitcase and carry-on bag
and headed down the hallway. As she left the cozy 1950s apartment building she'd lived in since her early twenties, she realized
Eustace had never spent the night there. He'd only come inside a
few times to pick her up. He always insisted on her sleeping at his
place, explaining, "I like to be the host."

Kim's friends had often cooed over Eustace being such a
gentleman. Kim thought how embarrassing it would be to tell
them how many truths he'd withheld from her.

Outside, the sky was cement gray and the temperature was
in the mid-40s. Kim remembered the tulips she'd seen next to
Phuket Sunset with Malia, and she thought how many of the
spring flowers would wither if the chilly weather continued. She
wanted heat in the South.

Fortunately, her taxi was waiting to pick her up. The driver
dropped her luggage in the trunk and opened a rear door for her.
While the car rolled along Kim's street, a Prius approached from
the opposite direction and passed them. Kim felt an ache in her
chest when she saw Malia's lovely face through the driver's side
window. Malia didn't appear to see her.

Kim knew she had time to go back to her apartment and say
goodbye properly. She could embrace Malia and tell her she would

miss her. Maybe Malia could even drive her to the airport. But then starting her journey would be that much harder.

The taxi driver must have noticed that Kim was turned around in her seat and watching the Prius brake in front of her apartment building. The man asked, "Do you want me to stop?"

Kim looked at him in the rear view mirror. "No. Please keep going."

2

Todd stepped out of the taxi and crossed the hot white sand in the direction of a model with a green parrot on each shoulder. She had high black hair and fluorescent-pink rings around her eyes. She wore a coconut shell bikini top and a fuchsia pencil skirt. Todd thought she might be that Czech girl he'd worked with a couple years ago in San Francisco. He'd felt old being paired up with her on that shoot. She was 18 at the time, and he was 30.

But no, he realized it wasn't the Czech girl as he reached the crew surrounding her. After almost a decade in the industry, he found all the models—both women and men—looking the same.

A smiling woman with gleaming silver hair approached him and touched his upper arm. "Todd Regan? I'm Macy. I'll be doing your hair today. It's an honor to work with you. I loved, loved, *loved* the Sin Tight campaign."

"Thank you."

Todd always appreciated people's compliments on those pictures, which had brought him much recognition and more than enough money. The 2008 campaign featured him posing oiled up in Sin Tight briefs with various large felines—an albino tiger, a yellow-eyed black leopard, a cheetah wearing a spiked collar. But that shoot was also possibly the climax of his career, and he hadn't done anything as impressive since.

"I haven't had a haircut in a while," he told Macy in an apologetic voice. He ran his fingers through his thick brown curls. "I've been really busy." He'd planned on visiting a salon near the clinic where he took his mother for her chemo infusions, but he was never able to get away from her bedside. Even when she slept, he didn't want to leave her.

"No worries," Macy said with a wink. "I'll make you look gorge."

"Regan?" A wiry, Italian-looking man in mirrored aviator sunglasses broke away from the crowd. "You were supposed to be here at 8. That was 30 minutes ago."

"Sorry," Todd said, sounding earnest. "My flight from LA didn't get in until about 2 last night. I accidentally overslept because my phone's alarm didn't go off. Anyway, I'm here now and ready to work." He stuck out his hand and asked, "Are you Rod the producer?"

The man frowned. "I'm Victor the art director." He didn't shake Todd's hand. "You can head into the changing tent. I'll have the stylist bring you some shorts to try on. You'll be shirtless in every shot."

"Sure," Todd said, trying to sound peppy for this prick. "I've got to say I'm pleased to be working with Cuba Gata. You guys are a terrific brand."

"We sure are," Victor said with sarcasm. He walked back toward the crew.

Macy placed a hand on Todd's back. "He doesn't know how lucky he is to have you here. I know, though. I'll do your hair as soon as you get changed."

Todd nodded and offered an appreciative smile. He glanced at Victor and saw the art director scowling at him. The man oozed disapproval.

Heading toward the purple-and-white-striped tent, Todd decided he should just be glad he was in Miami. His mother would be fine while he was away. He should treat this three-day job as a mini-vacation. The weather app on his phone predicted sunny skies and temperatures in the low-80s even though it was only the end of March.

Inside the tent were racks of clothes and a couple folding chairs. Todd peeled off his tank top and stepped out of his flip-flops. He lifted the flap covering a tent window and peered out at the sea, which was an emerald color far prettier than the Pacific's dark blue.

Todd told himself another reason not to worry was that Cuba Gata compensated very well—enough to cover some of what he paid for his mother's meds and the caregiver he'd hired to stop by her small house in West LA while he was working.

He remembered coming back to California from that ski-wear shoot in the Rockies and finding his 72-year-old mother on her kitchen floor, dressed in her nightgown and lying beside a half-eaten package of turkey she'd pulled out of the nearby refrigerator. A large bruise blossomed on her right knee.

"It's nothing, Toddy," she'd said as he helped her to the bathroom. "I must have fainted. One of my pills can make me dizzy. It only happened a couple hours ago. I didn't call because I knew you were coming over soon. You shouldn't be disturbed after working so hard."

Working so hard. Todd knew the opposite was true. He'd barely modeled during the months his mother was receiving chemo for her breast cancer, and since the end of her cycles two months ago he'd only had the skiwear shoot. He was supposed to work on a cologne campaign in New York at the end of February, but the job mysteriously fell through. While his agent insisted people still wanted him, Todd was starting to doubt.

"Todd?" Macy spoke from outside the tent. "I told the stylist I'd bring you your first pair of shorts. She'll be coming with the rest."

"Thanks," Todd said, reaching outside to receive a pair of white linen shorts. He put them on. "Are you going to do my hair in here?"

"Yes." Macy sounded hesitant. "Victor said he wants to look at you first."

"'Look' at me?" Todd asked with irritation. He stepped outside the tent and saw Victor striding toward them. "What does he have to look at? He already saw my body shots."

"Don't let him get to you," Macy said. "He's just super-critical. You and I have been around long enough to know those types."

Todd nodded. He was somewhat embarrassed a middle-aged woman had assigned him the status of weathered model.

Victor came within a few feet from Todd and stopped. The art director folded his arms over his chest. He still wore his sunglasses, but Todd could tell he was eyeing his torso.

"This isn't going to work."

"The shorts?" Todd asked. "I'm not crazy about linen myself."

"You. You're too heavy. That's not the upper body I saw in your portfolio."

Todd glanced down at his stomach. He wasn't ripped like he'd been in his mid-twenties, but his stomach seemed flat enough. He grew anxious as he recalled all those carbs he'd eaten during the months his mother was receiving chemo. Sandwiches instead of lean meats and salads. An occasional scone. Walnut and chocolate chip cookies his mother had baked to make her feel like her normal self again.

"It's probably water weight," Todd said. "But I'm going to be sweating a lot under this sun." He glanced at Macy, and he was relieved to see her nod in agreement.

"No," Victor said. "This isn't water weight." He reached out and pinched Todd's waist.

"Don't touch me!" Todd stepped back from the art director.

"I'm going to have to release you from this photo shoot."

"Wait," Todd said, dumbfounded. "You're actually firing me?" No one had ever released him from a shoot before.

"Look, I don't have time for drama," Victor said.

"What about my airfare? And the hotel in South Beach?"

"Have your agent work it out with the corporate office." Victor turned away from him and headed back toward the crew. Todd saw the model was no longer in her bikini. She cupped her hands over her breasts while a hose sprayed her with pink water.

"Fuck this scene," Todd said. He headed back inside the tent to fetch his clothes.

"I'm so sorry, Todd," Macy spoke from outside. "Can I buy you a drink when I finish the shoot? I'd be happy to give you a haircut, too. No charge."

"Thanks," Todd said as he picked up his tank top from the chair. He glanced down at his stomach again, and now he thought he saw a slight curve. "I'm going to pass. I think I just need to get out of this city."

Wanting to walk off his rage, Todd headed up Ocean Drive in the direction of his hotel. It wasn't long before his stomach was grumbling. He knew he was near that diner all the models and telenovela actors frequented. He soon found the place—Romeo's—which took up the bottom floor of a lime-green Art Deco building on 10th Street. The 1930s building was wedged between two gleaming white condo towers.

Inside, he sat at the counter and ordered a cafe con leche, huevos rancheros, and a side of chicken apple sausage.

"And a cheesy biscuit, too," he told the waitress before she could leave him. Now that he was a model without a job, he would pork down whatever the hell he wanted.

While waiting for his food, he glanced around Romeo's and saw the usual beautiful patrons. A twenty-something bottle blonde with pouty lips made brief yet meaningful eye contact with him and then went back to looking at the man sitting across the table from her. A sexy Latina lady gave him a wink before sliding her purse strap over her shoulder and sauntering out of the restaurant.

He felt a stirring in his groin as he considered taking a woman back to his hotel room this afternoon. He hadn't had sex in a few months because he'd been so distracted by his mother's health. He'd had some dates while she was going through chemo. They'd mostly been with hot-bodied women he met in bars when he was out with friends. The LA ladies gladly talked about their exercise routines and their budding careers, and some of them asked which famous models he'd worked with in the past. But when he brought up his mother's discovery of a hard, pea-sized lump under her right breast, they went quiet and picked at their low-calorie dinners.

Todd sensed someone else in Romeo's was watching him. He looked to his left and checked who occupied the other stools at the counter. Past an elderly couple sharing a plate of chicken and waffles was a beefy bald man who couldn't have been older than 35. The man wore a pastel-blue suit, a white shirt, and a pink tie. He stared at Todd with a lopsided grin.

Todd immediately looked down at his mug of milky coffee. He often caught men ogling him, and he usually found the attention flattering. But he was always careful to show them he wasn't interested.

This man, however, didn't seem to get the message. He came over and sat on the stool beside Todd. "Morning," he said, holding out his hand. "Guthrie Toll. Talent scout." The stranger had a slight Southern accent.

Their eyes met while Todd pumped his hand. Todd didn't detect any dishonesty. He also sensed Guthrie's interest in him wasn't sexual.

"Todd Regan. I'm a model."

"Not surprised about that," Guthrie said, smiling again. "You've even got the beauty mark thing." He touched his cheek in the same location where Todd had his chocolate chip-sized mole.

"Huevos rancheros and sausage," the waitress said, reaching between the two men to set down a pair of plates. Another server trailed behind her and brought Todd a biscuit that was the size of a fist.

Todd gave Guthrie an embarrassed smile. He knew no model should be eating this much for breakfast. "I've been fasting for a photo shoot," he lied. "I flew in from LA a few days ago."

"You go ahead and enjoy your food," Guthrie said, grinning again. "I apologize for bothering you. It's just that I'm helping cast a movie that's going to be filming in Georgia, and you've got the look my clients want. But I don't want to interrupt your breakfast."

"Stay," Todd said. He hoped he didn't sound too desperate. He was relieved someone thought he had something to offer besides excess fat. "What kind of a movie?"

The man pointed at the steaming huevos rancheros. "Don't let your breakfast get cold."

Todd noticed a circular tattoo on the back of the man's pointing hand. It looked like a lizard—no, an alligator—with its snout close to its tail.

"It's a horror movie," Guthrie said. "Kind of experimental, but with a lot of depth to it. Set during the Civil War."

"Horror's hot right now," Todd said, forking egg and tortilla into his mouth. One of his favorite shows was *Fang Gang,* about werewolves living in New York in the 1980s. He'd even dressed up as one of the main characters last Halloween.

"It's a low-budget, nonunion film. But they're offering the lead actors a lot."

Todd listened with raised eyebrows.

"They're paying 25K for a week of filming. And you'd get a 5K cash bonus for going to Savannah in the next few days. My clients would cover your hotel until the shooting begins in about two weeks—mid-April—and, of course, during the filming. They need to have the actors ready to start at any time, so that's why you'd need to go to Savannah now."

Chewing biscuit, Todd thought how helpful $25,000 could be—both for his mother and himself. That was what he made in three months, and only if he was receiving steady work.

But what was he thinking? He wasn't an actor. He'd taken a single acting class in Santa Monica about seven years ago, and all he remembered from it was some dumb exercise where you would clap your hands at another student and say "zip," "zap," or "zop."

Todd took a sip of coffee. "This all sounds great, but I don't have any acting experience."

"You've got the look, though," Guthrie said. "Like I said, this movie's experimental. No script for the actors. No rehearsals. My clients don't want people with experience, union membership, or agents."

"I've got an agent," Todd said, "but she's for my modeling work."

"You wouldn't need to involve her in this."

"No, I wouldn't." Todd didn't think she deserved any cut considering she'd found him so little work lately.

"Do you have any concerns about being away from your wife or family for that long?" Guthrie asked, looking searchingly into his eyes. "I'm afraid they couldn't join you."

"I'm not married. Single at the moment. My only family is my elderly mother."

"So you're interested," Guthrie said, sounding pleased.

Todd nodded. He knew there were things to work out—extending the caregiver's visits to his mother, fabricating some story to keep his agent from booking him until late April. "I am."

"Can you come to a party tomorrow night? My clients would like to meet the candidates I've selected, and then they'll decide who's right for the role."

Todd didn't want to reveal his disappointment. He'd thought he'd already gotten the part. "I'm always game for a party," he said. He ate more huevos rancheros and considered not finishing the guacamole on his plate.

"Before I leave you," Guthrie said, "I've got just a few routine questions. My clients have me ask these of all the candidates. They want a good personality match for each character."

"Shoot," Todd said. He set down his fork and pushed the plate away from him.

"When was the last time you cried?"

Todd gave an embarrassed grin. "Um, a few months ago?" It had been when his mother had lost the last of her hair during chemo. "Are you wondering if I could cry in front of the camera?"

"Don't worry about it," Guthrie said. "Next question: Would you rather be a saint or a martyr?"

"Martyr. They make more interesting characters in movies."

Guthrie stared at him intently. "Have you ever had a near-death experience where you felt like you left your body and you could see everything happening to you?"

Todd considered the latest strange question. "I was in a skateboarding accident when I was 15." He remembered it was the year after his parents divorced. His father had just moved to Chicago with his new wife. Todd was drinking Olde English and trying out skateboarding tricks with his friends at the skate park in Venice Beach, and he fell down a ramp and hit his head. "I was unconscious for a long time, and they took me to a hospital."

"And did you feel like you left your body?"

Todd shook his head. He recalled waking to find his mother sitting by his hospital bed. She'd told him he had to be more careful because she couldn't ever lose her one and only son. "You're my golden boy," she said.

"Good," Guthrie said. "Now let's say you're walking on a path in a dark cave...."

"Okay?" Todd was starting to feel uncomfortable.

"Someone who seems hostile or frightening is walking toward you. What do you do?"

"Hide," Todd said, sounding certain.

"You wouldn't confront him?"

Todd laughed warily. "I'm a lover, not a fighter?"

Guthrie smiled. "So you'd let him pass."

"Sure."

Guthrie gave Todd a congratulatory pat on the shoulder. "I'll see you at the party tomorrow night, buddy. Let me write down the address." He pulled his wallet out of his pocket. He started to remove a business card, and Todd spotted the word *Minister*. Guthrie quickly pushed that card down and removed another, which read:

Lights, Camera, Actors
Guthrie Toll
Talent Scout
305-555-3423

Todd didn't ask him if he was a minister on the side. Todd didn't want to pry. He watched Guthrie write on the back of the card, and he once again noticed the man's tattoo.

"I like the alligator."

Guthrie smiled widely and handed him the card. "I do, too. Have you been on an airboat tour in the Everglades yet?"

"I've been meaning to." Todd was bending the truth again.

"There are wild gators everywhere," Guthrie said with a glimmer in his eye. "They're in the grass, under the trees, floating above their holes. Did you know there are about 1.5 million gators in the state of Florida?"

"Wow," Todd said.

"Just think how many of them are watching us and we have no idea they're there."

Todd found the thought unsettling.

"Tomorrow night," Guthrie said. He shook Todd's hand and headed toward the door.

Todd took one last, small bite of biscuit and motioned for the waitress. He wanted to get back to his hotel so he could work out in the gym.

The address on the gatepost of the pink Mediterranean villa matched the address on the card Guthrie had given Todd. The house was in Miami Beach and only a ten-minute walk from Todd's hotel. With an ornate gate, lattice windows, and tile roofing, the villa had elegance, but it wasn't extravagant. Whichever indie filmmaker lived there clearly wasn't struggling. The front walkway led Todd past palm trees and a gurgling tiered fountain.

Back at the hotel, he had Googled Guthrie Toll and found a website for the man's business. Even though the site was basic, the numerous headshots on the "Talent Pool" page gave Todd the impression that Guthrie wasn't trying to scam him. This house only made the man seem more legitimate.

The front door opened before Todd could knock.

Guthrie stood inside the villa. "Hey, buddy," he told Todd. His suit was similar to the one he'd worn yesterday, except this one was pastel-green rather than pastel-blue. His face appeared flushed and sweating.

He must have guessed Todd's thoughts because he said, "Sorry I'm out of breath. I just helped move something heavy. Come on in."

Todd entered a foyer with a marble floor and a high, arched ceiling. To the right was a staircase rising to a dim second-floor landing. Past the foyer, a hallway stretched toward the windowed doors at the rear of the villa. The doors were open and afforded a view of a lighted pool. Shadowy figures mingled beside the water.

Guthrie handed Todd a pair of beige swimming trunks. "My clients would like you to put these on. They want the guests to enjoy the pool. You don't mind, do you?"

"Um, not at all." Todd thought of the incident with the art director yesterday, but he was feeling more confident today. He'd gotten plenty of crunches in since his embarrassment at the beach. "Are you going to introduce me to the clients before I change?"

"You'll meet them later," Guthrie said, bringing him into a hallway that intersected the main one. There were a few closed doors, and Guthrie pointed to one on the left. "That's the bathroom. Just leave your clothes in the closet. I can put your valuables somewhere safe if you'd like."

Todd hesitated before handing over his phone and wallet.

"You can trust me," Guthrie said. "I'd like you to get this role. I'll see you out back."

The only decorative object in the bathroom was a pink, lotus-like flower in a vase on the rear of the toilet. Todd peeked inside the medicine cabinet and saw it was empty.

After putting on the swimsuit, he brought his bundle of clothes and shoes to the closet and found that the shelves held a couple other men's outfits. He wished the clients could have seen him in his diamond-patterned Dolce & Gabbana shirt. He always received ooh's and aah's on that one. He hung the shirt on a hanger.

When he opened the bathroom door, a woman came out of the room across the hallway. She was an attractive redhead in her early twenties. Her wavy hair nearly reached her waist, and her tight green dress only covered her upper thighs. Like Todd, she was barefoot.

Todd glimpsed a large portrait hanging on the wall behind her. It was an old, black-and-white photo of a pretty but unsmiling woman. She had a 1920s-style short haircut and black mascara, and wore a sleeveless, beaded dress. She stood on a stage in front of a dark curtain. A red candle flickered on a small table beneath the portrait.

The redhead quickly shut the door behind her. "Hiya, Tarzan," she said, eyeing Todd's chest. "You look like you're headed for a swim."

Todd glanced down at his torso. Thankfully, his stomach was feeling flat and hard. He grinned at the woman and held out a hand. "Todd Regan. I'm auditioning for a part in a movie. Do you know the filmmakers?"

The woman offered her hand, which was surprisingly hot and damp. "I know the owners of the house, but I don't talk shop with them. I'm just here for the party. My name's Orchid." She motioned toward the main hallway. "Shall we?"

Strangely, all the doors along the hallway were shut. Near the rear of the villa, the hallway opened into a cavernous area with a kitchen on the left and a dining room on the right. A few guys who looked like they were about 19 clustered around the kitchen island. They were thin and wore T-shirts and jeans—clothes that seemed too casual for a movie industry party in Miami Beach. One of them gave Todd a weird, blank-eyed stare, as if he were looking right through him. While passing by, Todd noticed the young man had the same alligator tattoo as Guthrie on his upper right arm.

The furnishings in the kitchen and dining room were taste-ful yet impersonal and too new-looking. Todd felt like he was in a staged home.

Orchid squeezed his hand. "You're dilly-dallying. Come on."

The walkway divided two squares of grass and led to the pool, which was the centerpiece of the rectangular backyard. Pot-ted flowers and ferns lined the ivy-covered wall that formed the perimeter of the yard. There were also a number of flickering tiki torches. The guests outside weren't much older than the ones in the kitchen. Todd scanned the crowd and found it was mostly female. The guests seemed to swarm around two other shirtless men wearing beige swimming trunks: a sandy-haired fellow who was more muscular than Todd, and a big-eyed French model Todd recognized from some of the major men's fashion magazines. Todd tried not to let the competition daunt him.

"What's the frown for, Tarzan?" Orchid hooked her arm around his and pulled him closer to the pool. "You're not a party pooper, are you?" She brought her lips to his ear and whispered, "I was hoping to have some fun with you tonight."

Todd tried not to let her words arouse him. He was wearing swimming trunks, after all. "I'm glad to be here," he said, displaying a camera-worthy grin. He remembered the clients could be watching. He glanced around to see who might be a director or producer, but everyone looked too young. Some of the guests were wild-eyed and abnormally loud. They reminded him of the addicts and street youth that hung out in downtown LA. But maybe they were just intoxicated.

"Sazerac?" Guthrie emerged from the shadows with a glass of auburn liquid. He handed the glass to Todd.

"What is it?"

"New Orleans specialty. It's got whiskey in it."

"Drink it fast, Tarzan," Orchid said. "Let it go to your head."

Todd sipped the drink, which tasted sweet, spicy, and lemony at the same time.

"When you finish that," Guthrie said, "you should get in the pool. The clients want to see how you take to water."

"Okay. Sure." Todd finished his drink and stepped to the edge of the pool. Suddenly lightheaded, he told Orchid, "See you soon?" He saw Guthrie walk off toward the house.

Orchid kissed Todd on the cheek and took his glass. "Make Mama proud." She pushed him, and he fell backwards into the water with a loud splash.

The pool cancelled the alcohol's effects and cleared Todd's brain. Underwater, he wondered about Orchid's words. *Make Mama proud.* Surely she was referring to herself, wasn't she? She couldn't know anything about his mother, or what she'd said to him before he left for Miami: "Don't worry about leaving me, Toddy. You need to go for your career. I know you'll do amazing work and make your mama proud once again."

Todd sank to the bottom of the pool, which was about seven feet deep, and then, using his leg muscles, propelled himself upwards and broke through the surface with perfect posture, ready for all eyes to be on him.

The guests were indeed watching, and they had become oddly quiet. Todd noticed Orchid had vanished. He also realized he wasn't alone in the water. The other bare-chested men were in there with him, and Todd felt less than special. He was just another ingredient in the competition soup.

Also floating in the pool were three large pink flowers—the same as the lotus-like one he'd seen on the back of the toilet. Green tendrils dangled from the flowers into the water.

He glanced at the French model, who looked as uneasy as Todd felt. Todd told himself to relax. He'd been to more outlandish parties than this in LA. Such functions were the norm in the film and fashion industries.

"Y'all ready for a game?"

The voice was Orchid's. She pushed past some of the onlookers until her toes were curled over the edge of the pool. She held a beach towel. The guests around her dispersed, and soon Orchid stood alone. Behind her was the walkway to the house.

"You three are the contestants," she told the swimmers. "Winner gets quite the prize. Come on out and stand over there." She pointed at a patch of wall past one of the squares of lawn.

Todd obediently climbed out of the pool, and Orchid handed him the towel. "You got this, Tarzan," she whispered. After drying off, Todd headed across the grass. He had no idea what the "contestants" would have to do next. Charades? A dance-off? When the two other swimmers stood to the left of him, Todd noticed a group of people coming from the kitchen toward the back door.

It was the trio of young guys he'd seen before. Two of them carried a massive, black turtle out to the backyard. The third wielded a white, curving cane.

"Mais qu'est-ce que c'est?" the French model murmured with concern. He stood between Todd and the sandy-haired man.

The creature was repulsive. It was the size of a small boulder, and it had a hooked beak that kept opening and closing. Its slimy-looking shell was covered with three ridges of spiky scales. Fat, bear-like claws and a pointed tail protruded from the shell.

The tail whipped from side to side as the turtle's carriers set it on the lawn. The reptile faced the three men in swimsuits.

Orchid crept up behind the turtle with a devilish grin. "Go on and pick the one you want," she told it.

Todd made eye contact with her, and he didn't like the crazed, almost malicious look on her face. All the other guests filled the lawn behind Orchid.

The beady-eyed turtle started in the direction of the contestants, its beak still snapping shut. The tip of the upper beak looked as sharp as any dagger.

"What if it bites us?" the sandy-haired man called to Orchid.

"They've been known to snap broom handles in half," Orchid said. "But we won't let her damage you boys."

Todd wasn't convinced. He glanced down at his bare feet. He wondered if he should head for the house. But he had a powerful desire to win whatever this game was after being a loser on the beach yesterday morning.

The sandy-haired contestant darted away from the others in the direction of the pool. "You guys win," he said, "I'm out." He did a cannonball in the water.

Todd glanced at the turtle, which was still coming at a steady pace. It made a hissing noise. The guy with the cane trailed behind.

Todd looked at the Frenchman's perspiring face. "You think the prize will be worth this?" he asked, giving a nervous grin.

"You can find out," the model said. He fled in the same path as the other contestant, but the turtle was too close.

It lunged at him and bit his heel.

The Frenchman howled and tumbled on the grass. Todd could see his heel was torn and his calf was slick with blood. The guy following the turtle shoved the cane between the reptile's jaws so it couldn't strike again.

Todd stepped toward the moaning man. "Are you all right?"

"Todd!" Guthrie called from the back door. "Come on inside!"

Todd hesitated. He looked down at the model, who was scowling at his wound. "Merde," the Frenchman kept saying. One of the turtle's handlers patted him on the head while another wrapped a towel around his ankle.

"Todd!" Guthrie repeated.

Todd reluctantly started toward the house. The guests had gone back to mingling with one another, and Orchid had disappeared once again.

"What the hell was that about?" Todd asked Guthrie inside the house.

"Oh, he'll be fine." Guthrie waved away Todd's alarm. "It's an old Southern tradition."

"A fucked-up tradition."

"Listen," Guthrie said, wrapping his arm around Todd's shoulder. He led him along the main hallway toward the front door. "What matters is you got the part. The clients want you in their movie."

"But I haven't met them yet."

"They saw you and they made their decision." He pulled an envelope out of his coat pocket and handed it to Todd. "Inside is the cash bonus I told you about. There's also information about the hotel where you'll be staying in Savannah. You need to fly out of Miami tomorrow afternoon."

Despite the bizarre accident outside, Todd was thrilled. He couldn't wait to tell his mother he now had a role in a movie and 25K coming his way.

Guthrie also gave Todd his valuables and motioned toward the bathroom. "Go on and get dressed. You don't mind if you show yourself out? I need to attend to our injured friend in the backyard." He stuck out his hand.

"Of course," Todd said, enthusiastically shaking Guthrie's hand.

After dressing, he thought of Orchid and where she might have gone. When he left the bathroom, he tried the door of the candlelit room where he'd first seen her.

The door was locked.

She seemed like a piece of work anyway, Todd told himself, remembering her deranged look. He left the Mediterranean villa a happier man than when he'd entered. He was almost at the street when he spotted the sign propped up against the backside of the gatepost.

The sign read *PROPERTY FOR SALE.*

3

Kim awoke to the sound of her cell phone vibrating against Eustace's urn. Both objects were on the night table next to her. Reaching for the phone, she remembered she was in her room at the bed and breakfast she'd checked into last night. The chamber also contained a small antique desk and chair, a dresser with a television on top of it, and a few hanging prints of brightly painted pineapples. This morning the room was surprisingly muggy, and Kim's pink tank top was soaked with sweat.

She saw the name *Malia* on the phone's screen, and she tapped the screen to send the call to voicemail. She set her cell back on the table, but further from her fiancé's remains this time. She wondered how a 5'11" man with a runner's build could fit in such a tight container, and then she began to cry.

"That's truly awful," a blond, big-haired woman had told her last night on the flight from Atlanta. The woman was pregnant and in her early thirties, and she sat in the middle seat while her preppy spouse had the aisle. The husband and wife watched Kim with pained, sympathetic gazes as she told them how she was taking her fiancé's ashes to the South.

"I don't know what I'd do if I lost Billy," the woman said, glancing at her husband. "I don't work, and we've got a couple little ones at home in Decatur. My mom's watching them while we're on our getaway trip to Charleston."

Kim and Eustace had never discussed having a baby. She guessed that if they'd eventually married and started a family, he wouldn't have complained about her quitting her job to raise a child. He'd never guilted her when she lost her job at Harborview Medical Center and was living off his income—wherever that income had come from. Instead, he'd only massaged her sense of self by repeatedly telling her, "You're a hell of a lot better than that last job."

The husband leaned over his wife's baby bulge and said to Kim, "What you've told us reminds me we can't ever take each other for granted. That can happen when you've been with someone for a while."

The couple kissed, and Kim frowned at the thought that she'd done much worse than take Eustace for granted. But she was going to respect his memory during this trip. She was going to reunite him with his family, and she was going to tell Malia they needed to end things—at least for now. Maybe they could eventually be together, but how would they be able to grow something that began with an affair and Eustace's suicide?

A gentle knocking sounded on the door of Kim's room.

She wiped her eyes with the back of one hand and cleared her throat. She moved the urn to a less visible spot on the rug beside her bed. Opening the door, she saw Cora, the owner of the Orange Tree B&B. They'd met last night, after Kim received her suitcase from the airport shuttle driver. Cora had been drinking mint juleps on the veranda with a couple guests. She was a pretty, wide-bodied woman with short white hair, a deeply tanned face, and light gray eyes. This morning she wore an orange-and-yellow striped dress that was perfect for her role at the B&B.

"You all right, honey? I thought I heard some tears in here."

Kim put on a smile. "Bad dream is all. I had a few of them last night."

"I've got a fresh pitcher of sweet tea downstairs. That'll wake you up. I'm afraid the breakfast hour has passed. I think there are some biscuits left, though."

Kim glanced at the antique clock above the desk and saw it was almost 10:30. She was meeting Teressa at her apartment at 4. "That's kind of you."

"I actually came up here to tell you the AC is on the fritz. We've never had problems with it before. It should be working by noon."

"I hope I didn't bring bad luck with me," Kim joked.

"Oh, I don't allow that in the Orange Tree," Cora said with a grin. "People don't worry when they stay with me. I see to it they enjoy themselves in the friendliest city in the U.S. of A."

Kim's heart felt a little lighter with Cora in the room. She told herself this trip would only be for the positive. She was fulfilling Eustace's last wish. She'd get to know more about him and where he'd grown up. And maybe she'd be able to start over in her own life.

"Come on down when you're dressed and we'll come up with a sightseeing plan for you," Cora said. "You've got a lot to see if you're only staying in Charleston for one more night."

After Cora closed the door, Kim pulled open the window curtains, filling the room with sunshine. She peered out at a charming street lined with historic houses and their lush gardens. She saw a church steeple in the distance. Before preparing for her shower, she set Eustace's urn in a patch of sunlight on her mattress.

"Bad luck be gone," she said as if it were her new mantra.

Kim struggled to maintain her cheerfulness as she wandered along East Bay Street. She was feeling anxious about meeting with Teressa. Did Eustace's sister blame her at least a little for Eustace's suicide? And what had Eustace told Teressa about her? Also disconcerting was the puzzled look on Cora's face when she'd mapped Teressa's address on her phone.

"I thought that building was condemned or something," Cora had said. "There used to be a couple shops in it. I didn't realize anyone lived there."

"That's the address she gave me," Kim said with a shrug. "What if I wrote it down wrong?"

Cora pointed at Kim's forehead and grinned. "You're too young to have worry lines, honey. You can call her if it's the wrong address. And besides, it's not a long walk from here."

Kim told herself to stop fretting and relish the warmth. It was only April 15, but the day felt like an August afternoon in Seattle. Of course, the air was more humid than what she was used to, but she was still comfortable in her short-sleeved blouse and jeans. She looked out at the placid blue waters of Charleston Harbor. "In that bay is Fort Sumter," Cora had told her, "where the first shots were fired in the Civil War." Overlooking the waterfront were regal, pillared mansions with spacious balconies. Some of the houses had bronze pineapples adorning their doors or gateposts. But what Kim found most appealing was the City Market. She was impressed by the indoor market's columned front, which resembled the entrance to a Greek temple. Inside, she passed dozens of stalls selling everything from candied nuts to sweet grass baskets to "low country lemonade."

She found the dining hall and ordered a container of barbecued pulled pork and coleslaw. She also allowed herself a small cup of lemonade mixed with rum. She set down the tote bag that held Eustace's ashes. The comfort food and alcohol utterly relaxed her, and she was grateful to be here and not be at the hospital, dealing with cancer. She wouldn't have to deal with it for nearly a week. She managed to momentarily let go of her regrets about her relationship with Eustace.

A passing woman carried a plastic bag that showed the words *PINEAPPLE EMPORIUM* and an illustration of the ubiquitous fruit.

"Excuse me," Kim said to the woman. She pointed at the bag. "Where can I find that place?"

She soon stood over a table lined with kitchenware that was either in the shape of a pineapple or decorated with its image: butter dishes, serving trays, salt-and-pepper shakers. Kim was particularly fond of a pair of pineapple mugs. She lifted them to feel their weight.

She thought of Malia sipping from one of the mugs at the tiny table in the dining nook of her apartment. It would be morning, and they would have woken up together. She forced the image out of her head, and she reminded herself she was on this trip for Eustace—and his family.

"You interested in those?" A grandfatherly man with glasses stood across the table from her. "I'll sell you the pair for $15. They make a great housewarming gift."

Kim became annoyed with herself when she realized she hadn't brought Teressa or any of Eustace's other family members presents from Seattle. She decided a gift from Charleston would have to do. "I'll take them. What's with all the pineapples in this city anyway?"

"They're a symbol of hospitality," the man said. "A 'welcome' if you will. The tradition goes back to colonial times."

"So does that mean my host will be sweet to me if I give her something that resembles a pineapple?" Kim asked with a grin.

The man winked at her. "She'll at least pretend to."

After leaving the City Market, Kim walked west, away from the harbor. The address Teressa had given her wasn't far outside the downtown core. But when Kim saw the two-story building, she understood Cora's previous bafflement. The tall, red door bearing the address number was between a couple empty storefronts. Kim peered inside the dusty window of one of the storefronts and noticed a ladder lying on the floor and a slew of empty paint cans.

Patches of cardboard blocked the window of the other storefront. Kim stepped back from the building and looked up at the second-floor balcony. The balcony's railing supported a number of almost alien-looking plants. Vines from one of the pots dangled spiky purple flowers above Kim's head. Someone spoke while Kim stared up at the flowers.

"White witch is up there, and I don't mean 'white' as in 'good.'"

Kim glanced to her right and saw a petite elderly woman in a turquoise dress standing on the sidewalk in front of the neighboring building. She held a broom that looked as if it had been in heavy use for decades.

Before Kim could respond, a younger version of the woman stepped outside the neighboring building. The words *Sadie Lady's Bakery* were above the door.

"Mama, what are you up to now? Why don't you come back in here and sit for a while?" The younger woman gave Kim an apologetic look.

"White witch pretends like she's doing nothing," the older woman continued for Kim, "but she's up to something. Her friends, too."

"Mama!" the daughter snapped. "In here now."

The mother nodded knowingly at Kim and entered the bakery with her daughter, her broom trailing behind her.

"Is that you, Kim?"

Kim looked up at the balcony again and saw a plump, dark-eyed woman smiling down at her. The woman had long black hair with bangs, and she wore a white sleeveless dress that seemed out of place among the peculiar plants. She couldn't have been older than 33 or 34.

"I'm Teressa," she said, sounding enthusiastic. "I'll be right down to let you in."

After opening the door, Teressa hugged Kim tightly. "I feel like you're part of the family."

Kim peered into Teressa's eyes, searching for some hidden sign of resentment or loathing. She only saw glee.

Teressa brought Kim up a narrow flight of stairs and into a small living room connected to a kitchen. More strange plants lined a shelf in the kitchen. A plant with thorny, leathery-looking leaves occupied the center of the coffee table in the living room. The thing reminded Kim of a Venus flytrap.

"You've got quite the green thumb," Kim said.

"The plants make this place more homey. As you saw, the downstairs of this building isn't much to look at. The landlord's renovating." She motioned toward a recliner in the living room. "Take a load off. Would you like something to drink? I've got iced herbal tea."

"Please," Kim said, remembering Cora's refreshing sweet tea from this morning. "It's getting hot out there."

Teressa eyed Kim's tote bag. "Did you bring it?" she asked in a hushed voice.

Kim removed the urn from the bag and carefully set it on the coffee table.

"Oh, you dear soul," Teressa whispered to Kim. Oddly, she showed no sign of grief. "Now you sit." She moved into the kitchen.

Kim lowered herself into the chair. She eyed a painting of a swamp sunset that hung on the wall across from her. The orange orb of the sun looked as if it were melting on the watery horizon. On another wall was a framed, ancient-looking photograph of a woman wearing a flapper dress. She had on a floppy hat and a jeweled choker. Behind her was New York's Flatiron Building.

"Is that a relative?" Kim asked, pointing at the photograph.

"That's Maman," Teressa said. She removed a pitcher of dark brown liquid from the refrigerator and filled up two glasses sitting on the counter. "My great grandmother. Mine and Eustace's, I mean. She was born in 1896." Teressa stirred the tea.

"Maman means 'mother' in French, doesn't it?" Kim asked.

"That's right. Maman was French Creole. Her family lived in New Orleans. She spent some time in New York as an actress before she went on to do greater things." Teressa brought the two glasses to the coffee table and set one in front of Kim. "It's got a little slippery elm in it. Good for the digestive system."

"Thank you." Kim eyed the glass, remembering the old woman's words about the "white witch." She told herself to drink the tea and not be rude. She tasted the cool liquid, which was somewhat bitter and surprisingly earthy. She tried not to grimace.

Teressa sat on a couch that was near Kim's chair. She touched the lid of the urn and sighed. Kim couldn't help thinking it was a sigh of relief rather than a sigh of sadness.

"You've done Eustace proud by bringing him home," Teressa said.

Kim felt her grief returning. The guilt was coming, too. She sipped her tea as a distraction. "I owe him that and more."

"You've been very good to him, Kim. Eustace couldn't ask for more."

Kim's eyes became glassy with tears. "Oh, I'm not so sure about that."

"I think your mama taught you well."

Kim wiped away a tear as it streamed down her cheek. "Actually, my mom was a pretty lousy wife—at least to my stepfather. I think she was good to my real dad, but he died when I was only 3." Kim had always suspected her dad's death from prostate cancer permanently unraveled her mom. After Kim's mom married her next husband—a charming advertising salesman who turned out to be a verbally abusive alcoholic—she developed the habits of hurling back insults at her spouse and talking to herself when she was alone. The unhappy pair died in a car accident during Kim's junior year at Western Washington University. When she received the news of her mom and stepfather's deaths, Kim wasn't surprised to hear that her stepfather had been at the wheel.

"Don't you settle for the kind of marriage I ended up with," Kim's mom had once told her. "When you meet the right man stick with him." Instead, Kim had cheated on her fiancé and saw his brain matter bits on the wall of his apartment.

Kim's tears began to flow. "I'm sorry," she told Teressa.

"No apologies." Teressa stood from the couch and placed a hand on Kim's shoulder. "Let me get you some tissue. That tea will make you feel better."

Kim lifted the drink to her lips despite its odd taste. She felt a little calmer after each sip.

When Teressa returned, she carried both a tissue and what looked like a greeting card. "Did you have any doubts about bringing Eustace's ashes to the South?" she asked.

Kim thought of how she'd wanted Malia by her side while she waited for her plane to Atlanta. She shook off the thought and told Teressa, "I want to grant Eustace's wish. He deserves that. He never let me down—and he lifted me up when I was at my lowest."

Teressa nodded and smiled. "I'm sure he did." She handed Kim the tissue and the card. Kim wiped her eyes and looked at the front of the card, which showed an illustration of two grinning, bumpy toads sitting side by side on a lily pad. Kim recognized Eustace's handwriting inside.

Dear Sister,

I wanted to share with you that Kim and I are engaged. She's a truly loyal and giving person, and I can't wait for you to meet her. I'd be lost without her.

Love,

Eustace

Kim winced at the words *I'd be lost without her*. She remembered Eustace dropping her off at her apartment one morning a few months ago, before she'd ever met Malia. He'd kissed her intensely, smashing his lips against hers. Kim had wondered about the reason for the passionate kiss. Afterwards, he stared into her eyes and said, "My life would go to hell if I didn't have you."

Kim sighed and handed the card back to Teressa. "And now I'm the one who's lost."

As Teressa placed the card on a table, Kim wondered why Eustace would write his sister about the engagement rather than call her on the telephone. Kim wanted to tell Teressa that Eustace had never even mentioned her, his brother, his aunt, or his grandmother. But she was concerned about hurting Teressa's feelings.

"There's something I wanted to ask you about," Kim said.

"I'm listening," Teressa said in a sugary voice.

"Did you know Eustace worked at a law firm in Seattle?"

"Uh-huh," Teressa said. She sounded as if she wondered where Kim was taking this conversation.

"Well, he didn't really work there," Kim said. "He lied to me. I found out after he died."

Teressa gave her a confused look.

"And he rented his place. He'd told me he owned it." She watched Teressa's face. Gone was the cheery expression of before. The woman's white skin flushed crimson with an obvious anger.

"Don't you think he'd have good reasons for lying?" Teressa asked. "You were just saying how he never let you down."

Now Kim's face was red from embarrassment. "I'm sure he had his reasons, but I can't figure out what they could have been."

"What help is it to wonder about the dead's past actions?" Teressa said. "All we can do is honor them—and their wishes."

Kim nodded and glanced down at the carpet.

"You help with research studies for a living, don't you?" Teressa asked.

Kim looked up at her. She was surprised Teressa knew about her profession.

"Well, sometimes life is like those studies, isn't it? The patients don't know exactly what they're getting into, but hopefully their being in the studies will lead to a cure, right?"

"Sure," Kim said, her reply sounding like a question.

"So maybe you just need to not think about things so hard and trust there's a reason for everything that's happened."

Kim wasn't sure if she agreed with Teressa, but she didn't want to upset the woman again. She faked a smile and said, "I suppose you're right."

"I was wondering if you could give me some time alone with my brother's remains," Teressa said in a softer voice. "I'm going to take my part of his ashes and just be with him for a bit. And then you can come back here and pick up the urn."

"Oh, of course," Kim said. She rose from her chair.

"You can come back in an hour or so. Don't spend too much time in the sun."

Before leaving, Kim glanced down at Eustace's urn. She realized she was relieved to get away from it for a while.

The air seemed muggier outside Teressa's apartment building. Kim squinted in the late-afternoon sunlight. She considered seeking refuge in the bakery next door, but a sign hanging in the window showed the place was closed. Her tote bag felt heavier even though it no longer contained Eustace's ashes.

"Shit," Kim said when she realized she'd forgotten to give Teressa the pineapple mugs. She decided she'd do it later. She left Teressa's street and shuffled along one lined with quaint houses. She didn't have the energy to admire all the porch swings, potted flowers, and ornate doorknockers.

Stumbling over a crack in the sidewalk, she had the idea Teressa had drugged her. But for what purpose would the woman do that? Kim decided she was merely jetlagged. After walking a few more blocks, she was grateful to find a park beside a small city lake. She planted herself on a bench shaded by a large oak tree. Shutting her eyes, she told herself she'd nap for just 15 minutes.

"This is wonderful," Kim sighed. She felt Malia's lips move down her sweaty neck. Malia's fingers were beneath Kim's tank top, playfully circling her bellybutton. The two women shared a quilt on the flowery bank of a brown, slow-moving river. Across the river was dried grass stretching to a small house that had been blackened by fire. A pair of dead-looking elm trees flanked the structure. Kim recognized the trees from her grandmother's backyard in Tennessee. Kim had wandered around those trees when she and her family first arrived at the house on their trip. Nana had warned her, "Watch out for the big ol' copperhead that lives back here."

Choosing to ignore the depressing view of the burnt house, Kim tried to look in Malia's eyes.

But she couldn't turn her head.

Eustace entered her field of vision as he walked past her toward the water. He wore the beautiful navy blue suit he'd worn so often to work, and he carried a shabby suitcase with a bloody towel dangling from it. He glanced back at her briefly. His black hair was sleek with product and perfectly parted. He gave her a wounded look, and then he turned back to the river.

"Wait!" Kim cried, rising.

"Don't go," Malia pleaded.

Kim attempted to turn to her again, but she couldn't. "I need to explain us to him," she said. She hurried after Eustace, who was now waist-deep in the muddy water. Kim entered the river and watched Eustace's head sink beneath the surface.

Kim dove in after him, hoping she'd be able to lift him to safety. The water was murky, and she could just barely see Eustace's figure sinking to the bottom. She swam toward him, and as she neared her fiancé, he began to disintegrate, as if he were made of bread rather than flesh. Panicked about losing him, she tried grabbing his arm.

Eustace's limb broke into tiny saturated bits and drifted downstream.

Desperately needing to breathe, Kim kicked her legs to propel herself to the surface. She stopped when she saw the form of a massive alligator floating above her, its thick tail slowly undulating.

She knew it was waiting for her.

Kim jolted awake with the thought that her foot had brushed against an alligator's tail. Her eyes shot open, and she saw her shoe rested on one of the oak tree's dark roots. She still possessed the vague idea that something horrible had happened. She sat up straight on the bench. The sky was now a twilight pink, and lights were blinking on in the houses surrounding the lake. Kim noticed her tote bag had fallen off the bench. When she dug through the bag in search of her cell, she realized that both of the mugs she'd bought were broken.

"Damn," she whispered. She wanted to curse again when she saw the time on her phone's screen: 7:38.

She'd slept for a little over two hours.

A crowd of people sauntered along the lakeside path that curved a few feet away from Kim. They stopped beneath a lamp. The fellow leading the group wore a top hat and black trench coat and carried a sign reading UNHOLY CITY TOUR.

While she picked up her tote bag, Kim heard a man mumble a question to the tour guide. The guide responded, "Yes, some say Savannah's got even more ghosts and ghouls than Charleston, but we've got our fair share of the diabolical. Did you know 50% of all slaves came through this city? Charleston was the capital of the American slave trade."

Unsettled and disoriented, Kim staggered away from the bench and started in the direction of Teressa's apartment. Night fell quickly. After taking a couple wrong turns onto poorly lit streets, she managed to find Teressa's building.

Teressa once again stood on the balcony, her elbows resting on the one stretch of railing that was clear of the weird plants. She looked serene. She didn't seem surprised by Kim's tardiness, and Kim had the suspicion Teressa had wanted her to be away for a long while. Kim once again recalled the old woman referring to Teressa as the "white witch." She wondered what had prompted that.

"I'm sorry I'm late," Kim said. "I fell asleep in a park."

"That's quite all right," Teressa sang. "We've got a slower pace in Charleston." She pointed at the sky. "Beauty of a moon tonight. It'll be full tomorrow."

Kim looked up at the bright orb, which had halos around it. The light actually hurt her eyes. She wondered again what had really been in that tea Teressa had given her.

"I'll bring the urn down to you," Teressa said.

"May I use your bathroom?" Kim needed to pee after her long nap.

"Oh, course you can." Teressa seemed startled by the request.

When they reached the living room, Kim sensed there was another presence in the apartment. The air was hazy, as if someone had been smoking inside. The space stunk like scorched meat. Kim remembered Eustace's neighbor saying his apartment had smelled of burning meat.

"I was doing some cooking while you were gone," Teressa said.

Kim didn't see any sign of a meal on the stove or counter. "What'd you make?" she asked, wanting to press Teressa.

"Nothing edible, it turns out," Teressa said with a wink. She motioned toward a hallway. "The bathroom's this way."

Sitting on the toilet, Kim glanced around the small, undecorated room. She peeked past the shower curtain and opened the drawers beneath the sink, but she didn't find anything unusual.

The only object that drew her attention was a box of black hair dye. Teressa was too young to be going gray. Kim had figured black was Teressa's natural hair color, just like it was Eustace's. But for all Kim knew Eustace had dyed his hair, too. Kim closed the drawer and flushed the toilet.

While washing her hands, she thought how she'd wanted to talk to Teressa about what it had been like growing up with Eustace. She'd planned on asking if Teressa had any photographs from his past. But now she just wanted to get away from this odd woman she no longer trusted and go to bed.

Kim found Teressa in the living room, waiting for her with Eustace's urn. Teressa carefully placed it inside Kim's tote bag.

"You feeling better, Kimmy?"

Kim managed a smile even though she loathed that nickname. Her stepfather had called her "Ms. Kimmy" when he was drunk and thought she was acting judgmental.

"I'm okay," she said, rubbing one eye. "What all was in that tea you gave me?"

Teressa shot her a surprised look, and then she offered a smile. "Slippery elm, like I told you. A bit of honey. There was some chamomile in there, too. Maybe that's what made you so sleepy."

Kim wasn't sure whether she believed Teressa. She stuck out her hand. "It was nice to meet you."

Teressa embraced her. "A real pleasure. I'm so grateful. Eustace would be, too."

Kim nodded. She started toward the staircase. On her way, she noticed the swamp painting was crooked on the wall. Teressa had either bumped into it or moved it.

"You'll be heading down to Savannah tomorrow?" Teressa asked. "Harlon's expecting you then. You told me over the phone you'd only be staying in Charleston for one night."

Kim nodded. "I'm renting a car in the morning. May I have his phone number and address?"

"Course!" Teressa said. "I almost forgot." She removed a pen and piece of paper from a kitchen drawer and began writing. She handed Kim the paper. "That's everyone's information on there. Harlon, Aunt Lizanna, Grandma Vess."

"Thanks," Kim said, depositing the paper into her tote bag.

"Did you tell a lot of people you were coming down south?"

Kim paused on one of the upper steps and looked back at Teressa. "Should I have?"

Teressa only laughed uncomfortably in response. She reached out and patted Kim's shoulder.

Her touch made Kim cringe.

The Orange Tree was even hotter than it had been in the morning. Kim didn't see Cora or any guests when she returned to the B&B around 9:30. She had no desire to talk to anyone anyway. Once inside her room, she set Eustace's urn on her nightstand and stripped off her clothes. She considered brushing her teeth, but she turned off her light and collapsed on the bed instead.

She guessed it was the middle of the night when she opened her eyes. The room was pitch black and even muggier than before. Her body ached with exhaustion, yet she couldn't go back to sleep because she heard a subtle scraping sound, like metal on metal.

It sounded like someone lifting the lid off Eustace's steel urn.

Kim's limbs tensed. She felt a chill despite the suffocating heat in her room. She didn't sense anyone standing beside her bed. She reached for her phone, which was on the nightstand, just next to the urn. She knew if she pressed the home button, the phone's screen would provide some illumination.

When the screen cast its blue light, Kim was able to see that nobody was there.

But she saw one side of the lid lift, and a thick index finger wiggled its way out of the container and curled over the edge.

Kim shrieked and recoiled from the sight. She ran from the bed to the light switch by the bathroom door. She flipped on the room's overhead light.

The lid was on the container again.

Kim cautiously approached the urn. She saw her reflection in a mirror above the night table. Her face and bare breasts were covered in sweat. She had pouches beneath her eyes.

"Just a nightmare," she whispered to her reflection. "Just a dream. There's no hand inside the urn."

Kim picked up the urn and bundled it inside her tote bag, which lay on the floor. She placed the bag within her suitcase and zipped up the luggage. She knew the urn's new location would help her sleep better.

Kim awoke to the sound of cool air blowing through a vent in her ceiling. The AC was working again. She felt surprisingly well-rested, and she saw she hadn't slept in too late today.

As if on cue, a knock sounded at her door. "Honey?" Cora called. "Breakfast hour starts now. I'm serving bacon and the best cheese grits this side of the Blue Ridge Mountains."

"Please save a place for me at the table," Kim responded. She was happy to be feeling normal again, and she was glad to be leaving today. After her experience with Teressa, though, she had reluctance about meeting Eustace's other family members. "I'll check out after breakfast," she said. "I should probably get on the road."

"I have something for you. Mind if I come in?"

"Sure."

Cora wore a bright yellow and white polka dot dress. She held a folded piece of paper. "Your friend stopped by and paid for your room this morning."

"My friend?" Kim asked with raised eyebrows.

"She left a note for you."

Kim unfolded the piece of paper and read the following:

Kim,

The least I can do for you is pay for your hotel room. Don't you dare try to pay me back. You are giving so much by bringing Eustace's ashes down here like he asked you to. Thank you from the bottom of my heart. And my whole family thanks you, too.
Grateful,
Teressa

Kim felt the warmth of appreciation as she read the note. She remembered her suspicion that Teressa had drugged her. She told herself the trauma of Eustace's passing had probably made her paranoid. It probably also caused her vivid nightmare.

Following a quick shower, she dressed and applied a little make-up. She wanted to look ladylike for breakfast with the other guests. She went to the night table to pick up her phone, and her eyes wandered to the edge of the table. Her heart began to pound, and then the phone slipped out of her hand and fell onto the carpet.

"This isn't possible," she stammered.

But she couldn't deny what she saw in the morning light: a sprinkled line of ashes showing where they'd spilled out of the urn last night.

4

"You look anxious."

Todd glanced up from his cell phone to see who spoke to him. A beautiful twenty-something woman with big brown eyes stood by his corner table in the Anti-Bellum Coffee Shop. Her curly, reddish-brown hair was tied up with a bright blue headband. She wore a yellow sundress and had a backpack over one shoulder.

"Is my angst so obvious?" Todd asked. "I guess you could say I've got a lot on my mind." He looked back at the screen of his phone, which showed the email from his mother's caregiver. The caregiver had written that his mother's strength was returning, but her dizzy spells were becoming more and more frequent.

"Tourists aren't supposed to be stressed," the woman said. She smiled widely, revealing adorable dimples.

"And it's also obvious I'm an out-of-towner," Todd said with mock defeat. He, too, was grinning now.

"I would have noticed you around if you lived here," the woman said. "You're too good-looking to miss." She blushed, as if she'd realized she'd gone too far with her flirting.

"Would you like to join me?" Todd asked. "I could use some company." Since arriving in Savannah 13 days ago—on April Fool's Day—he'd only interacted with a couple people who were involved in the movie. A spacey-eyed woman in a butterfly-collar shirt and cords had stopped by his hotel to take his shoulder and waist measurements. "For your costumes," she told him, and she didn't say much else. The following week a short, extremely shy guy with a military crew cut had visited him twice—once to take some profile shots for the make-up people and the second time to deliver a book with the title *Homes on Fire: Personal Accounts of the Burning of Atlanta*. "The director wants you to read this," the man told Todd.

Growing bored with the book, Todd called Guthrie to confirm the filming was definitely starting mid-April, like he'd said. Guthrie responded, "They'll get in touch with you when they're ready for rehearsals. Remember this is an experimental film."

What Todd remembered instead was that he'd get 25K for only a week of work. And that he didn't have to pay for his hotel room.

The woman placed her backpack on the chair across from Todd's. "I can sit with you for a while before my class starts, but you've got to drink something other than that." She pointed at Todd's Perrier. "I'll go order."

She left for the counter before Todd could offer to pay.

Todd looked down at the green bottle of sparkling water in front of him. His stomach had needed the help after last night's 11 o'clock dinner: fried hushpuppies, alligator bits, an oyster po' boy sandwich, and a couple pints of cheap American beer. He'd been trying to eat healthy over the past two weeks, hoping to define his abs for his time in front of the camera. But after another lonely day with no news of the movie, he had to indulge himself. Plus, he wanted to get out of his hotel room at the Mansion Garden Inn. During the past few nights when he'd gone to bed, he'd heard what sounded like someone pacing above his room. He wouldn't have thought much of the footsteps if he hadn't overheard other guests talking about how the hotel was supposedly haunted. Also, Todd knew nobody should be walking above him when his room was on the top floor of the five-story building.

"You look worried again." The woman had returned with two glasses of an iced, caramel-colored drink. She set the glasses on the table. "Maybe I should be giving you booze instead. But you've got to try some New Orleans coffee. This is the only place in town that serves it." She moved her backpack from chair to floor and sat across from Todd. He hoped he wasn't too obvious in noticing her crossing her long, toned legs.

"I should have paid for this..." Todd looked in her smiling eyes, waiting for a name.

"Iola. Iola from NOLA."

"I'm Todd—from the LA that's not Louisiana. I've never been to New Orleans." He sipped the coffee, which was the perfect blend of bitter and sweet. He smacked his lips in pleasure.

"It's chicory that sets it apart," Iola said of the coffee. "The milk and sugar aren't bad either." She sipped her own drink.

"You're a student?" Todd asked.

"I'm at SCAD—Savannah College of Art and Design. I'm getting my MFA in Furniture Design."

"Nice," Todd said, impressed. "You'd probably be horrified by what's in my bachelor pad."

"Oh, I don't know," Iola said, tapping a finger against her chin. "I tend not to notice a man's furniture if I'm interested in him." She blushed again.

Todd found himself turned on by her mix of aggression and naiveté.

They both sipped their coffee until Iola asked, "So what's a Los Angeleno doing in Savannah? I'm guessing you didn't come for the nightlife."

"A role in a movie," Todd said, thinking his response sounded silly. He wondered if he was the one who'd been acting naïve—or gullible—with his expectations around the part. He told Iola about Guthrie approaching him after the botched modeling job in Miami, the strange party, the past two weeks in limbo. And, before he could stop himself, he shared about his mother's cancer and his attempts to be there for her as much as possible. He mentioned he should probably be with her right now.

Iola was silent. Todd regretted that once again he'd said too much and burdened a woman with his cancer talk.

Iola finished the last of her coffee, and then she stared deeply into his eyes. "You've had to deal with a lot. It's important that you've been there for your mom, though. She'll remember that. People always remember who was there for them when they were sick."

Todd looked at her with raised eyebrows. None of his dates had shown such empathy, and Iola wasn't even a date—yet.

"I really hate to say this," Iola said, rising from her chair, "but I've got to get to class. Advanced woodworking. We're talking about beds today."

"Would you like to go out with me?" Todd blurted. "Dinner, or a walk, or anything?"

Iola smiled as she picked up her backpack. "A model's never asked me out. I'm in. When?"

"Got plans tonight?"

"I guess I do now." Iola unzipped the rear pocket of her backpack and pulled out a cell phone. "What's your number? I'll text you later about where to meet. I can pick the place since we're on my turf."

After she left, Todd finished his coffee and headed outside. Though it was late morning, heat was beginning to saturate the city's Historic District. He wandered through the square near his hotel. Before, he'd found the massive oak trees oppressive with their dark, crooked limbs that blocked out the sun. Now the trees seemed protective, and he appreciated the small fountain gurgling in the middle of the square. He pictured Iola and himself sharing one of the benches near that fountain.

Todd's ringing phone interrupted the pleasant thought, and he hoped Iola might be on the other end of the line.

Instead, a man with a thick Southern accent greeted him. "Todd Regan? My name's Harlon. You and I are going to be in a movie together. You all set to rehearse?"

When Harlon's '80s Chevy truck rumbled across a high bridge over the Savannah River, Todd realized they were leaving the city. Harlon hadn't said anything since picking Todd up at his hotel, so Todd decided to end the silence. "The rehearsal isn't in Savannah?"

"Naw," Harlon said, staring ahead at the road with an intense gaze. He couldn't have been older than 30. He had thick black hair and a mustache that made him resemble a younger Burt Reynolds. Todd decided he was handsome in a backwoods kind of way. His dark features contributed to his good looks, but he needed a haircut, and his right eye seemed a little more open than his left one. He turned that right eye on Todd and said, "We're going to the film set. It's an old plantation outside of town."

"Old plantation," Todd said, nodding in approval. "That's a good setting for a horror film. Any idea about what parts we're going to play?" He was suddenly nervous he was actually going to be acting.

"We'll talk about that later," Harlon said, sounding dismissive.

The truck soon sped along a freeway with forest on either side. Judging from the road signs, Todd guessed they'd entered South Carolina. He grew concerned that he wouldn't be back in Savannah in time for his date with Iola, but he reminded himself how much he'd wanted to start work on this film. He tried to focus on the Southern scenery.

"Are there any swamps around here?" he asked. He had no sense of the geography in this part of the country.

"Biggest swamp is south of the city, about two hours' drive. Okefenokee Swamp." Harlon gave him a crooked grin. "You like swamps?"

"I've never been in one," Todd said. "I guess I'd like to see one."

"We'll get you in one soon enough," Harlon said, slapping Todd's thigh. Todd was surprised at the formerly quiet man's enthusiasm.

"I spend a lot of time in the swamp," Harlon said. "It's the most powerful place. Gives me energy."

"For your acting," Todd said, now thinking he understood Harlon. "The inspiration of nature."

Harlon grinned more widely and looked as if he might start laughing. "That's right. For my acting. Some people got human nature for inspiration, and I've got swamp nature."

Todd wondered what would fuel his own performance in the movie. He worried money wouldn't be enough.

About fifteen minutes later, Harlon steered the truck off the freeway, and they drove along a road bordered by pine trees and green pastures. Harlon turned onto a narrow lane. Enormous oaks on both sides of the road created a canopy that lasted for about half a mile. Spanish moss dangled from the limbs like the hair of monstrous women. Even though it was only afternoon, the shade from the trees made it feel like evening. On the trunk of one oak was a sign with peeling paint and an arrow pointing in the direction the truck was traveling. The sign read *SUGARWELL PLANTATION.*

Todd figured the plantation was a tourist destination when he saw the two buses parked at the end of the lane. But as the truck neared the vehicles, Todd realized people must have been living inside. Sun reflectors and blankets covered many of the buses' windows. The windows that were clear afforded views of piles of clothes, plants, and canned foods. On the side of one bus was a mural of black snakes swimming on the surface of what looked like a pond or a lake. Todd didn't spot anyone around the vehicles.

The sight unnerved him. "Homeless people?" he asked.

Harlon frowned, as if he disapproved of the term. "Homeless people don't have homes. Those people have their own kinds of homes, don't they?"

Todd disagreed, but he didn't say anything. Instead, he eyed the white plantation house they were approaching. The huge, box-like structure was four stories tall with three red chimneys protruding from its flat roof. Seven windows lined each floor of the house. Pillars stretched from a fourth-floor balcony to the top of the front stairs. As the truck neared the fountain in the center of the house's circular drive, Todd was able to discern the building's state of decay. Some of the windows' blue shutters were either lopsided or rotting. A brown mold covered portions of the pillars and the underside of the balcony. Graffiti darkened the front door and walls surrounding that entrance. Todd thought he saw a noose hanging inside one of the first-floor windows.

"Spooky place," he said.

Harlon didn't reply. He drove around the fountain—which contained murky water and empty beer cans—and took the truck onto the overgrown lawn that stretched past the right side of the house. He parked next to an old blue Buick. The vehicles were near a well with a mossy stone covering.

Todd noticed a man and woman emerge from a copse of trees. They both looked like they were in their early twenties, and they could have been brother and sister if not twins. The sandy-haired man and woman were pale with big, gazing blue eyes that made them look feral. The woman wore a short green-and-purple floral dress and held a clipboard to her chest. The man was in jeans and a T-shirt advertising the 1970s movie *Logan's Run*. He carried a camera and a tripod.

Harlon reached behind Todd's seat and pulled out a black plastic garbage bag bulging with something. "Come on out and meet Jack and Rayna."

Todd shook their hands. "Happy to be working with you," he said. He guessed they were too young to be anything more than interns. Maybe they'd fetch lattes or lunch for the crew. Todd glanced around to see who else would be joining them, but he didn't spot anyone. He did see a row of wooden cabins through the trees. "Where are the other actors?" he asked Harlon.

"Just us today." Harlon gave him a hard pat on the shoulder and handed him the plastic bag. "Rayna will show you where to put on your costume. You and I are going to be rehearsing an important scene. Jack will film us."

"But where's the director? I haven't even met him yet." Todd regretted his antsy tone of voice.

"You'll meet him soon enough," Harlon said. "He wants you to try being in your character first. He might intimidate you if he's standing right by you, watching over you."

"Makes sense," Todd said, even though it didn't really. He reminded himself this was an experimental film. He wasn't in some Hollywood blockbuster. And he couldn't have expectations when he'd barely acted before. At least he'd be making a lot of money. He stepped toward Rayna. "Let's go."

In the shade of the trees, she told him, "I saw that advertisement with you and the panther when I was a teenager."

Todd didn't bother telling her there'd been no panther in the Sin Tight campaign. He'd posed with a tiger, a leopard, and a cheetah. He even recalled the cheetah's name—Royal—and how the 20 or so people on the set had clapped when the animal raised its paw for him to shake at the end of the shoot.

And here he was today, rehearsing for a movie he knew practically nothing about with a total of three backcountry-type strangers and not a director in sight.

"That was a cute picture," Rayna said, walking ahead of him toward the cabins. "You've turned yourself into a Ken doll in the flesh."

"Excuse me?" Todd asked, offended.

She glanced back at him. "With this movie, we're going to make you a god man—a real star."

Each of the cabins had a few stairs leading up to a small covered porch. Rayna climbed the stairs of one of the middle cabins and opened the door for Todd. "You can put your clothes and shoes in the bag when you're done changing," she said.

"All right," Todd muttered, still slightly annoyed by her comparison of him to a Ken doll. He entered the cabin, which had a dirt floor, mattress-less bunk beds, and a single window on the rear wall. The air inside the cabin was hot and stale. Todd almost asked Rayna if there was somewhere else he could change, but then he saw the canvas chair in one corner. A rectangle of tarp was beneath it, and next to it was a small table holding a water bottle and an energy bar. Most satisfying of all was that the chair displayed the name *TODD REGAN*.

Todd opened the bag so he could change, but he hesitated when he saw its contents.

A Confederate soldier's uniform.

Todd held up the gray wool coat and the similarly colored trousers. The bag also contained an undershirt, a gray cap with a black brim, and a gold-buckled belt. He wondered what kind of Confederate soldier he'd be. Hopefully, a heroic one fighting for his family, and not some slavery-loving fiend. If he was the latter, he wondered what Iola would think of him playing such a role. He wasn't sure, but he guessed she was mixed race.

This is just a horror movie, Todd reminded himself. *Not an ad campaign for the Old South or the Ku Klux Klan.* Surely, this character would stretch his acting abilities. He shouldn't dismiss the role until he knew exactly what it was. Iola could be impressed by him playing a daring part.

He draped the costume over one of the bunk beds and took off his shirt, shorts, and sneakers. He found the uniform fit him well, but the wool made the cabin feel that much stuffier. Luckily, the pants had pockets for his wallet and phone. He looked down at his bare feet and wondered if Rayna would give him boots.

Leaving the cabin with his bag of clothes, he found her sitting on the edge of the porch. She'd pulled her long, unkempt hair over her right shoulder. When she glanced back at him, Todd saw that familiar alligator tattoo on the rear of her neck.

"I've been seeing that tattoo a lot lately," he said. "Is it a film company thing or something?"

Rayna pushed her hair over her shoulder, concealing the tattoo. She gave a faint smile. "We creative people got to stick together. Maybe we'll convince you to get one, too." She stood and took the bag of clothes from him. She started toward the house, and Todd remained on the porch.

"I don't have any shoes," he said.

"It's best that you're barefoot for this scene."

Despite his annoyance, Todd walked along the path leading through the trees. He was careful to avoid sticks and rocks. He reminded himself this wasn't modeling work. Actors had to get dirty sometimes.

Harlon and Jack were waiting for them by the well. Its cover now lay on the grass. Not far from the well, the camera sat atop the tripod. Todd noticed Harlon still wore the Western shirt and jeans he'd had on before.

Harlon gave him a satisfied grin. "You look like the Southern gentleman of days gone by."

"Where's your costume?" Todd asked.

"You don't see me in this scene. I'm just here in spirit—your brother's spirit, actually. I'll be playing your brother in later scenes."

"Okay," Todd said, feeling uneasy about his performance. How would he get into the head of this character? He had no siblings in real life. Of course, he'd always wanted a brother.

"Just relax," Harlon said, as if he detected Todd's thoughts. He motioned for Todd to come join Jack and him by the well. Jack held a rattle that consisted of a wooden handle and a cluster of dark brown seedpods.

"What's that for?" Todd asked.

"Soundtrack," Jack said, as if it were obvious.

Todd peeked into the well, but its depth and darkness prevented him from seeing anything inside. He asked, "What's at the bottom?"

"Bugs, probably," Harlon said. "Maybe some bones. And the heart of this plantation."

Todd frowned at the gaping hole. "So where do you want me?"

Harlon stepped closer to him and turned Todd's body until he fully faced the well and the distant house. Harlon stood behind him and hooked a sweaty, muscular arm around his neck.

Todd's body stiffened. "What the-?"

"It's just part of the scene," Harlon said in a soothing voice, "to get you to that mental space where you need to be." Todd didn't like that he could feel Harlon's breath on the back of his neck.

"Camera time," Harlon said, and Jack disappeared from view.

Todd looked up at a large window on the top floor of the house. He saw the tattered remains of lace curtains.

"General Sherman and his troops have burned Atlanta and are heading toward the sea," Harlon said. "When you came here to your home after fighting up north, you found out the Union army killed your brother on its path to Savannah. Your brother was a much better man than you are—a more important man than you are. You know your brother's spirit is here, and you can feel him gripping on to you like I am now." Harlon tightened his hold around Todd's neck. "You want to let your brother have control of your body for a while. You know he deserves that favor."

Todd heard Jack begin shaking the rattle somewhere behind him. "What are my lines?" Todd asked, wanting to get through this as quickly as possible.

"Come into me, brother," Rayna spoke. "It's your one line, over and over."

"Come into me, brother," Todd repeated. Saying the words again and again somewhat calmed him.

"More force!" Rayna snapped. "Come into me, brother!"

"Come into me, brother!" Todd said.

Harlon's hold became even stronger. He pushed Todd up against the side of the well. Growing more uncomfortable, Todd touched Harlon's forearm to pull it away from his neck.

"Don't break the moment," Harlon said, his arm remaining locked.

Todd feared that Harlon was going to hurt him—or do worse, like send him over the edge of that well. Todd had the thought that if something happened to him, his mother would have nobody to take care of her.

"Go with it," Harlon whispered into his ear. "Show us you can do this."

"Again!" Rayna said. The rattling became louder.

"Come into me, brother!" Todd said.

"That's right, guy," Harlon said.

Todd decided he would prove he could act. He would earn all the money Guthrie had promised him. He would step up to the next level in his career, and once he was there his mother would be secure for the rest of her life. "Come into me, brother!"

"You're rocking this," Harlon whispered. "Just trust yourself—and trust us." He leaned into Todd's back, bending his upper body over the side of the well. The rattling increased in volume, as if the instrument were right next to Todd's ear.

Todd looked up at the window once more and thought he saw the curtain trembling. He soon stared into the blackness of the well. "Come into me, brother! Come into me, brother! COME INTO ME, BROTHER!"

And then Todd felt someone lift him. He heard himself repeating the words, but he was outside his body, floating upwards above the well, above the property. He saw the grass was now manicured. The house's pillars were without mold. The fountain in the middle of the drive was clean and bubbling. A woman in a pink gown stood on the house's balcony with a little girl. Slaves moved about the row of cabins. Todd looked down at the well and saw himself still in Confederate uniform. But Harlon was no longer behind him. Instead, a gaunt, lizard-like man stood with his arm around Todd's neck. The man wore a black shirt, a red vest, and a skinny necktie. He had two puffs of gray hair on either side of his balding head. He looked up at the hovering Todd and smirked malevolently.

Todd plummeted from the sky toward the mouth of the well.

"She gets into town day after tomorrow. You two are going to make sure she gets here."

Todd recognized Harlon's voice.

"You awake, Todd? Come back."

Todd cracked open his eyes and saw Harlon gently slapping his cheek.

"Come back, brother," Harlon said.

Todd found himself propped up against the side of the well. Jack and Rayna stood side-by-side in the shade of the trees. Jack held the camera and tripod. He no longer had the rattle with him. Rayna gripped Todd's bag of clothes.

"You got so involved in the part you passed out," Harlon said. "It might have been my chokehold, but I had to pull you back. You were heading into the well."

Todd remembered that creep's smirk and the view of the plantation. He must have imagined all that in some hallucinatory dream. What else could it have been?

"You were great, though," Harlon said. He looked at Jack and Rayna, and they both nodded in agreement.

"I was?" Todd touched his neck, expecting it to feel bruised. Surprisingly, it wasn't tender. "That was quite a hold you had on me," he told Harlon with a hint of irritation.

"We wanted to push you to see what you've got," Harlon said. "And you've got a lot. A+ performance." He held out a hand and helped lift Todd to his feet.

"I did it," Todd said, sounding bewildered.

"You did." Harlon led him toward the trees. "Soon enough it'll be the real deal."

"I think I'm ready," Todd said, nodding. He received the bag of clothes from Rayna and started in the direction of the cabins. He was feeling oddly confident until he stepped on a rock that cut the bottom of his foot.

"You all right?" Harlon asked Todd. They were in the truck again, crossing the same bridge they'd been on this morning.

Todd's foot ached, and he was still woozy from losing consciousness on the plantation. He thought of all the strange things he'd seen while unconscious, and the sensation of floating above the plantation. He recalled Guthrie asking if he'd ever had an out-of-body experience.

"I probably just need to eat something," Todd said. The sky had a pinkish hue. Evening was on its way. Todd remembered he was supposed to meet Iola tonight. He hadn't even checked his phone once while he'd been at Sugarwell. He pulled the phone out of his pocket and saw a text message on its screen:

I know a place that has good bbq and the best coconut cake. Interested?

YES, Todd texted. Then he noticed Harlon frowning.

"Who's that?"

"Someone I'm going on a date with tonight."

"You won't have much time for dating," Harlon said, his eyes once again on the road ahead. "If you want to bang a lady tonight, go for it. But that's about all you're going to have time for. This movie's going to keep you busy."

Annoyed by the comment, Todd became quiet. He wondered if Harlon always banged rather than had sex or made love. He realized he'd had enough of the good ol' boy for the day. He said, "Maybe when I meet the director he can tell me exactly how busy I'll be. Then I'll decide what to do with my spare time."

Harlon grinned at him. "Aw, come on. Don't be sore. I'm just saying you don't want to have any distractions while you're working. Especially distractions of the female persuasion."

"Okay, thanks," Todd said in a dismissive voice. He took a quick peek at his phone and saw the latest text:

Where are you now? I can just meet you.

Todd decided he didn't want there to be any tension between Harlon and him. After all, they were going to be playing brothers. "Listen, I'm not sore," he said. "I'm just tired is all. Thanks for driving me to the film set today. This movie's a great opportunity for me."

"For us all," Harlon said, sounding as if he wanted to add an "Amen" to his words. He steered the truck onto a freeway exit ramp.

"Have you been in many movies in the past?" Todd asked.

"Some," Harlon said, nodding. "But none as cool as this one." He turned to Todd. "Before I take you back to your hotel, I'd like to stop by my place and give you something. It's a little gift from the film crew."

Todd wanted to focus on setting up his date with Iola, but he knew he needed to show some gratitude to Harlon. "That's nice of you guys," he said. He tried not to look down at his phone as Harlon drove them into Savannah's Historic District.

The truck passed a palm tree-lined cemetery that spanned a couple blocks, and then Harlon made a left and pulled the truck in front of a three-story brick apartment building located on a corner. A staircase with a wrought-iron railing led up to the front entrance. Todd spotted a nearby street sign.

"Mind waiting down here?" Harlon asked. "My place isn't ready for company, but you'll be seeing it soon enough."

"Of course I can wait." Todd watched Harlon ascend the stairs, and then he quickly typed his message for Iola:

I'm on E Oglethorpe Ave — near a cemetery

Ellipses immediately appeared on the screen, showing that Iola was writing him back.

Colonial Park Cemetery. I'm 10 mins away. Meet at the entrance? Arch with an eagle over it.

Todd would have liked to shower and change for Iola, but he didn't want to make her wait. He was eager to see her again. He typed, *I'll be there.* He stepped out of the truck and stared up at Harlon's apartment building. Even though night had fallen, few of the windows were lit. The evening air was warm enough, but the setting of the dark building and the nearby cemetery made him shiver. He was relieved when he heard the building's front door shut.

Harlon approached him with a thick envelope in hand. "We figured you were sick of waiting for us to get the movie going. Here's a little something to make up for lost time." He handed Todd the envelope.

Todd could feel the cash inside. "Really? That's generous." The extra cash helped dispel some of his concerns about the bizarre happenings earlier in the day.

"You deserve it," Harlon said, making a thumbs-up motion. "We're happy to have you on board."

"Thank you much," Todd said, pocketing the cash. He considered putting the money toward something for his mother—maybe an extravagantly expensive bathrobe and slippers, or an overnight trip to Catalina when she was feeling stronger. He held out his hand to Harlon. "I think I'm going to walk back to my hotel. It's not far, and I'd like to see the neighborhood at night."

Harlon's tight handshake was painful. "You sure, brother?"

"I am."

Harlon patted him on the shoulder, and Todd felt Harlon's hand creep toward his neck.

"Remember the line?" Harlon asked.

Todd tried to shake off his discomfort from Harlon's touch. He offered a hearty, "Come into me, brother!"

"That's it," Harlon said, withdrawing his hand. "We'll do some more rehearsing tomorrow. I'll call you to let you know what time."

Todd stepped in the direction of the cemetery. "Good night."

"Don't spend any of that money on your lady tonight," Harlon said. "And kick her out of bed as soon as you're done. You'll need sleep."

"Aye, aye," Todd said, trying not to be annoyed. He walked away without looking back.

The cemetery was closed. Todd leaned against the locked gate beneath the arch, peering in at the lamp-lit graves. A few of the tombstones were crooked and looked as if the elements had been eroding them for centuries.

"It's pretty in the daytime."

Todd turned around and saw Iola standing on the corner. She wore sandals and a sky-blue sleeveless dress that revealed the smooth bumps of her knees. Her hair was untied, and the curly strands stopped just above her shoulders. Her dimples appeared again when she smiled. Todd found her even more attractive tonight.

He felt like kissing her, but he hugged her instead. Her blush was apparent despite the evening dim.

"You don't seem anxious anymore," she said.

"I just finished my first rehearsal for the movie. It was an interesting day, to say the least."

"Congratulations."

Todd recalled with embarrassment that he was wearing what he'd had on when he met Iola this morning. "I would have changed for our date. I just left the guy who took me to the rehearsal. He's an odd one. He lives right over there." Todd pointed in the direction of where he'd come from.

"Which building?" Iola asked, her eyes round.

"The one on the corner." Though dark, the structure was visible in the glow of a street lamp.

Iola's smile was gone.

"What's wrong?" Todd asked.

"Let's walk and talk," she said, tugging on his arm. "The barbecue place is near River Street."

Iola was quiet for the first part of their walk. They passed ornate, cheerfully lit mansions with spacious verandas and plentiful gardens. Occasionally, Todd spotted a flickering gas lamp. He guessed this neighborhood must have looked much the same in the 19th century. He imagined what the ruinous Sugarwell plantation looked like after dark.

"I have to confess something," Iola said. "I didn't just happen to see you in the Anti-Bellum Coffee Shop. I followed you there."

Todd watched her troubled face while listening intently.

"I first saw you on Abercorn Street. You were with a short man wearing a Texas Rangers tank top."

Todd thought of the shy guy with the crew cut. The man had taken Todd outside his hotel and into a nearby square for some of the profile shots.

"I'd seen that man before," Iola said, "when I was looking for my friend Allimay after she disappeared. She was involved with a cult that met at the apartment building you just came from. I saw that man come out of the apartment building a few times. I wanted to check if you were part of that cult, too."

"I'm not in any cult," Todd said, sounding defensive.

"I know. I could tell soon after I met you. There's something very innocent about you. You've got a brightness inside of you."

Todd appreciated the flattery. He wasn't used to people complimenting him on anything deeper than his looks. "That guy you saw me with is part of the movie," he said. "What kind of a cult was this?"

Iola said she didn't really know. Allimay had called her about a year and a half ago, after Iola had started at SCAD. They hadn't talked in years even though they'd grown up together and been like sisters. Allimay said she was in Savannah for a few days. They met for lunch, and Allimay told Iola how she'd been involved with these people, and she'd come up from Louisiana for some teachings at that apartment building. She said the people had helped give some meaning to her life, but she was getting away from them. She didn't like being the only black person in the group. And she said they were obsessed with swamp energies or entities or something.

Todd thought of the comment Harlon had made earlier about the swamp being the most powerful place.

Iola continued: "Allimay said the main teacher was this woman nobody ever saw, but supposedly she was able to communicate with the swamp entities, and she was 120 years old."

"Crazy," Todd said.

"Yup. And that was the last time I saw or heard from her." Iola sighed. Her face took on a deeply pained expression. "She disappeared, and her family and the detective they hired couldn't find her. I told them about the apartment building Allimay had mentioned, but neither they nor the police came up with anything." Iola's voice cracked when she said, "I'm assuming she's dead."

"Do you think they're still in that building?" Todd asked.

"I don't know. I just want you to be careful."

As they descended a staircase to the cobblestones of River Street, Todd wondered whether Harlon and the other film people were connected to the cult. Even though Harlon had made that comment about the swamp, he hadn't hinted at wanting Todd to join anything. Todd glanced at the dark water of the Savannah River and thought about the tattoo of the alligator trying to bite its own tail.

He recoiled at the memory of what Rayna had said to him: "Maybe we'll convince you to get one, too."

5

Kim was picking at a clump of hash browns and melted cheese on her plate when her cell phone rang. A knot formed in her throat as she read Malia's name on the screen. She wanted so badly to hear her voice, and yet she knew she couldn't allow Malia to distract her from her journey. She was already feeling distracted enough. It was time to tell Malia she was going to press pause on their relationship.

She glanced around the Waffle House to see who else was in the restaurant. A few heavyset and hairy trucker types ate by themselves in booths, and two lavender-haired elderly women chatted over pieces of pie. Kim decided she'd have more privacy outside.

She pushed away her plate and took the call. "Hi, Malia." She left cash on the table and headed out of the restaurant to the parking lot. She hit a wall of heat.

"Where are you?" Malia asked. "I hear lots of cars."

Beyond the parking lot was the busy US-17, which Kim was taking from Charleston to Savannah. "I'm on the road," she said, glancing at her white Ford Focus rental car. The car was in a parking space directly in front of the restaurant. "I'm still in South Carolina. I should be in Savannah in about half an hour."

"How's it going?" Malia asked, concern apparent in her voice.

Kim wanted to tell her about seeing a finger poking out of Eustace's urn last night, but she knew she'd sound crazy. And she felt like she'd somehow become weaker if she blabbered about all that. She needed to be strong. She still had three more cities to visit, and she couldn't go running home. She was going to do the one thing Eustace had asked of her. "It's going okay, I guess," she said. "Eustace's sister was a little odd."

"How so?" Malia asked.

"I'd rather not talk about it."

Malia hesitated before saying, "Sure." She sounded disappointed. "Hey, I just bought a couple cartons of eggs for Easter. It's next Sunday, you know. I was thinking you could come over and we could dye eggs together."

"I don't know if I'll be back by then," Kim said without emotion. It hurt her to be so cool to Malia.

"Well, who says we can't dye eggs after Easter?"

"Listen," Kim said, "there's something I wanted to tell you." She headed for her car, thinking she'd turn on the AC for the conversation. She noticed two people occupied the vehicle next to hers. The car was a weathered blue Buick that looked at least a couple decades old. The man and woman inside were young—maybe 22 or 23. They were as pasty-skinned as any Seattleite in the winter. They both looked at Kim with piercing blue eyes, and then they turned to each other and kissed.

Kim decided not to sit in her car. She didn't want to be close to the strange pair in case she became too emotional during her conversation. She walked toward the side of the Waffle House. Glancing back at the couple, she saw they were still making out.

"You there?" Malia asked. "What is it?"

"I'm here." Kim walked beneath a willow tree next to the restaurant. She was grateful to be in shade. She was sweating, but she didn't know if it was from the temperature or her nervousness. "I've decided I can't be with you, Malia. At least not right now. I need to focus on doing what Eustace asked of me. I owe it to him."

"But you're coming home eventually," Malia said. "What about then? Are you just going to pretend we weren't getting as close as we were?"

"I can't think about then." Kim's throat tightened again. She told herself she wasn't going to cry. "I just know I betrayed Eustace, and you and I were together when I should have been with him."

"But you didn't love Eustace," Malia said.

The words stung Kim because they were true. And not only did she not love him; apparently, she barely knew him. She was silent, overwhelmed by her thoughts and emotions.

"Do you think he would have wanted to stay with you if he knew how you really felt?"

Kim didn't like Malia making assumptions about what Eustace would have thought. She pictured his urn locked in the blackness of the trunk. She hadn't wanted to put his ashes back there, but she was still troubled by what she'd seen last night.

"Kim?" Malia asked, sounding impatient. "I'm sure what you're going through must be so hard, and so horrible. But things will get better eventually, and there's a future for you—for us. A beautiful future. I'm sure of it."

"I'm sorry," Kim said. "I've made up my mind. I can't talk more about this now."

"Kim, wait-"

"I'm hanging up, Malia. Goodbye." Kim clamped her eyes shut, holding in the tears.

She heard someone clear his throat, and she glanced at the side of the Waffle House. The young man from the Buick leaned against the building. He held up a lighter to a cigarette protruding from between his lips. He wore a tight gray T-shirt with a snakeskin pattern on it. He grinned at Kim.

Kim was disturbed he'd chosen a spot so close to her. She was suddenly self-conscious about whether he'd been listening to her conversation with Malia. She knew the South wasn't the gay-friendliest of regions.

She started for her car. Rounding the corner of the restaurant, she saw the pale woman sitting on the hood of the Buick.

The woman wore a tie dye tank top and Daisy Dukes. Her feet were bare and dirty. Kim wondered if the couple was following her for some reason.

The woman smirked at her.

Kim hurried to unlock the driver's side door. She sensed the woman staring at her as she pulled out of the parking lot. She tried not to make eye contact. "Just white trash wanting to stir up trouble," she grumbled to herself. Back on the highway, she checked her rear view mirror to make sure the Buick wasn't behind her. She didn't see the vehicle.

While driving, she kept hearing Malia's wounded voice in her head. She was crying by the time she saw the sign reading, *Welcome to the Peach State.*

Although it didn't have the charm of the Orange Tree B&B, Kim's hotel was located right next to the Savannah River, and her room had a view of the water and the immense Talmadge Memorial Bridge, which she'd crossed to get into town. The concierge told her The River Inn had once been a cotton warehouse. Directly below Kim's window was a cobblestone street leading past a praline shop on the corner. Kim considered going down there to buy a large dose of sugar and fat for her blues. She was about to pick up her purse when her phone started ringing.

She didn't recognize the number. "This is Kim."

"It's Teressa."

Kim grimaced. She told herself to be polite—and speak some words of gratitude. Eustace would have appreciated that. "Teressa, I wanted to thank you for paying for the B&B. That was too much. I'm going to mail you a check."

"Nonsense," Teressa said. "You're doing so much for Eustace—for our whole family. I called because I sensed a little tension between us before you left Charleston. I wanted to say I'm sorry if I caused that tension."

"No need to apologize," Kim said. "It was probably just my jet lag and...losing Eustace."

"Course it was," Teressa said. "I also wanted to say that thanks to you bringing me my brother's ashes, I can feel his presence again. I sensed him in the apartment last night. It's a wonderful feeling."

Kim glanced at Eustace's urn, which she'd set on the chair by the closet, and she thought about that finger curling over the edge of the urn. Why couldn't she feel Eustace's soothing presence around her? Maybe because he'd never affected her in that way, even when he was alive? His presence had given her a sense of security and reassured her she was doing the right thing—the conventional thing—with her life, but it had never truly soothed her.

"I'm glad you can feel him," Kim spoke into the phone. "That must be reassuring."

"Anyway, I'll let you get on with your day. I know Harlon can't wait to see you."

"I'm looking forward to it, too," Kim lied.

With her tote bag over one shoulder, Kim climbed the stairs to Harlon's apartment building at around 6 p.m. Eustace's urn kept bumping against her hip. Although the day's heat had diminished, Kim's palms were sweating. She'd tried calling Harlon to ask when she should come over, but she'd gotten his voicemail. She left a message saying she'd try stopping by.

Standing in the doorway, she noticed the apartment buzzer system had 12 buttons on it, yet only a few had names next to them. She located Harlon's last name—*Grable*. She looked toward the cemetery across the street and breathed deeply. *You're going to be a good fiancée and hand over Eustace's ashes to his brother,* she told herself. *And you're going to refuse any strange tea he offers you.* She pushed the button for Harlon's apartment.

Peering through one of the door's glass panels, she saw an attractive young redhead bounding down a flight of stairs.

The twenty-something woman flung open the door and squealed, "Welcome to Savannah!"

The woman had long wavy hair and wore a tight green dress and black heels. She looked like she was dressed for a date. Kim felt a little dowdy in her loose-fitting Mexican blouse, jeans, and pumps. She held out a hand. "I'm Kim."

"Orchid," the woman said. "Harlon's wife. C'mon in." She took Kim by the hand and led her up to the third floor. Kim withdrew her hand at the top of the stairs.

"Did you drive here from your hotel?" Orchid asked.

"I walked."

"You see so much more of the city that way. And this is a pretty enchanting town." Orchid was beaming. She pointed at a door. "Right in here."

Harlon and Orchid's apartment was sparse in comparison to Teressa's—and it seemed to lack a feminine touch. When Kim entered, she saw an old suede rocking chair, a black leather couch, and a coffee table with a small stack of hunting magazines on it. There were few prints on the walls—mostly photographs of what looked like dilapidated barns. Kim spotted a pale rectangle on the wall above the rocking chair, as if a painting had previously hung there.

"Evening," someone said in a booming voice.

Kim saw a man with a moustache walking down the hallway. The door directly behind him was closed. He was darkly handsome, and as he stepped out of the shadows of the hallway, Kim noticed he had a black eye. There was a pouch beneath his other eye, as if he hadn't been sleeping enough.

"I'm Harlon," he said. He gave her a slanted smile.

Kim guessed he wasn't going wherever his wife was because he wore a faded red T-shirt, cargo shorts, and boots with no socks.

"Good to meet you, Harlon," she said. She shook his hand, which showed more veins than most.

"Please, have a seat," Harlon said, motioning toward the couch. She hesitated before sitting, and he sat right next to her—a little too close. His smell was pleasant, though. The smoky scent reminded her of incense or those tiny Indian cigarettes she'd occasionally puffed on in college. Orchid perched on the edge of the rocking chair, still smiling at Kim as if she were a celebrity visiting their home.

"Sorry I look like this," Harlon said. "It's been a rough weekend."

"Harlon's cousin Sander is visiting us," Orchid interrupted. "He and Harlon went rafting for their hunting trip. The boat tipped and they both got injured."

"Oh, I'm sorry," Kim said, taken aback. "I hope you guys are okay."

"We're alive," Harlon said. "Me and my cousin both." He winked at his wife.

"Sander's resting," Orchid added. "He's Aunt Lizanna's son. You'll be seeing her next, won't you?"

"Yes," Kim said. "In Pensacola."

"I hope Teressa treated you well," Harlon said.

"Why yes," Kim stammered, "she did." She regretted fumbling her words.

"My sister's the hotheaded one in the family," Harlon said. "Sometimes she lacks grace. She always means well, though."

"I enjoyed meeting her," Kim tried to say with enthusiasm.

Orchid told Harlon, "Sweetie, you need to make sure Sander's awake by the time Kim and I get back."

"'Get back?'" Kim asked. "Are we going somewhere?"

"We're going to have some girl time, of course," Orchid said. "I took the night off from my waitressing gig. I want to show you Savannah. And Harlon would like to spend some time with…." She gave a respectful glance toward Kim's tote bag.

"Oh," Kim said. "Of course." She considered how Teressa had wanted her to leave her apartment, too. Kim thought about insisting she stay with the urn, but how rude would that seem? And did she really need to guard Eustace's ashes? After all, she'd come to the South to spread them. Plus, Harlon looked like he'd prefer a nap to her company.

Kim smiled politely and handed the tote bag to Harlon.

"This means the world to me," he said, sounding sincere.

Orchid rose from her seat and walked to the door, her heels clacking loudly on the hardwood floor. She took her purse off a hook by the door and blew her husband a kiss. "We probably won't be back before dark."

"Why would you?" Harlon asked. "This city's so much more interesting at night."

Kim stood and smiled at Harlon.

"Watch out for my wife," he said. "She's a bad girl."

Kim was pleased to hear him add, "Eustace told me you're just the opposite."

Savannah's Historic District seemed sleepy on this warm Sunday evening. Kim and Orchid strolled past grand homes that were over a hundred years old and had more character than any houses Kim had seen before. They walked through squares sheltered by massive, ancient-looking trees. Kim loved how Spanish moss was often dangling over their heads. It made her think of mistletoe.

Orchid hooked her arm around Kim's at one point and led her to the side of a building that had a waterspout shaped like a catfish. "Cute, isn't it?" Orchid asked.

Kim found her touch comforting, and she thought how she could have been exploring this neighborhood with Malia. She sighed when she recalled their conversation from earlier today. Perhaps it would turn out to be their last one ever.

"What's eating you?" Orchid asked.

Kim was startled by her intuition. She slipped her arm out of Orchid's and stepped toward the waterspout, pretending to examine it. "Why would you ask that?"

"I'm a little psychic," Orchid said. "A very wise and very old woman taught me my tricks. I use them to help people when I can."

Kim shot her an awkward smile. "Thanks for offering, but I'm fine. Really." She tried to will away the ache in her chest.

"It's all right not to be fine, Kim, considering everything you've been through." Orchid approached her and rubbed her back in a gentle circling motion.

Kim appreciated the affection. She turned to Orchid. "Did you ever meet Eustace?"

"Afraid not. Harlon told me how much Eustace loved you, though. I can see you're something special."

Kim blushed. She suddenly thought how much she wanted a drink. She knew she'd had that lemonade and rum at the City Market yesterday, and she normally tried to stay off alcohol because of her stepfather's drinking problem. But she needed to feel a little numb.

"I was thinking we could go to a restaurant or a bar," Orchid said. "You hungry?"

"I'm actually thirstier than I am hungry," Kim said with a guilty grin.

Orchid took her to a riverside tavern that was only a few blocks from Kim's hotel. The place was dim and small, and it smelled like seafood and cigarettes.

"They've got fish 'n' chips if you want any," Orchid said.

Kim shook her head as she eyed a painted portrait of a pirate with a pointy moustache and goatee. At the bottom of the picture was the name *Jean Lafitte*. "Hey, where's that Pirates' House restaurant?" she asked. She'd read about the restaurant before leaving Seattle. Built in the 18th century, the old pirate hangout was supposed to be one of the city's main tourist attractions.

Orchid shrugged. "Haven't heard of it. You sure that's in Savannah?"

Kim thought her response was odd. But for all Kim knew Orchid and Harlon could be new residents in the city. "Maybe I've got the name wrong," Kim said with a shrug. "Have you guys lived here long?"

"Harlon has," Orchid said. "I moved here about a year ago, after we got married. I'm a Florida Keys girl."

"I've always wanted to go to the Keys," Kim said. She almost said she'd heard they were as beautiful as Hawaii, but she didn't want to talk about Hawaii and keep thinking about Malia.

"I'd love to take you there one day," Orchid said, sounding sincere. "Maybe during your next visit to the South."

"Maybe," Kim said. She appreciated Orchid's offer, but she doubted she'd ever see Eustace's family again. She'd give them Eustace's ashes during this trip, and then she'd try and move on to whatever was next in her life.

"What's your poison?" Orchid asked, stepping toward the bar.

"Anything stronger than beer," Kim said. "Thank you." She glanced around at the crowd, which seemed like a mix of tourists and residents. A jukebox played a Diana Ross song, and a man and a woman danced in one corner.

Orchid handed Kim a glass. "Whiskey sour." She clinked her own glass against Kim's and said, "To family."

"To family—and to Eustace." Kim drank quickly, and she hoped her thoughts of Malia would disappear with the alcohol. She bought the next round. They talked about Kim's trip thus far, and Orchid asked her, "So what'd you think of Teressa?"

"She's...interesting." Kim instantly regretted the adjective, realizing she sounded critical of Orchid's sister-in-law.

Orchid laughed. "She's a weird one. You can say it. I say it to Harlon all the time, and he agrees with me."

Kim chuckled and sipped her drink. "Well, I think you're a fun one," she said.

"Aw," Orchid said. She gave Kim's cheek a quick pinch. She told Kim how glad she was to get out of the apartment tonight.

"It's been hard hosting Harlon's cousin. Sander's—how should I put it—got an intellectual disability."

"Oh," Kim said, her own brain fuzzy from the whiskey sours.

"He barely speaks. He stares off into space a lot. It's been worse since the rafting accident. I think it seriously spooked him falling into the water like that. We really need to get him back to Aunt Lizanna's tomorrow. You said on your voicemail that you're not leaving until Tuesday, right?"

"That's right," Kim said, taking another sip. She hesitated before asking, "Were you wanting me to bring him to Pensacola with me?"

"Harlon would kill me if he knew I was talking to you about this. He's planning on taking Sander tomorrow, but he doesn't get off of work from the post office until 4, and it's over six hours to Pensacola. And I'm worried about his own health after the accident. He hit his head pretty hard when the boat tipped over."

"His eye looked bad," Kim said with a nod.

"But if you drove Sander, you'd have to leave town a day early."

Kim thought how she'd like to show Eustace's family her loyalty. And she really did like Orchid. She raised her glass and slurred, "I can take him to Pensacola. I could use some company on the long drive."

Orchid hugged her tightly and didn't let go. Kim didn't want her to let go. She appreciated the human warmth and the way Orchid's hair smelled of strawberries. Eustace never had a scent, and he was always so stiff when they hugged.

"Harlon and I will pay for your room cancellation fee. You can spend the night at Aunt Lizanna's. She's got a big ol' house with plenty of room."

Orchid fetched them a third round of drinks. This one was a heavy pour of tequila. As Kim swallowed the alcohol and the remains of her good judgment, Orchid said, "Now you can tell me what's been eating away at you."

Kim thought of her conversation with Malia. "I just feel like I've been making a lot of mistakes. I've always wanted to have my life in order and not be like my mom, but I'm wondering if that's impossible."

"Honey, I know what it's like not to want to turn out like your mama."

Kim barely heard her. She still heard the pain in Malia's voice. She told Orchid, "Whenever I think I'm doing the right thing, I start thinking I'm doing just the opposite." She had the drunken thought, *The road to hell is paved by good fiancées.*

Orchid reached out and stroked the side of her head, bringing her out of her daze. "Honey, I think you're doing just the right thing right now—for yourself, for Eustace, for our whole family."

The jukebox began playing a Taylor Swift song.

"Oh, please come dance with me," Orchid said. "I love this one."

Kim followed her into the corner, and they danced closely beneath another pirate's portrait. Kim closed her eyes and felt Orchid take her hands. They occasionally bumped hips as they danced. Kim was feeling a little dizzy when she heard the man speak.

"Hey, Red."

Kim opened her eyes and saw the stranger was addressing Orchid. Potbellied and wearing a polo shirt and khakis, he looked like a middle-aged fraternity brother. He held a pint of frothy beer.

"Hey, Red!" he repeated more loudly.

Orchid gave him an icy look that surprised Kim. In those eyes was no sign of her former sweetness.

"You should stay away from Thorner," the man said.

"Who?" Orchid sounded disgusted.

"Thorner. White bald guy? Well over six feet? I saw you with him this morning near the cemetery. You two were carrying a huge albino snake."

"I don't know what the fuck you're talking about."

"Well, I know I went to high school with Thorner and he's always been into dark shit. You're way too pretty for-"

"Fuck off before I hurt you," Orchid hissed. She grabbed Kim by the wrist and pulled her toward the entrance. "Let's get out of here."

As they descended the stairs outside the entrance, Kim nearly fell. She braced herself against the stairway's railing and laughed. "I think I'm drunk. What was that guy talking about?"

"Local yokel," Orchid said in a dismissive voice. "These pigs will come up with anything so they can snort around a girl."

Kim descended the stairs and walked toward Orchid. She was swerving. "I've got to get Eustace's ashes," she murmured.

Orchid placed her hands on Kim's shoulders, balancing her. "You can get them tomorrow morning before you leave for Pensacola. You're sure you're okay with going?"

"'Course,'" Kim said, snickering at how she'd just sounded like Teressa.

"I got something for you," Orchid said. She reached inside her purse and pulled out a postcard showing a steamboat on the Savannah River. "Ever heard of drunk writing?"

Kim smiled and shook her head.

"It's like drunk dialing, except you write to somebody instead of call them." She handed Kim the card and had her sit on one of the steps. "Go ahead and write to somebody. Anybody. I'll mail it for you."

Kim took the pen and placed the postcard on the step. She felt Orchid looking over her shoulder. Kim wrote:

Save some eggs for me.

In the address section, she wrote, *Malia Kai.*

But she didn't know Malia's address. And she reminded herself she should be trying to forget about Malia. She crumpled up the card.

"What'd you do that for?" Orchid asked, sounding irritated.

Kim pressed a hand against her forehead and shut her eyes. She felt like she was on a rocking boat. "She and I aren't…friends anymore."

"She's someone special," Orchid said.

Kim looked up and saw Orchid was smiling smugly, as if she'd just solved a puzzle or won a game.

"I need to go to bed now," Kim said. "I haven't been sleeping well." She wandered off in the direction of her hotel. She paused once to call to Orchid, "I'll come get the ashes in the morning."

"And Sander," Orchid said.

Kim squinted in the morning light outside her hotel. She put on her sunglasses as she walked to her rental car. Now she just needed something for her headache. She chided herself for getting drunk last night and nearly saying too much about Malia. How wonderful would that be if Harlon found out she'd cheated on his brother with a woman? And why the hell did she offer to drive Harlon's cousin to Pensacola? With this hangover, she'd want silence on the six-hour drive. What was she going to talk about with a complete stranger who wasn't fully there mentally?

Eustace would be grateful you're helping out his family, she told herself while parking across the street from Harlon and Orchid's apartment building. And she should be grateful, too. When she'd checked out of her hotel, she learned that Harlon had paid not only for her cancellation fee but also for the one night she'd stayed in her room.

Kim fixed her hair in the rearview mirror and added a little lipstick. She couldn't do anything about the gray smudges beneath her eyes. "Well, I declare!" she said in an exaggerated Southern accent. "You do look a little peaked, my dear."

Orchid opened the apartment building's front door for her and brought her upstairs. Today Orchid dressed more casually—a

T-shirt, skinny jeans, flip-flops. She showed no signs of a hang-over, and she was as friendly as ever.

"I'm not going to let Harlon pay for my hotel," Kim told her in the hallway outside the apartment. "Teressa paid for my room in Charleston. Eustace's family can't keep spoiling me like this."

"Oh, yes we can," Orchid said, wagging a finger at her. "Harlon will get mad if you try and pay him back. You're doing us a huge favor."

"It's nothing," Kim fibbed. "I'm going to Pensacola anyway."

Inside the apartment, Orchid sang, "We're here."

While they waited for Harlon, Kim wandered across the living room and glanced out a window. She saw the building had an inner courtyard with a large circular fountain, a couple marble benches, and some lemon trees. A few branches had broken off one of the trees. "That looks like a pleasant place to sit," she said.

"We were just out there yesterday morning," Orchid said. "Sander needed some sun. Didn't you, Sander?"

Kim turned toward Orchid and saw Harlon standing in the living room with a stunningly handsome man who was about a foot taller than him. The man looked as if he were around Kim's age. He had curly brown hair and eyes with longish lashes. A mole on his cheek accentuated his features. He reminded Kim of someone—maybe an actor she'd seen in a movie or a TV show or a commercial.

"Happy Monday," Harlon said. "This is my cousin Sander."

"Pleased to meet you," Kim said. She left the window to shake Sander's hand. When she neared, she saw he had a dark purple bruise around his neck. His pink collared shirt hid most of the discoloration.

Harlon must have noticed Kim's look of concern because he said, "The bruise is from a rope that got wrapped around his neck during the accident. We're lucky it didn't kill him."

"Yes, I'll say," Kim replied. Sander barely lifted his arm, and Kim shook his limp hand. He looked back at her with glazed eyes that didn't seem to fully register her. Something about those eyes reminded Kim of Eustace.

A phone started ringing, and Kim, Harlon, and Orchid all glanced around them for the source of the noise. Kim realized it was coming from beneath the couch, which was just behind her.

"Oh, that's mine," Orchid said. She quickly lowered herself onto her knees and reached under the couch. When she fished out the phone, Kim saw it had a scratched screen. The name *MOTHER* was on that screen.

Orchid laughed and said, "Mom always calls Monday mornings." She pressed a few buttons on the sides of the device until it became silent.

Kim noticed a tense look on Harlon's face.

He went to a table and picked up Kim's tote bag. "Here are the ashes. Thank you so much for bringing them."

The urn felt lighter. Kim wondered how many ashes he'd taken, and exactly what he'd done with them. "I'm sorry I didn't make it back last night so we could spend some time talking," she said. "I would have loved to hear more about your family and what it was like growing up with Eustace."

"You'll hear about all that from Aunt Lizanna. Don't worry about not coming back. I understand you two had some fun. I told you my wife's a troublemaker." He winked at Kim, and then he hugged her. "We'll walk you out to your car."

Outside, Harlon gave her a driving map with Aunt Lizanna's phone number on it. "She knows you're coming today," he said.

Kim thanked him profusely for paying for the hotel. During their conversation, she occasionally glanced at Sander. He'd shuffled rather than walked out of the apartment, and now he glanced around the street like he was surveying an alien world.

"He might need to sleep a lot," Harlon told Kim. "Just let him."

Orchid nodded in agreement.

"I'll try not to play my death metal music too loud," Kim joked, but neither Harlon nor Orchid laughed. Kim hugged them again and then opened the car door for Sander. He gave her a brief look of recognition, as if he momentarily understood who she was, and then he got inside the car.

Kim had rounded the corner and was driving parallel to the cemetery when she heard someone call, "Todd!"

A pretty woman in her early twenties ran alongside the car. She banged her fist on one of the doors.

"Hey!" Kim said, stepping on the brake pedal. "Don't hit my rental car."

The woman ignored her. "Todd," she said, looking at Sander through the partially open passenger-side window. Sander turned toward her, but he made no sign of recognizing her. He didn't bother rolling down the window.

"His name's Sander—not Todd," Kim said. "I'm taking him home to Pensacola."

The woman shook her head. "Todd, you were supposed to meet me at the fountain two nights ago. What'd they do to you? What happened to your neck?"

Kim was losing her patience, and her headache had worsened into a throbbing pain in one temple. She glanced in the rearview mirror and saw an old blue Buick creeping around the corner.

That couple really was following her.

"I need to go," she told the woman. "I'm sorry. He's not who you think he is."

"Todd!" The woman tried the door handle. Luckily, it was locked. Kim pressed her foot on the gas and sped past the cemetery. She took a sharp right turn, losing sight of her pursuers.

6

"You saw him, too? The ghost has been showing himself lately."

Todd heard the man's voice coming from the hallway out-side his hotel room. He lay in his bed in his underwear. He'd only woken up about 10 minutes ago. He hoped he'd remembered to hang the *Do Not Disturb* sign on the door handle. The man speaking must have been a hotel worker cleaning rooms.

Todd heard a woman murmur a question, and the man responded, "We think he's an indentured servant from the 18th century. One of those European folks who agreed to serve a master for some years to pay off the passage to the New World. Wealthy folks 'round here used indentured servants before they used slaves. Anyway, back when there was a mansion here instead of a hotel, an Irish servant died in a really horrible way."

The woman spoke, but Todd couldn't make out her words.

The man continued, "So you've heard about it. Well, that's one of the stories about why the brothers killed him. But I've also heard there never was a sister for him to seduce. I've heard the teenagers clubbed him to death because they found the servant eating alone at their family dining table, and I've also heard they did it because they were just plain bored rich kids and there wasn't much to do in Savannah at the time. What's the same in all the stories is the brothers chopped him up with a hatchet and buried his body parts in different areas of the property. That's enough to keep someone from resting in peace."

The tale gave Todd goose bumps, and he pulled the comforter up over his body.

The woman said something else, and the man responded, "The ghost hasn't shown himself to anyone in a long time. He must be getting worked up over something—or someone. Normally, people just feel a cold spot in the elevator or they notice some of their toiletries are missing or they hear him walking on the roof at night."

Todd frowned. He'd heard the footsteps above him again last night, only it had sounded like someone was dancing rather than walking. The noise had kept him awake for a while, but he was so pleased about his first date with Iola that he'd managed to fall asleep. He was still happy this Saturday morning. He and Iola were going on a picnic. He glanced at his clock and saw it was nearly 10 o'clock. Iola would be picking him up in half an hour. He climbed out of his bed to go shower, and he paused when he heard the man speak again.

"He's not going to harm anyone. Ghosts show up because they want attention. They're not trying to scare us. They're trying to communicate with us. Sometimes they're even warning us."

Todd shook his head and continued into the bathroom. He bravely yanked open the shower curtain and said, "Come on, Todd. Ghosts are bullshit."

Todd told Iola about the specter while she drove them out of the city center to Bonaventure Cemetery. Today she wore a green ruffled blouse and a short gray skirt. He tried not to gawk at her smooth, sunlit thighs while he talked to her.

"I'm not surprised your hotel is haunted," she said. "Practically every building in Savannah is. I don't pay much attention to the ghost stories, though." She took one hand off the steering wheel and patted him on the leg. "I care more about the living."

"That must be why we're going to a cemetery for lunch," Todd joked.

"It's not your average cemetery," Iola said.

Twenty minutes later, after leaving Iola's Fiat and wandering past the Bonaventure Cemetery gates, Todd was in complete agreement with her. Mossy oaks, lush ferns, and dwarf palmettos were everywhere, giving a greenish tint to the light in the cemetery. Crossing the grounds—which, Iola said, covered nearly 100 acres—they passed pillared tombs and statues of winged angels and forlorn-looking women.

Todd's phone started ringing while he peered down at the stone figure of a soldier sleeping in a fetal position on a grave. Todd recognized the local number.

"Hey, Harlon," he answered.

"Rehearsal time, boy. You ready?"

Todd turned to Iola and mouthed the word, "Fuck." She gave him a questioning look.

"I'm sorry, but I can't come over right now," Todd spoke into the phone. He searched for an excuse, and he remembered the laundromat around the corner from his hotel. "I'm in the middle of a couple loads of laundry. I didn't hear from you this morning, so I didn't think we'd meet up until this afternoon."

"Can you be here by 1?" Harlon asked, sounding disgruntled.

"One o'clock?" Todd looked at Iola.

She grinned and shook her head. She held up a couple fingers.

"How about 2?" Todd asked.

"No later," Harlon growled before hanging up.

Todd truly did regret not being available, but he was feeling less keen about his acting gig after what Iola told him about that cult. He also felt like this date with Iola was important. He went to her and wrapped an arm around her waist. "I guess I'm being a bad actor," he said.

After winding past dozens of graves, they reached a bluff overlooking the Wilmington River. The sun beat down on the blue water while a ceiling of Spanish moss shaded Todd and Iola. She removed a picnic blanket from her backpack.

"Thank you for taking me here," Todd told her while he helped unfold the blanket. "I'm starting to realize why people love this city so much."

"I can't say I love it more than I love New Orleans or else I'd be a traitor," Iola said, lowering herself onto the blanket. She reached inside her backpack and pulled out wrapped sandwiches and bottles of root beer. "But the cities are almost neck and neck. I don't think I'll ever leave the South. I don't care what my mom says."

Todd sat beside her. "What does she say?"

"She moved to Denver after she divorced my dad. She tells me it's a much more open-minded place. She claims to have been fed up with Southern white men, but I think she was really just fed up with one—my dad."

"He's still in Louisiana?"

Iola nodded. "He's not a bad man. He's just bad with his finances. He tends to make all his money disappear in casinos. But he promised he'd quit by the time I finish school. He wants to help me when I start my furniture design business."

"I'm sure you'll do fine, help or no help."

Iola unwrapped the sandwiches. "I hope you like fried chicken. I usually only eat greasy Southern food when I'm with out-of-towners." She smiled and added, "Not that I don't like eating it."

Todd bit into the sandwich and savored the combination of meat, pickle, and aioli. "Love it," he said, no longer caring whether he had six-pack abs. After all, he wouldn't be showing any skin in the movie if he were going to be wearing a wool coat.

He was on his second bite when he noticed a bald man who seemed to be staring at them from across the cemetery. The towering man stood next to a distant grave marker that was in the shape of a cross. A woman appeared from behind the cross, and the pair walked in the direction of Todd and Iola. The man was leading.

Todd set down his sandwich. As they came closer, he saw the bald guy resembled a skinhead in his Confederate flag T-shirt and red suspenders. He wore black jeans and boots that reached halfway up his shins. He was glaring at Todd.

Todd stared back at the man. He'd never been in a fight in his life, but he was willing to take on this racist beast to protect Iola.

The woman had long, wavy red hair. Her purple tube top and tight jean shorts revealed her narrow waist and curving hips. She was oddly familiar.

"No way," Todd whispered to himself.

She was that woman from the party in Miami.

"Your name's Orchid, right?" he asked her as the pair neared.

Orchid passed her friend and approached Todd and Iola with a smug look on her face. She stood over them, her flip-flops on the edge of the picnic blanket. She looked down at Iola with disapproval. "You sure move fast, Todd," she said.

"Excuse me?" Todd asked. He glanced at Iola and saw the confusion on her face.

"I didn't think those two days we had in Miami made me anyone special," Orchid said, "but I'm surprised to see you up to the same tricks with another woman so soon after that." Orchid looked at Iola again. "Todd took me on a picnic, too."

Todd stood, accidentally knocking over his bottle of root beer onto the grass. "I don't know what you're talking about. We barely met at a party, and that's the only time I saw you. What are you doing here anyway?"

"Visiting my friend Thorner, of course." She motioned toward the bald man. "We grew up together. He's like a brother to me, and brothers don't like guys disrespecting their sisters."

Thorner nodded. He was still glaring at Todd.

"I haven't disrespected you," Todd said, frowning. "What you said isn't true. I don't know what you're up to here, but-"

"Have you kissed him yet?" Orchid asked Iola. "I'm not even going to mention what kind of a lay he is, but I can tell you he's a lousy kisser. That's probably why he has to jump from girl to girl."

"You can get the hell out of here," Iola snapped.

Todd shot her a surprised look. He wondered if she'd believed everything Orchid was spewing.

"We'll go," Orchid said. She stepped off the blanket, and Thorner started back toward the graves. Before joining him, Orchid turned to Iola. "Ditch him, sister. There are much better rides in the amusement park."

Todd stared at them in disbelief until they disappeared behind a tomb. He stepped back to return to his place on the blanket, and his shoe landed on his sandwich. "Damn it," he muttered.

Iola stood. "Let's go," she pleaded with him. "No sense in pretending this picnic isn't ruined."

As they walked back to the Fiat, Todd assured her that Orchid had been lying. He told Iola how the woman had been at that weird party in Miami, and how she'd helped orchestrate the challenge with the turtle. "I barely even talked to her," he said.

"Don't worry about it," Iola said, but Todd couldn't shake his awkward feeling.

He was quiet with worry as Iola pulled the car out of the parking space, and his limbs tensed when the vehicle passed a weathered bus parked in a field not far from the cemetery. He saw sun reflectors in the dirty windows and a Louisiana license plate. The bus resembled one of those that had been at the Sugarwell Plantation yesterday.

"What is it?" Iola asked. She took her eyes off the road and looked in the direction of the bus.

"Nothing," Todd said, trying not to reveal his dread. "Just a coincidence." Yet he wasn't sure about his words. Too many coincidences were occurring: Orchid showing up at the cemetery,

Harlon living in a building that had housed cult members. Todd had the depressing thought that maybe he'd made a major mistake by coming to Georgia. Rather than rising in his career, perhaps he was falling into some kind of trap.

He would have consoled himself with the fact that he'd at least met Iola, but he figured he'd never see her again after the excruciating incident in the cemetery. When she slowed the car to a stop in front of his hotel, he said, "So I guess today was our last date."

She gave him a perplexed look. "Why would you say that?"

"You mean you're still up for seeing me? You actually trust me?"

Iola slipped her hand into his. "I know you didn't have anything with that woman. She was lying. She said you took her on a picnic, too. But you didn't take me on a picnic. I took you." Iola leaned over and kissed Todd on the lips.

Todd was beaming. "I'd really like to get together with you after my rehearsal tonight."

Iola squeezed his hand. "Definitely. I want to make sure you're safe."

"I'll be careful," Todd said. He grinned. "I can handle cult members. I'm used to being around warped people after working in the fashion industry for so long."

"I'm serious," Iola said, poking him in the stomach. "How about we meet at the fountain in Lafayette Square? It's on Abercorn, below Colonial Park Cemetery. Eight o'clock all right?"

Before leaving the car, Todd said, "Thank you for believing in me."

Todd tried calling his mother's landline while he crossed the lobby of the Mansion Garden Inn. He stopped walking when the caregiver answered.

"Hi, Tammy, it's Todd." He stood in front of a framed black-and-white illustration of the Savannah riverfront. In the picture,

19th-century laborers unloaded massive sacks of cotton from a boat. "Can my mom talk right now?"

"I'm sorry, but she's sleeping. She was having dizzy spells again this morning."

"They're not getting any better?"

"I'm afraid not. I know she'll feel better when she hears you called, though. How's the movie going? She and I have both been wondering. She's so proud of you."

"It's going great," Todd said, feigning confidence. "Please tell her that. I'll try calling again tonight."

"She could call you when she wakes up."

Todd thought how angry Harlon would be if he took a call in the middle of rehearsal. "I'll call her," he said. "And Tammy? Please give her my love."

Todd checked the time on his phone as he approached the door of his room. It was 1:13. He could relax for 20 minutes before heading over to Harlon's. He looked forward to eating the half a sandwich Iola had given him before he left the car.

He swiped his key card in the reader on the door, and a little red light blinked. He tried again multiple times, but the door still wouldn't open. Giving up, he started back down the hallway toward the elevators. He planned on asking the front desk for a new card.

He was waiting in front of the elevators when he noticed the figure at the end of the hallway. The ceiling light above the man wasn't working, so it was difficult to see his features. He had black hair and an extremely pale face. Todd thought he saw dark circles around the man's eyes. The man wore what looked like a white linen shirt, and he had on blue breeches, white stockings, and shoes with buckles on them. Behind him was a doorway leading to an unlit hotel room. The man stared at him.

"Hello?" Todd asked in a nervous voice. He thought of the tale about the indentured servant, but he told himself he wasn't looking at a ghost. There was no such thing. Surely, the man was in costume.

The man didn't respond. He stepped backwards into the shadows of the room, and he pointed at his chest and then at Todd. He motioned for Todd to join him in the room.

Growing anxious, Todd repeatedly pressed the button for the elevator. He looked toward the man again and gasped.

Floating in the darkness of the hotel room was a naked, limbless torso splattered with blood.

The elevator doors opened, and Todd jumped inside. Before the elevator descended, he heard a door slam shut down the hallway.

Todd's forehead was covered in cold sweat by the time the elevator reached the lobby. *That wasn't real,* he told himself as he started toward the front desk. *That was your nerves, your imagination.*

"Are you all right, sir?" a plump, raven-haired woman asked from behind the front desk.

Todd breathed deeply to collect himself. *Your nerves,* he repeated in his head. "My key card isn't working," he told the woman.

"What room are you in?" she asked with a smile.

"505."

"Oh, you're Mr. Regan." She looked at her computer monitor and then glanced up at Todd. "You're all checked out."

"What?"

"A Mr. Harlon Grable paid your bill today. He's the one who originally reserved your room. He said you'll be staying with him."

"But what about my stuff? My suitcase is in the room."

The woman shook her head. "Mr. Grable took your things."

"You let him in my room?" Todd asked, outraged.

The woman stared up at him with remorse. "I'm sorry, sir. He told us you gave him permission."

Todd kept hitting the buzzer for Harlon's apartment until a red-haired man with a tattooed face opened the door. The skinny, malnourished-looking fellow was dressed in a desert camo T-shirt and dirty jeans. Todd was momentarily speechless while he took in the many tattoos covering the man's head. He saw a sinking ship, a vulture, cypress trees, the words *Bayou Baby.* On one side of his neck was the familiar alligator tattoo.

"I'm here to see Harlon," Todd told him.

The man brought Todd to a third-floor apartment where Harlon sat in a rocking chair, his bare feet up on a coffee table. He wore a Confederate uniform, and he held another, folded uniform in his lap. Beside the rocking chair were Todd's suitcase and carry-on bag.

"You're a little early," Harlon said.

"That's because I couldn't get into my hotel room," Todd replied with annoyance. He remembered the gruesome torso down the hallway from him, and he forced the memory out of his head. That hadn't been real, and he couldn't allow any distractions. "Why'd you take my stuff without telling me?"

"You were getting too comfortable there. We need to keep you on edge for the movie. Oh, and I figured your laundry was all done because your suitcase seemed full."

Todd tried not to blush when he remembered his lie about the laundromat.

"This is Bird, by the way." Harlon pointed at the man with the tattooed face, who was now setting up a tripod in the center of the living room. "He's going to do some of the camerawork."

Todd nodded coolly at Bird. He then went back to scowling at Harlon. "I don't think I'm up for rehearsing today."

"What do you mean, brother? You're just pissed off about the hotel, aren't you?"

"What I mean is I haven't met a director. I don't know the title of the film. And now I'm starting to question whether this movie's even going to happen."

Harlon laughed loudly, and Bird added a chuckle.

"It's already happening," Harlon said. "And you were awesome yesterday."

Todd wondered if he could be overreacting. Maybe Iola's story about the cult and the appearance of Orchid at the cemetery had made him paranoid. He'd been less than sane today. After all, he did see a limbless man floating in a hotel room.

"*The Skin That Fits,*" Harlon said in a calming voice.

"What?" Todd asked.

"That's what we're calling the movie: *The Skin That Fits.*"

Todd was actually impressed with the title.

"The director comes first thing tomorrow," Harlon said. "If he doesn't show, you're welcome to walk. But I'm asking you to stay with us here, in this apartment, tonight."

"Why can't I be at the hotel?"

"You and I need to bond before tomorrow. We've got a scene together in the morning—in front of the director—and it's one of the most important ones."

Todd still felt uncomfortable with the situation, but he figured he could talk to Iola about it when he saw her at the square tonight. And he didn't want to ditch the movie on day two of rehearsing. He needed that money more than ever with his mother's health deteriorating like it had been. He had no siblings or other family members to help him with the bills, and what if his mother soon had to move into an assisted living facility? Plus, there were the costs associated with her house: the recent hike in her property taxes, the long overdue roof repairs, the rogue jacaranda tree that should go because it was threatening her neighbor's fence.

"I'll think about spending the night," he told Harlon. "Should we get on with the rehearsal?"

"You betcha, brother. We're going to do a dialect test in a few minutes. Here's part of the script."

While Harlon reached for some papers on the coffee table, Todd noticed a painted portrait on the wall behind the rocking chair. The man in the painting was the reptilian-looking fellow Todd had seen during his hallucination at the plantation. The man had the same long, narrow nose and pointed chin and patches of gray hair on either side of his head. He even wore the same red vest and skinny necktie.

Todd pointed at the picture with a shaky finger. "I've seen him. It was when I passed out during the rehearsal yesterday."

Harlon smiled and sat up straight in the rocking chair. "Everything's working then. You're already opening up to the dead."

"The dead?" Todd remembered the floating torso and the tale of the indentured servant.

"That's Grandpappy in that portrait," Harlon said. "He was part of my family. He was the biggest patriarch in the family, actually. He died in 1921."

"Why would I see him?"

"Because he wanted you to. That rehearsal helped you tap into your abilities—the abilities you need for this movie. Every great artist needs to be able to see through that veil to death and the afterlife."

Todd felt like Harlon was complimenting him, but the flattery didn't help his discomfort. He would have preferred never having seen that man.

"I think we've chit-chatted long enough," Harlon said. He handed Todd the script. "Hold on to this."

Todd glanced at the top piece of paper. Various words appeared in yellow highlighting: *Yonder, chaperone, cane fields, bride.*

"I'll show you where we'll be sleeping tonight." Harlon stood and tucked the extra uniform under one armpit. He picked up Todd's luggage.

Todd wondered at the word "we," but he didn't say anything. He followed Harlon down a hallway and into a small room with two single beds, each pressed up against a wall.

"We're sharing a room?" Todd asked with dismay.

"Tomorrow's the big scene with the two brothers," Harlon said. He set down the luggage by one of the beds. "We need to stay in each other's company until then. Tomorrow you let your brother's spirit enter your body."

Todd couldn't help but shake his head. He decided he'd spend the night with Iola. Surely, he wouldn't lose his acting job if he refused to share a bedroom with Harlon, would he?

"Don't worry," Harlon added. "You may be pretty, but you ain't my type of girl. Now get dressed before we listen to you speak like your character." He handed Todd the uniform. Before leaving the room, he added, "I'll let you keep your shoes on this time."

When Todd returned to the living room, he noticed a camera was on the tripod and Bird was in the kitchen, placing a small paper package in the refrigerator. Todd wondered if it was meat from the grocery store or a butcher shop. His stomach grumbled, and he regretted throwing away his half a sandwich on the hurried walk to Harlon's apartment.

"I haven't eaten since this morning," he told Harlon, hoping he would offer something.

"It's good you'll have an empty stomach for this rehearsal. Food will make you lazy." He pointed at the hardwood floor. "Sit."

Todd lowered himself onto the floor with the script, and Harlon sat directly across from him. Their knees almost touched. Bird approached the pair with a ceramic bowl, and Harlon instructed, "Your phone goes in there. We can't have any distractions."

Todd reluctantly pulled his cell phone out of his pocket and deposited it in the bowl. He knew his mother was supposed to call, and Iola might text him.

"Pick something to read," Harlon said, tapping the script with one finger. "Something that's highlighted."

Harlon glanced down at the paper. "Window," he said. He noticed Bird move behind the camera and point it in his and Harlon's direction.

"Say win-DOH," Harlon instructed.

Todd repeated the word.

"Now wind-UH."

"Winduh," Todd said.

"Good," Harlon said. "Now another one."

"Naked."

"Say NEKK-id."

"Nekkid."

"That's right," Harlon said. "You need to let go, though. Breathe like this." He inhaled and exhaled quickly, as if he were blowing up a balloon as part of a race.

Todd imitated him.

"Faster," Harlon said. "Faster!"

Todd felt himself growing lightheaded with the rapid breathing.

"Make room for he who comes," Bird spoke from across the room.

Todd glanced at the tattooed man, and Harlon snapped, "Don't look at him. Look at me. And keep breathing. This is going to help you get into character."

Todd did as he asked. He began to feel dizzy. The room grew dim, and Todd saw a green glow coming from behind Harlon's head.

Bird once again chanted, "Make room for he who comes."

"Breathe faster!" Harlon barked at Todd. The green light was growing stronger while the room became darker.

Todd couldn't stop the breathing when he tried. He felt a sensation at the back of his neck. It was as if his skin were splitting without any pain. He watched his right arm lift. He wasn't consciously moving it. He gave Harlon a panicked look.

"Don't be scared," Harlon said.

Next, Todd's left arm lifted. Todd wasn't controlling or even feeling his body. His entire being seemed to be trapped in his head.

"You're doing beautifully, brother," Harlon said.

Whatever controlled Todd's body made him move into a standing position. The room was now entirely dark except for the green glow behind Harlon's head. Todd watched in terror as tendrils of green light slowly wrapped around Harlon's face, forming a glowing mask.

Todd whimpered when he saw Grandpappy's face appear where Harlon's had been.

"Make room for he who comes," Bird said, and then the green light became blackness.

Todd slowly opened his eyes and saw Grandpappy's portrait on the wall. The dead man seemed to be staring down at him. Todd was lying on his side on the floor. He heard footsteps behind him, and then he felt a hand on his shoulder.

"You did it again, boy," Harlon said. "Passed right out."

Todd lifted his body into a sitting position. He felt like he'd been working out at a gym for hours.

"You went through what you had to go through," Harlon said. "You were great."

"At what?" Todd asked, sounding skeptical.

"Giving up control. Being the kind of vessel actors need to be. We'll do more with the dialect tomorrow morning, before the director gets here. We'll ease up on the breathing, though."

Todd wanted to ask about the green glow, but he thought he'd sound crazy. Surely, the quick breathing had triggered the visuals and the idea that someone or something else had seized control of his body. When he was in a sitting position, he noticed the apartment's windows were dark. It was night already.

"What time is it?" he asked, thinking of his 8 o'clock date with Iola.

"8:15," Harlon said.

"I need to go," Todd said, standing as quickly as possible. A wave of dizziness almost made him fall.

Harlon looked at him with a furrowed brow. "That's not going to happen."

Even Bird—who was removing the camera from the tripod—seemed offended by Todd's declaration.

Todd remembered Harlon's disapproval of his first date with

Iola. "I just want to go out for a short walk," he told Harlon. "I need some air. I'll be back soon enough." He planned on finding Iola at the fountain in Lafayette Square. He'd tell her what had happened as part of the rehearsal today and ask if he could spend the night. She'd help him decide what to do next. He couldn't think properly in this airless apartment.

"A walk around the block is fine," Harlon said, motioning toward the door. "But no further than that."

Todd staggered toward the exit in a daze. His body continued to ache. He told himself he'd get used to moving when he was outside. He managed to fake a smile for Harlon and Bird before leaving.

Once he was on the sidewalk, he felt like running away from the apartment building. He hobbled across the street to the sidewalk bordering the cemetery, and then it hit him. "Shit," he said, glancing down at his outfit.

He still wore the Confederate uniform.

And his cell phone was still upstairs.

He didn't want to go back up there. He needed to see Iola. He needed her clarity, and he wanted to hold her.

He ignored some passersby who snickered at his outfit. He kept his eyes on the distant square, and as he approached that square, he thought he saw Iola standing by the fountain. He started to run in her direction, but he lost his balance and fell against a tree. He was about to call Iola's name when someone yanked him backwards by the collar.

He reeled around and saw Bird.

"Your mama needs to talk to you," the man said. "She called your phone. She's in a bad state."

"My mother?" Todd asked, instantly worried. He glanced at the fountain, but he no longer saw anyone beside it. He started with Bird in the direction of the cemetery.

7

Sander stirred in his seat when Kim turned off the freeway in Tallahassee. With the exception of a bathroom break, Kim had been driving for about four hours. Sander had slept the entire time. It was almost 3 in the afternoon.

"I'm getting hungry," Kim said. "How about you?" She glanced at Sander, who appeared to have fallen back asleep. His pale skin had a grayish tint to it. Despite his sickly coloring and stiff posture, he was remarkably handsome.

Kim focused on the road ahead, watching for restaurant signs. Even though she'd driven for so long and her blood sugar was plummeting, she was in good spirits. She was pleased with herself for helping Eustace's family. After she returned to Seattle, they would remember her for both delivering Eustace's ashes and driving Sander all the way to Pensacola. Maybe these deeds made up a little bit for her betrayal of Eustace during their engagement. She glanced over her shoulder to make sure Eustace's urn still sat upright in the middle of the backseat.

She pulled the car into the small parking lot of a taco shop and partially lowered Sander's window to wake him. A blast of muggy air and the smell of grilled meat entered the vehicle. Kim touched his forearm, which was surprisingly hard. His long eyelashes fluttered.

"I'll get us some food," she told him, and then she left the car.

Kim glanced outside the taco shop's front window while she waited for her carne asada plate and the chicken burrito she'd ordered for Sander. The sky was clouding up. Sander remained motionless in his seat. Kim kept eyeing the road, expecting to see a blue Buick roll into the parking lot. She hadn't spotted the couple during her drive to Florida. She'd noticed a red car that appeared in her rearview mirror a few times, but she decided she was just being paranoid. She hadn't seen it in the past couple hours.

Kim now saw movement in her car. Sander was frantically slapping his hand against the windshield.

"I'll be right back," Kim said in an alarmed voice to the woman who'd taken her order. She ran across the pavement, feeling a few heavy raindrops on her head. She opened Sander's door.

"Can't breathe in here," he said in a raspy voice. His eyes were closed and his eyelids twitching. "Too confined. The helping hands aren't helping."

Kim remembered the words *HELPING HANDS* on that box in Eustace's apartment. "Sander," she said in a firm voice. "Sander, wake up!"

He lifted his arm to smack the windshield again, and Kim caught his hand.

"Sander!"

He opened his eyes, but he didn't look at her. He gazed through the windshield.

Kim reminded herself of Orchid's words: *intellectual disability*. She wasn't sure about what to do or say.

"Señora?" The woman from the taco shop stood in the entrance. "Your lunch."

"I've ordered us food to eat in the car," Kim told Sander. "Do you like Mexican?"

He still stared straight ahead of him with glazed eyes.

"Stay here." Kim gently shut the door and went to fetch their meal. When she came back outside, rain fell more heavily.

She hurried inside the car, wondering what she should try and talk about with her awkward passenger. She had over two hours of driving ahead of her. She didn't say anything because Sander was asleep again.

And he had Eustace's urn in his lap with the lid off.

Kim found the lid between his feet. She placed it on the urn. She didn't like glimpsing Eustace's powdery remains inside. She carefully lifted the container and set it inside her tote bag, which was on the floor behind Sander's seat.

Before opening the bag of food, she watched Sander's face. She wondered what would happen when he awoke and saw the urn was no longer there.

He wouldn't hit her, would he?

Kim turned onto Aunt Lizanna's street at around 6 o'clock. Thankfully, Sander still slept. The rain had stopped, but dark clouds continued to loom overhead. The suburban neighborhood was about a mile from the Gulf, and while the homes were humble, the yards were large. Kim was trying to read an address on a brick lamppost when a car swerved around her and braked in the road.

It was a red Fiat—the same car she'd seen during her journey to Pensacola.

Kim stepped on the brake pedal and tightened her grip on the steering wheel. She wondered if she should try driving around the Fiat.

The driver's side door opened, and the woman who'd chased after Kim's car in Savannah stepped out. As the woman approached, Kim saw her face in the headlights. She appeared a little less desperate than before. Now she just looked dejected. She soon stood outside Kim's door.

Kim rolled down the window. "What do you want?" She sounded frustrated.

The woman glanced past her at Sander, who somehow had remained unconscious. Her eyes met Kim's. "I'm sorry I startled you. My name's Iola, and I'm not trying to cause any trouble. I'm here because of my friend."

"You actually followed us?" Kim asked.

"I managed to catch up to you on the freeway—but I also knew the way you were going to get to Pensacola. It's how I drive home to New Orleans."

"Iola, I told you his name is Sander. He's not the man you think he is." Not that Kim knew much about him either. She still wondered why he'd had Eustace's urn in his lap.

Iola peered inside the car at Sander again. "That's Todd. I should know. I kissed him two days ago. He was supposed to meet me Saturday night, but he never showed. Those people in that apartment building brainwashed him or something. I can tell you're not one of those people. You seemed too surprised by me in Savannah."

"Who do you mean by 'those people'? Harlon and Orchid?"

Iola nodded. "I think they're in some sort of a cult. The cult members did something to my friend Allimay, and now they've done something to Todd."

"A cult?" Kim asked. "Are you kidding me?"

Iola shook her head. "I'm very serious." She stepped closer to the window and said, "Todd!" Her eyes were tearing.

"He's not going to respond," Kim said, glancing at Sander. His head was slumped forward, and his square chin almost touched his chest. "I've been with him all day, and he hasn't spoken to me once."

"That proves they did something to him."

"Well, they told me he's out of it because he was in a boating accident." Kim wondered about Iola's accusation, and then she dismissed it. If Harlon and Orchid had actually done something to "Todd," why would they introduce him to her and put him in her car?

"Are you involved in the movie?" Iola asked. "Todd was supposedly going to be in some film they were making."

Kim shook her head and rubbed one bleary eye. "No movie. Listen, I'm pretty exhausted myself, and I'm almost at my destination. I don't know what else I can tell you."

"Who's he seeing?" Iola said, sounding suspicious.

"His family. I'm staying with them for a night or two."

"You're not from the South, are you?" Iola asked.

"Seattle."

Iola nodded like she'd proven a point. "Would you please do me one favor?" She reached inside her pants pocket and handed Kim a business card. The card identified her as *Iola Benoit – Furniture Designer.*

Iola asked, "Would you call me so we can talk more about this? I'm going to spend the night in a motel nearby. I can talk or meet you at any time."

Kim recalled some of her stranger experiences with Eustace's family. She remembered her suspicion that Teressa had drugged her and that man's claim that Orchid had been carrying an albino snake. "Okay," Kim said, nodding. "I'll call you."

Iola gave an appreciative smile. That smile dropped when she glanced at Sander once more. "Goodbye, Todd," she said.

It began to pour as Iola returned to her car. The rain soaked the young woman's yellow blouse, giving her a defeated look. She made a U-turn and waved at Kim as she drove past the rental car.

Kim waved back.

Aunt Lizanna's house was a few blocks away from where Kim had left Iola. A picket fence bordered the trimmed lawn that gently sloped up to the beige ranch house. Palm trees lined both sides of the structure. To the right of the home was a white church with a spire and a sign out front reading *Cane Road Baptist Church.*

Aunt Lizanna's home reminded Kim of the rambler where she'd grown up in a middle-class neighborhood in Kent, Washington. She recalled hugging her mother after Kim's stepfather had completed one of his drunken verbal assaults. "We have the normal American home," her mother had said. "Now I just want us to have the normal American life."

"Sander," Kim said. "You're home."

Sander didn't stir.

Kim reached for his hand, but she withdrew her fingers when she felt the coldness of his skin. She had the frightening thought he was dead, but then she saw his chest was moving with his breath.

Someone tapped on the driver's side window, making Kim flinch. She turned around to see a bald man in a pastel-blue suit and pink tie standing in the rain. Kim opened the door so she could talk to him.

"I'm Guthrie, Lizanna's boyfriend. Let me help you."

"I can't seem to wake Sander."

"I'll get him moving. You go on inside, where it's dry." Guthrie came around the car and opened Sander's door.

Kim popped the trunk so she could retrieve her suitcase.

"I'll grab your bag for you," Guthrie said. "You go on and get. You've done enough today already."

Kim was glad he appreciated her efforts. "If you insist," she said. "Thank you." She lifted her tote bag off the floor in the rear of the car. Before leaving the vehicle, she watched Guthrie hold a vial of something beneath Sander's nose. The smelling salts or whatever it was he used took effect immediately. Sander lifted his head and blinked repeatedly. He didn't appear to notice the urn was missing from his seat. He turned toward Kim and gave her the same look of recognition he'd given her in Savannah. Again, his eyes reminded her of Eustace's.

"He knows me."

"Sure he does," Guthrie said. "You've been together in a car all day. Now get before the rain soaks you."

Kim ran up the walkway to the house. The door opened, revealing a thin but fit-looking woman with a dark tan and long silver hair. In her hair was a string of red glass beads that were a little too weathered to be fashionable. Kim guessed she was in her mid-fifties—much older than Guthrie, who couldn't have been 40. She wore a plain violet dress that matched her eyes. Those eyes seemed to peer deeply into Kim's, as if she were inspecting her soul.

"So glad to meet you," the woman said, holding out a hand. "I'm Aunt Lizanna."

"Thanks so much for letting me stay here, Lizanna," Kim said as she shook her hand.

"Please call me Aunt Lizanna. I feel like I'm your aunt since I was Eustace's."

Kim smiled. "Of course I will." Aunt Lizanna's eyes had left her and were taking in Guthrie and Sander, who came up the walkway.

Aunt Lizanna looked gravely concerned. "I don't like his color," she said.

Guthrie had his arm around Sander's waist. Aunt Lizanna took her son's hand and snapped at her boyfriend, "Leave him be. You bring her suitcase inside."

Kim smiled gratefully at Guthrie as he passed her and entered the house. She turned to Aunt Lizanna. "Sander slept almost the whole way down here. I'm assuming Harlon told you about the boating accident."

"He did," Aunt Lizanna said, eyeing her son's face. She put on a smile for her guest. "A mother always worries, you know. I'm sure he's going to be just fine, though." She motioned for Kim to enter her home.

Beyond the entranceway was a living room with minimal furniture: a couple mid-century sofas, a coffee table, a low-backed chair, a TV set. Side-by-side above a fireplace mantle were painted portraits of a skinny, balding man in 19th-century attire and an elegantly pretty woman with a 1920s-style hairdo and black pearls around her neck.

"I know who that woman is," Kim said, pointing at the portrait. "Teressa told me about her—Maman—Eustace's great grandmother."

"That's right," Aunt Lizanna said. She now had her arm around Sander's shoulder.

Guthrie approached them along a hallway. "I put your suitcase in your room," he told Kim. He glanced at her tote bag. "Are the ashes in there?"

Kim removed the urn.

"May I?" Guthrie asked, holding out his hands.

Kim gave him the urn, and he went to set it on the mantelpiece, just below the portraits.

"This is the special place in our home," he said.

A door opened on the other side of the living room, and a lean young man who wasn't much older than a teenager stepped out of the doorway. He had messy blond hair and wore a tight orange T-shirt with the word *HOTLANTA* on it.

"This is Kilby, my other son," Aunt Lizanna told Kim.

"Nice to meet you, ma'am," he said, coming over to shake Kim's hand. He then turned to his brother. "Welcome home, Sander." He sounded oddly reverent when addressing his sibling.

"How was the drive?" Aunt Lizanna asked Kim.

"Good," she chirped, not wanting to be negative. "A little long, but that was to be expected." She considered mentioning Iola, but she decided against it. First, she wanted to talk to Iola more. She also wanted to see if she had any suspicions while staying in this house. So far, she had a warm, comforting feeling among these people.

"I've got pork chops on the stove," Aunt Lizanna said. She pointed toward a dining room that was to the right of the entrance. Kim could see a doorway connecting the room to a kitchen.

"Dinner will be ready in half an hour," Aunt Lizanna told Kim. "Why don't you get settled in your room and have a shower if you like, and then we'll all sit down together. We're happy to have family join us."

"I'm happy to be with you," Kim said.

Kim had just dropped her wet towel on the carpet of her bedroom floor when she heard Sander's voice coming from the room next to hers. Her small, cube-like chamber contained a single bed and a suede beanbag chair. The only decoration was a little painting of an orange grove. She cupped her ear against a patch of wall next to the painting so she could listen to Sander.

"Where are the helping hands?" he moaned. "I don't see them. I don't see the green fire." He began sobbing.

"Sander," Aunt Lizanna snapped. "Remember what we taught you. Remember what you're going to...." Her voice trailed off, and then there was silence. Kim had the thought Aunt Lizanna was aware of her listening.

Kim soon heard a gentle knock on her door. She quickly moved away from the wall and snatched the towel off the floor to cover her body.

"Kim?" Aunt Lizanna asked. "Pork chops are ready. How 'bout you?"

"Be right there." Kim dressed in a hurry. She glanced at her cell phone, which lay on her bed. She thought of how Iola had asked her to call.

This is a family's house—not a cult center, she reassured herself. But she decided she'd phone Iola when she was certain that nobody could overhear her. She headed down the hallway toward the dining room.

She was surprised to see Sander sitting at the table. The only empty seat was next to his. Kim smiled politely as she lowered herself into that chair. Aunt Lizanna and Guthrie sat at the ends of the table while Kilby was across from Kim and Sander. Kim could hear the pouring rain outside the dining room window.

"Green beans?" Aunt Lizanna asked, offering her a bowl of the steaming vegetables. Kim reached in front of Sander for the bowl because he wasn't moving. He stared down at a small pork chop and a glob of mashed potatoes on his plate. His skin looked more blue than gray now.

"We thought you two should sit together because you calm him," Aunt Lizanna told Kim. "Thank you for taking such good care of Sander."

"It was nothing," Kim said, spooning beans onto her plate. "I was coming to Pensacola anyway." She reached for the platter of pork chops.

"That's a long way for you to drive," Aunt Lizanna said. "At least you got to see some more of the South. I always feel more connected to a place when I drive through it."

Kim nodded. She remembered how on the family trip to Tennessee, her mom had driven her and her grandmother around the area where Nana lived. They popped inside small-town shops and stopped by the homes of Nana's friends. Her grandmother had told her, "Your ancestors walked these roads, and so some part of your soul knows these roads, too."

"I've always felt connected to the South," Kim told Aunt Lizanna. "Even before I met Eustace. My mom was from Tennessee."

"Blood ties are the strongest," Aunt Lizanna said in an assured voice. She raised her eyebrows and gave Kim a sympathetic look. "I hope you haven't been too lonely on your trip."

Kim thought of Malia's smile, and the way she always hugged her so tightly.

"What with Eustace being gone and all," Aunt Lizanna added.

Kim felt a twinge of guilt when she realized she'd been thinking of Malia instead of Eustace. "Of course I miss him," she said. She worried she sounded defensive. To change the topic, she asked, "What was he like when he was growing up? Nobody's told me that."

"Independent," Aunt Lizanna said with confidence. She glanced at Sander, but Kim didn't notice any change in his demeanor. "Smart. Gifted. Special."

"Helping hands," Sander suddenly spoke. He sounded angry. "But I'm still stuck in here, where it's dark! It's dark!"

"Do you want to take him to his room?" Aunt Lizanna asked Guthrie.

Guthrie nodded. He set down his fork and picked up his napkin. As he wiped his mouth, Kim noticed the tattoo on the back of his hand.

It was the same as Eustace's—an alligator trying to bite its own tail.

"Eustace had that tattoo." Kim blushed when she realized her tone was suspicious.

"That's right," Aunt Lizanna said. "Guthrie copied him because he liked it so much."

"That's right." Guthrie left his chair and moved toward Sander. "I said, 'I've got to have that, too!'" His words sounded disingenuous.

Kim nodded. She decided she'd ask Iola if she'd ever seen a tattoo like that on anyone in Savannah.

"Another thing about Eustace when he was growing up," Aunt Lizanna said. "He was always kind of a trailblazer—and everyone followed him."

Kim would never have guessed that about her fiancé. She'd always found him to be reserved.

"I think it's time for bed, buddy," Guthrie told Sander. "You've got to sleep off that boating accident so you can do some more fishing—or hunting."

Sander remained silent. Fortunately, he didn't resist when Guthrie took hold of his arm and guided him out of his seat.

"The good news is the rain's going to stop tonight," Aunt Lizanna told Kim. "It's going to be a beautiful sunny morning tomorrow. Kilby's planning on taking you to the beach so you can see the spring break scene. It's quite a spectacle. It'll be even more so since the college kids have been stuck inside because of the rain."

Kilby nodded dutifully and smiled at Kim.

"Are you going to stay here?" Kim asked Aunt Lizanna. She remembered how Teressa and Harlon had both remained at home with Eustace's ashes while she'd gone out somewhere.

"Guthrie and I have some long-overdue chores we need to attend to," Aunt Lizanna said. "Would that bother you if we didn't come with you?"

"Not at all," Kim said, putting on a smile for Aunt Lizanna and Kilby. She thought of Iola's request again, and she decided she'd definitely call her tomorrow.

Sometime in the middle of the night, Kim awoke to the sound of her bedroom door clicking shut. She couldn't see what time it was because there was no clock on her nightstand. She could only see a tall, shadowy figure approaching her from the doorway. As the person entered the moonlight that came through her window, she recognized Sander. He was naked except for black briefs. He reached out toward her with both hands.

"Maman," he said in a needy voice. "Maman."

"Sander," Kim spoke, startled. "What are you doing in here? Go back to bed."

"Maman!" Sander sat on the foot of her mattress and then moved to lie on top of her.

Kim tried to push him away, but his body was heavy and his limbs oddly rigid. "Sander!" she screamed.

Her bedroom door flew open and Aunt Lizanna and Guthrie rushed into the room.

"Sander!" Guthrie barked. He pulled Sander off the bed and led him out of the room. Aunt Lizanna momentarily stood by Kim's mattress.

"I'm so sorry," she said. "We appreciate your patience with him. We're also grateful for all you've done for us. Eustace is so lucky to have you." She wandered toward the doorway.

As she left, Kim wondered why she hadn't used the past tense. Eustace *was* lucky to have her. He didn't have her anymore.

In the morning, Kim sensed Aunt Lizanna wanted her out of the house. Aunt Lizanna wasn't exactly rude to her, but the woman busied herself with folding laundry in the living room, and she didn't offer Kim breakfast.

"Kilby's going to take you to a good breakfast spot near the water," Aunt Lizanna said. "I've got towels and sunscreen and a beach umbrella for you two in a bag by the door."

Kim noticed Sander still wasn't up when they left the house. She'd listened for him through the wall after she'd put on shorts and a shirt over her swimsuit, but he didn't make a sound.

"You remember to keep your tank top on," Aunt Lizanna told Kilby when they headed down the walkway. "You know the doctor doesn't want you exposing that place where he removed the mole. And make sure Kim doesn't get sunburnt. We can't have her turning into a lobster before she goes to New Orleans."

The sunshine and heat had indeed returned, and the day felt tropical even though it was only 9:30.

"I'll come back here if I start to turn red," Kim said.

"Kilby's got other options for you than this boring house," Aunt Lizanna said. "There's the lighthouse—or the Wentworth Museum. They've got all kinds of historical artifacts there. Much more interesting than old Guthrie and me."

"Oh, I doubt that," Kim said. When she reached the car, she glanced back at the house and thought that once again Eustace's family had arranged her exit after she'd delivered his ashes.

Kilby certainly wasn't interesting. He had little to say while he sat across the table from Kim in the Prawn Palace, a small, thatched-roof restaurant with a view of the Gulf. And his mirrored aviator sunglasses annoyed Kim because she felt like she was looking at herself while she ate her crab eggs benedict.

"So are you in school?" she asked when it was clear Kilby wasn't going to ask her a question.

"I take some classes here and there." He took another massive bite of his shrimp po' boy sandwich. Mayonnaise dripped down his chin.

"You're working then?"

"Sure, I'm working."

Apparently, he wasn't going to volunteer information about where he worked. Kim was glad he was eating so quickly. She wouldn't need to keep trying to have a conversation once they were lounging on the beach. She wondered why Aunt Lizanna would think Kilby would make an amusing tour guide for a woman who was nearly 30.

She asked, "So are you planning on moving out of your parents' house?"

"I already moved out."

Kim stopped cutting her English muffin and watched Kilby. "You don't live in the house?"

"Oh," he said, looking flustered. "I mean yeah, I live in the house. I don't know what I was talking about." He shoved the last of the sandwich into his mouth.

Kim stared at him for a moment, confused. She wasn't done with her meal when he placed a wad of cash on the table and asked, "Wanna go to the beach now?"

She put down her knife and fork. Relieved, she said, "Yes, let's get out of here."

She would have appreciated the beach if there weren't so many spring breakers crowding it. The stretch of white sand was littered with oiled, buffed, bronzed, and nearly naked bodies. All the voices drowned out the sound of the aqua-green water lapping at the shore.

Kim remembered one particularly gray morning in Seattle when Malia vowed to take her to Hawaii someday. Malia wanted to show her all her favorite beaches from when she grew up. But Kim now thought with a sigh that she was sharing her sunny beach experience with a boy bore.

"Wassup, cutie?"

Kim looked to her right and saw a trio of blond beauties in T-shirts with Greek letters on them. The sorority sisters were addressing Kilby. Kim supposed she would also find him to be cute if she were a vacuous 21-year-old. She noticed two of the girls held large Slurpee cups, and she suspected there was more than sugar and ice in the drinks when she saw the way the girls were swaying on the sand.

"How y'all doing?" Kilby asked them.

Kim stepped back, not wanting the girls to think she was his mom.

"What's with the wife beater?" the prettiest one asked. "You shy, or is that just how guys dress on the Redneck Riviera?"

Kilby glanced at Kim and then back at the girls. "I can't-"

"Take it off," said the girl who seemed drunkest, and then all three chimed, "Take it off!" The girls swarmed around him, and one of them yanked up his tank top, exposing his abs.

"Hey, no!" he said, grinning.

A second girl helped pull the tank top up past his head. The girls fled with the stolen piece of clothing, and Kilby pursued them. He gave up the chase after only a few steps.

That was when Kim saw what was between his shoulder blades. Instead of a wound from a mole removal, there was a large, circular tattoo of an alligator chasing its tail.

The same tattoo as Guthrie's—and Eustace's.

Kim had trouble breathing. She realized Aunt Lizanna hadn't wanted her to see that tattoo. And Aunt Lizanna hadn't wanted her in the house. But what were Aunt Lizanna and Guthrie doing in that house?

Kim needed to know. She pretended not to have noticed the tattoo. "I'm going to find a bathroom," she called to Kilby.

"Wait," he said, but she continued toward the ramp that would lead her from the beach to the street.

"I'll meet you by the rainbow umbrella," she said, pointing at an umbrella that sheltered another gaggle of college girls. "Make some friends."

She quickly pushed past bodies to get to the ramp. As she moved, she grew hot with an unexpected anger. She was pissed Aunt Lizanna had concealed the truth about the alligator tattoos. She was furious about Sander invading her bedroom, Eustace lying to her about working at a law firm and owning a condo.... She glanced behind her once and saw Kilby attempting to follow her. When she was at the top of the ramp, however, she lost sight of him.

Kim considered calling Iola, but before she met with her she wanted to see if anything was happening inside the house. This was her chance to find out what exactly Eustace's family did once she'd left the premises. Maybe she was taking a risk by surprising Aunt Lizanna and Guthrie like this, but her insistence on knowing was greater than her fear. Plus, her car keys were in her bedroom. She'd left them there so she wouldn't lose them at the beach.

She hurried along the sidewalk until she found a parked yellow cab. She told the driver the name of Aunt Lizanna's street.

Aunt Lizanna's neighborhood was peaceful and bright with sunshine. Few houses had cars in front of them. Kim figured most residents were at work on this Tuesday morning. A couple blocks away from Aunt Lizanna's, she noticed a dilapidated bus parked on the street. Ratty quilts covered some of the windows, and on the side of the vehicle was a painting of a vulture.

The taxi driver pointed at the bus and joked, "Must be lost."

"I'd say."

No car was parked in Aunt Lizanna's driveway, and all seemed calm. After leaving the taxi and ascending the walkway to the house, Kim heard the sound of a gardener trimming shrubs on the side of the Baptist church. She peeked through one of the house's front windows. She didn't spot anyone in the living room or dining room.

She wondered if she was being paranoid coming here, but she reminded herself Aunt Lizanna hadn't wanted her to see Kilby's tattoo. And Iola had mentioned a cult. Before trying the front door, she reached inside her purse and removed her phone and the card Iola had given her.

She texted Iola: *I'd like to meet you. Where? My name's Kim by the way.*

After sending the message, she turned the door handle.

The door was unlocked.

Kim quietly shut the door behind her and peered down the hallway, wondering if Aunt Lizanna and Guthrie could be in their bedroom. She didn't hear anyone. She turned toward the living room and noticed Eustace's urn was no longer on the mantelpiece. The portraits above the mantelpiece were also missing.

She hastened down the hallway and retrieved her car keys from her room. She looked into the bedrooms on either side of hers. They both contained unmade beds, and she was surprised to find that they were nearly as sparsely furnished and decorated as hers.

She returned to the living room and glanced around the space. Her eyes widened when she spotted the stack of photo albums on one of the shelves of the TV stand. Upon removing the albums, she saw each one had a small label on its front: *Alabama Kin, Mississippi Kin, Sander....*

She opened the *Sander* album and gasped. Horrified, she dropped it on the carpet. She collected herself and kneeled. With a shaking hand, she lifted the cover of the album and realized she'd really seen what she'd thought she'd seen.

A photograph of a sandy-haired teenager with a slit throat. He was lying on a lawn, and crouching beside him was a woman wearing a fish head mask. Even though the woman wore a mask, Kim sensed she was smiling at the camera. Among the brown and silver hair protruding from the lower part of the mask was a string of red beads.

"Fill the shell!" Aunt Lizanna cried out in the next room. Kim dropped the album again and glanced at the door through which Kilby had come last night.

"Fill the shell," Aunt Lizanna repeated, "and take what is yours."

Kim cautiously approached the door. She placed her ear against its surface.

"It's yours, Sander," Aunt Lizanna said. "Sander the heir. Sander the successor."

Kim turned the doorknob and cracked open the door. The large chamber appeared to be a rec room. Kim saw a couch with the man and woman's portraits upright on its cushions, as if they were serving as an audience. Next to the couch was a table supporting what looked like an alligator skull. Opening the door further, Kim spotted a plate on the carpet. Two dismembered, burnt-looking hands lay on the plate. Kim began to feel nauseous, and her own hand was trembling even more than before. She kept pushing the door open until she saw Sander, and then she froze.

He was on all fours on a muddy tarp in the center of the room, dressed only in his underwear. He stared down at the floor. Aunt Lizanna kneeled over him, shaking out the contents of Eustace's urn onto his back. His skin was covered in dirt and ashes. Fortunately, both his hands were intact. Surrounding the tarp were Guthrie and the weird couple who'd followed Kim in the blue Buick.

"Look!" the young, pale woman said. She pointed at Kim.

Aunt Lizanna glared at Kim. "Grab her!"

Kim tore through the living room, not looking behind her. She tripped on the two stairs that led up to the entranceway, and she came down on the hardwood floor with a bang. Her cell phone slid out of her purse. As she grasped for the phone, Kilby opened the front door. He gave her a bewildered look.

"Get her phone," Guthrie told him. The bald man placed a meaty hand on Kim's back, pressing her against the floor.

"Let me go," Kim said, trying to lift herself. She wasn't able to rise. She felt like a fool for letting herself get caught. She should have paid attention to the warning signs and what Iola had told her.

"We'll let you go," Aunt Lizanna said from the living room. "But you'll be going where we want you to go."

Kim managed to look in the direction of the living room. She saw Aunt Lizanna standing by the door to the rec room. The pale couple stood in the center of the living room, staring at her with icy blue eyes.

"Anything on the phone?" Aunt Lizanna asked Kilby.

"A message," he said. *"Sunshine Coffee Shop in 15 minutes. Meet you at the bar."*

"Go there," Aunt Lizanna told the couple. "And have the bus follow you." They walked past Kim without looking at her and left the house.

"Please," Kim said, "I just want to go home."

"You're going to New Orleans," Aunt Lizanna said.

Guthrie released his hand from Kim's back. She grabbed her purse and stood. She tried to snatch her phone out of Kilby's hand, but he lifted it above his head, out of her reach. He tossed it to Guthrie.

"You can't make me go anywhere," Kim hissed at Aunt Lizanna.

"I suppose not," Aunt Lizanna said, folding her arms. "But there's this very steep staircase your friend Malia goes down to get to her car after work every day. Imagine if she tripped on that staircase. The poor pretty thing could easily break her neck."

"Malia," Kim whimpered, shaking her head. She thought of Orchid watching her write Malia's name on that postcard.

She asked, "If I go to New Orleans you'll leave her alone?"

"Course we will," Aunt Lizanna said. She opened the door to the rec room further. "But I don't understand why you wouldn't want to go to New Orleans with your future husband."

Kim was speechless. Finally, she asked, "My future husband? You know my fiancé's dead."

"Is he?" Aunt Lizanna asked. She peeked inside the rec room. "Sander, come on out."

Sander slowly entered the room, caked in a layer of mud and ash. He no longer shuffled when he walked. He seemed more cognizant than before. He gave Kim a grateful look and smiled. "Kim, my helper. My chaperone."

"Eustace?" Kim asked. Her eyes began to tear. Even though that wasn't Eustace's body, that was his voice. And that was the way he had so often looked at her.

"His name was Sander before he took on the false name Eustace," Aunt Lizanna said. "Sander's spirit now has a new home."

Kim shook her head, not believing what was happening. "That's impossible," she whispered. Eustace couldn't be back. It was an ugly thought, but Kim knew she didn't want him back.

"The swamp made it possible," Aunt Lizanna said, nodding. "Now are you going to be by your fiancé's side voluntarily, or are we going to have to force you?"

Kim looked at Eustace and saw he was awaiting her response. She felt sick again. When the nausea passed, she spoke. "I'll go with him to New Orleans."

But she knew she was only going for Malia's sake.

8

"Where's my cell phone?" Todd asked as he entered Harlon's apartment. He felt physically exhausted, and he had trouble focusing. He braced himself against one wall. He tried not to look at Grandpappy's portrait. "I need to call my mother back."

Bird trailed him inside the apartment.

Harlon shut the door, and then he pulled Todd's phone from one pocket of his gray Confederate trousers. "She said she'd try again tomorrow. She wants to rest tonight."

Todd grabbed the phone out of Harlon's hand. He checked the recent calls and saw his mother had indeed phoned. Bird hadn't lied about her calling. He also noticed Iola had texted him. *Where are you? At Lafayette Sq now,* she'd written.

"Did my mother say anything else?"

"Just that she's not doing well," Harlon said, "and she wanted to talk to you. You shouldn't have wandered off. I told you to stay near here."

Todd squinted down at the phone's screen again, wondering what he should tell Iola. Her text now looked fuzzy.

"I thought that rehearsal would wipe you out, buddy," Harlon said. "Why don't we call it a night? Tomorrow's a big day for you."

Bird stepped beside Todd and slipped his cell phone out of his fingers. Todd didn't have the energy to resist. He tried to reach for the phone again, but sudden dizziness made him cease the effort.

"Let's not worry about things," Harlon said. "We'll put the phone back in the bowl, and you'll hear it if it rings. Right now you can't let it distract you. You need to rest."

Todd watched Bird deposit the phone in the bowl on the kitchen counter. Todd stepped toward that counter, but he retreated back to the wall after he thought he was going to faint. "Why am I feeling like this?" he asked in a weak voice.

"You've connected with the afterlife," Harlon said. "That takes a lot out of you. Now come on and get in bed." Harlon hooked his arm around Todd's and led him down the hallway toward the room with the twin beds.

Todd lay down on one of the mattresses, still clothed. He didn't want to spend the night here. He wanted to stay at Iola's. He couldn't hold on to that thought, though, because the ceiling was slowly spinning. He wondered if he should insist on calling his mother. But he closed his eyes, and sleep washed over him like a wave.

Todd still felt submerged when he awoke sometime in the middle of the night. Moonlight came through the window, illuminating the bedroom. Harlon lay on the bed across the room from Todd's. Harlon still wore his uniform. Todd shuddered when he realized Harlon was staring at him.

"How you doing, brother?"

Todd attempted to sit up, but his body was too weak.

"Just go back to sleep," Harlon said. "Our pivotal scene's in the morning."

"My mother," Todd said.

"She hasn't called, and she won't for a long while. Remember that we're three hours ahead of her here in Georgia."

Todd looked toward the door, worried he wouldn't hear his phone if it rang. The door was closed, and propped up against it was the portrait of Grandpappy.

"What the hell?" Todd asked, gaping at the picture.

"I thought I'd bring him in here since you two have connected."

Todd's vertigo was returning. He lay back on the bed, feeling defeated. "This is crazy," he muttered.

"This is our movie," Harlon said with pride. "Just sleep and we'll do our scene in the morning."

Todd looked at Harlon again, and he wasn't able to discern his features. He saw a dark head staring at him, and around that head were a few swirling orbs of green light, like fireflies. Todd didn't want to see what he'd seen earlier tonight, so he shut his eyes.

"You're seeing him, aren't you?" Harlon asked. "Does he look old, or are you seeing him when he was younger, when he ran the plantation?"

Todd heard Harlon talking about Grandpappy, but his voice soon faded and Todd viewed a sprawling plantation bordering swampland. A much younger version of Grandpappy stood on the front stairs of the main house. He must have been in his twenties, and he was thin rather than gaunt, with a full head of hair that was a blend of blond and brown. He gazed at the expanse of the property. A gray-haired woman in a dark purple hoop skirt stood beside him.

"Son," she said, "you're master now that your father's passed. I know your new responsibility will quell your rebelliousness and end your gambling and whoring."

Todd witnessed a succession of scenes in the swamp. The day the young Grandpappy strolled among the towering cypresses and heard voices promising him even greater power in exchange for human sacrifice. The evening he slit a slave's throat near a bayou and saw green fire dancing in the surrounding trees. Grandpappy undressing in the warm rain and lying on the muddy ground, reveling in his new, impressive strength. He shouted praise to some power for helping him survive yellow fever when nearly all his house slaves had died from the disease.

Todd found himself in the tight, hot quarters of a riverboat. He listened to Grandpappy bargain with the infamous pirate Jean Lafitte for more slaves.

"It seems I can hardly supply you with enough," the pirate said, stroking his bushy, black moustache. "And I've heard from other planters that the Africans are all disappearing."

"They're serving their purpose," Grandpappy said, and Todd somehow knew all the slaves would end up mutilated sacrifices in the swamp.

Todd observed the youthful appearance Grandpappy maintained over two decades, and the young followers he gained as a result of his miraculous health and the esoteric teachings he offered them. While his hair remained golden and his skin without wrinkles, his plantation fell into disrepair as his slaves either fled from their wicked master or met their deaths in the swamp.

Todd heard Grandpappy address his followers as they walked among the abandoned slave quarters. Grandpappy informed them he'd received a message from the swamp about dead slaves not being enough anymore.

"Sacrifice has so much more of an impact if there isn't a victim—only an individual willing to die."

Todd could hear the low voices rumbling through the dining rooms and salons of Louisiana and Mississippi plantations. There were rumors about the young members of wealthy families maiming themselves or giving their lives in dark rituals in the swamp. Nobody responded to the rumors, however, because the South was collapsing under the weight of the War.

"Sherman's almost here."

Todd opened his eyes and saw the bedroom was bright with Sunday morning sunlight. He felt surprisingly well-rested and clearheaded. "Sherman?" he asked.

"General Sherman and his troops," Harlon said. "Those who are responsible for your brother's death. Your brother's spirit is right around you now, and he's begging to get inside. Are you ready to give him control?"

"Oh, right. The scene." Todd sat up in bed and set his bare feet on the floorboards. His energy had returned. He'd always had amazing photo shoots when he felt this way, but he wasn't ready to get in front of a camera. Last night had been too bizarre. And why had they taken his phone? "I want to call my mother."

"It's 4 in the morning on the West Coast. You can call her later." In a more forceful voice, Harlon asked, "Are you ready to give your brother control?"

"Come into me, brother?" Todd asked. The words irritated him. He knew he couldn't do the scene this morning even if the director finally appeared. He needed to see Iola and talk to her about all these strange happenings and visions, and then he could make up his mind about whether he was still willing to be in this movie.

"I'm just going to use the bathroom," he told Harlon.

He moved Grandpappy's portrait so he could open the door, and he found a bathroom directly across the hall. After urinating, he inspected his reflection in the mirror. He looked uncannily good this morning. Sure, his hair was messy, but wasn't that the norm for a soldier in the Civil War? Even though his appearance was ready for filming, all he wanted to do was get his phone. He rinsed his mouth out with hot water and headed down the hallway toward the living room.

The foul, charred smell hit him when he was passing the kitchen. On the kitchen counter—near the bowl that held his cell phone—was the butcher paper he'd seen yesterday. The paper was unfolded and had reddish-pink stains inside. The stench grew stronger and reminded him of rancid meat.

Todd noticed Bird sitting on the living room floor. The tattooed man looked pensive, as if he were meditating or praying. In front of him was a large plate filled with a mound of dirt and two severed hands.

"Holy shit," Todd said, scowling.

The man glanced up at him with a look of surprise, but then his gaze became steely. "Good morning, brother Todd."

"'Brother Todd'?" Todd looked down at the plate again and spotted a couple maggots writhing in the soil. Those hands weren't part of a movie prop.

Bird began to clap his own hands and sang, "Make room for he who comes...."

Todd snatched his phone out of the bowl and rushed toward the front door of the apartment.

Someone punched him in the back of the arm and the phone fell to the floor and slid under a couch in the living room. Todd reeled around and faced Harlon.

"It's time for the scene," Harlon said, and then he hooked his arm around Todd's neck in a chokehold. "Say your line."

Todd tried to pull Harlon's arm away from him, but he couldn't. He was barely able to breathe.

"Say it!" Harlon tightened his hold. "'Come into me, brother!'" Todd began to choke.

"Say it!" Bird repeated.

"Come into me, brother," Todd croaked.

"Louder," Harlon said.

"Come into me, brother. Now let me go."

"Bird, it's time," Harlon said.

Bird shot up from the floor and came over and grabbed Todd's ankles. Harlon released his arm from around Todd's neck and slipped some kind of a hood over his head. Harlon took hold of his wrists, and Bird lifted his legs into the air. The two men carried Todd somewhere.

"Let go!" Todd shouted, kicking his legs and pulling his arms. The men didn't lose their holds.

Todd heard the front door open and shut. He could tell the men were taking him down the stairs leading to the building's entranceway. Terrified, he continued to struggle. He wasn't able to free himself. His face was sweating beneath the hood. Soon he was going down a second flight of stairs. Another door opened and shut, and sunshine warmed Todd's body. Bird let go of his ankles, and Todd was in a standing position once again. Harlon removed the hood.

Todd stood trembling and breathing rapidly in an inner courtyard. He glanced up at some of the surrounding apartment windows, but he didn't see anyone. There was a fourth man in the courtyard, however. Thorner—the massive bald fellow who'd accompanied Orchid in the cemetery yesterday—stood near a circular fountain. He had an albino boa constrictor curling around his shoulders. The reptile looked like six feet of white muscle.

"Help me!" Todd yelled, looking up at the windows again.

"Nobody else lives here," Harlon said with a sneer. He stepped toward Todd and once more locked his arm around his neck. He forced Todd to move toward the fountain.

"Please," Todd wheezed.

"Say your line," Harlon said, "and everything will be fine."

"Come into me, brother," Todd spoke in a scared voice. "Come into me, brother." While repeating the words, he glanced around in search of a weapon or an escape route. Beyond a potted lemon tree was another door to the building. If he could only reach that door, he could find his way to the main entrance and flee into the street.

"Keep at it," Harlon said.

"COME INTO ME, BROTHER!" With all his strength, Todd stepped to the left and broke free from Harlon's hold. He swung at Harlon, hitting him in the eye. Groaning, Harlon stepped back. The man pressed one hand over his face.

Todd ran toward the entrance, but Harlon caught up to him and pushed him into the lemon tree. Branches broke as he fell. The brick courtyard scraped his knees despite his wool trousers.

Harlon's arm was around his neck again, and Harlon dragged him back toward the fountain. Soon Thorner stood in front of Todd and positioned the snake so its head was inches away from his face. Todd stared at the pink eyes and darting tongue with horror.

"What do you people want from me?" he asked.

"Just what you promised us," a woman said. "Your beautiful body."

Todd saw Orchid approach from the building. She was grinning widely.

"Please," Todd told the group. He tried to ignore the snake. "I haven't done anything to you."

"But you're going to do so much for us," Orchid said.

Thorner pulled the snake away from Todd, and Orchid took the reptile's place. She held up a cupped hand, which was filled with ashes.

"You got this, Tarzan," she told Todd. "Make Maman proud."

She blew the powder into his eyes, and Harlon released Todd. A fiery pain instantly consumed Todd's body. He howled, and then he collapsed onto the bricks, rubbing at his burning eyes. He thought of his mother, and how she'd be destroyed if something happened to him. No mother should have to outlive her child.

"Up we go," Harlon said.

Todd tried to look at Harlon as he stood, but with the ashes in his eyes, all he could see was a pink and gray blur. When Todd was upright, Harlon shoved him hard, and he tumbled into the fountain. The water was surprisingly cold.

"Please!" Todd said, but someone's hand was around his throat, pushing his head beneath the water. Todd looked upwards while he writhed in the fountain. The water helped his vision a little, and he could see the blue sky and Harlon's determined look as he held Todd's head underwater. Todd tried to grasp the fountain's edge to pull himself upright, but his hands kept slipping.

He managed to bring his head above the surface at one point, and when he did so, he spotted someone in one of the apartment windows.

It was the pale-faced indentured servant from the hotel. The phantom stared down at him with empathy. Disappointment suddenly darkened his face, and he retreated from the window.

Harlon dunked Todd's head again.

Then someone dropped the snake into the fountain, and Todd saw its winding body above him. The snake's movement dimmed the sun, and all was going dark. Beyond the snake were Harlon and Thorner and Orchid's shadowy faces. Todd pictured Grandpappy staring down at him, and to get that horrible image out of his head, he thought of his mother smiling at him from the rocker in her living room.

"You've made your mama proud again," she told him in a soft voice.

And then there was blackness.

*

Iola experienced déjà vu as she stared up at the brick apartment building near Colonial Park Cemetery. She'd stood on this sidewalk while she was looking for her friend Allimay. Now she was searching for Todd.

When he didn't respond to any of the texts she'd sent him last night from Lafayette Square, she hurried to his hotel. She asked the woman at the front desk to try calling his room. The woman told her Todd Regan had checked out that afternoon. Baffled, Iola returned to her apartment and waited for him to call or text. She kept waking throughout the night, and each time she opened her eyes she checked her phone.

He never contacted her.

And now here she was again, in front of that building she'd tried to avoid since Allimay had vanished a year and a half ago.

When she and Allimay were teenagers in New Orleans, they went on double dates and attended as many raves as possible. Iola had always felt like the older sibling, dissuading Allimay from the overly self-destructive behavior that was her way of rebelling against her family's wealth. Allimay's father was the founder of the Nut 'n' Banana Company, which produced some of the most popular cookies in America. Allimay got into drugs and thug boyfriends, and Iola finally tired of counseling someone who seemed addicted to chaos. Iola guessed that joining the cult was Allimay's ultimate way of acting out.

Iola hated herself for refusing to let Allimay sleep over when she came to Savannah. "It'd be for just one night," Allimay had pleaded when they ate lunch together. "I'm skipping the teaching tonight, and I want to hide out from anyone who comes looking for me at my hotel. I'm heading back to New Orleans in the morning."

Iola didn't feel like watching Allimay slip down some booze or pill spiral in her apartment. She'd seen that enough times when they were younger. She gave an apologetic smile and said, "I'm really sorry, but I've got to study for a major exam tomorrow. Couldn't you just stay in a different hotel?"

Allimay's mother called Iola the next week asking if she'd seen her daughter. Iola pointed the police to the apartment building where Allimay had received her teachings, but the cop that interviewed her told her there was no proof of a cult operating there.

Iola knew the people who'd been inside this building were responsible for her friend's disappearance, though—and now they were responsible for Todd's. She wasn't going to fail Todd like she'd failed Allimay. She took a deep breath as she ascended the staircase that led to the building's front door. Most of the buttons on the buzzer system were blank. The only names on the buttons were *Grable, Snope, Zarania.* She pressed the *Zarania* button.

Nobody answered. There was also silence after she pressed the other two buttons with names on them. Iola noticed that one of the small square windowpanes that framed the door had a crack in it, and that pane wasn't too far from the door handle. She worried about breaking into the building on her own, but she didn't know anyone brave or stupid enough to help her—and she might not have another opportunity. She glanced at the street and the apartment windows above her to make sure no one was watching, and then she kicked the damaged pane with her shoe, clearing out the glass. Her hand fit easily through the space, and, with some straining of her arm, she turned the handle on the inside of the door. The door opened.

The wood-paneled entrance hall contained a table with a vase of dried purple flowers on it. Above the table was a rectangular mirror that reflected the fear on Iola's face. She started toward the stairs that were to the right of the table, but she froze when she heard footsteps beyond the wall. She saw there was a door to the left of the table, and she guessed a second stairway went down to a basement.

Iola didn't have time to run upstairs or leave the building. The door swung open, and a man with thick black hair and a moustache backed into the entrance hall. He wore a Confederate soldier's uniform. The man glanced behind him at Iola, and his eyes widened.

"Wait!" he called for whoever followed him up the stairs. "Stay there."

Iola watched the doorway through which the man had come. Why did the person on the stairs have to wait? Could that person be Todd?

Iola stepped toward the man. "I'm looking for my friend—Todd Regan. He came to this building yesterday for a rehearsal for a movie." She glanced at the man's outfit again. "Are you one of the actors?"

The man stared at her without speaking. One of his eyes was bigger than the other. There was something angry—something hateful—about the way he looked at her. Iola grew more anxious the longer the man eyed her, but she forced herself not to look away.

"Todd's no longer in the movie," the man finally spoke. "We decided he wasn't right for the role. He left here last night. I don't know where he went."

"I was supposed to meet him near here," Iola said. "He never showed." She once again looked at the doorway. Who could be waiting on the stairs?

"How'd you get in here anyway?" the man asked.

Iola's eyes met his, which seemed to be burning with rage. She suspected he was a man capable of violence. "Someone buzzed me in."

"Oh, really? Who?"

"I pressed a few of the buttons. I-"

"You can go now," the man said in a firm voice. "I told you what you need to know."

Iola nodded and headed toward the front door. She still wanted to see who was coming up the stairs. As she opened the door, she glanced at the shards of glass on the carpet. She hoped the man wouldn't notice them.

Outside, she crossed the street and stood on a corner of East Oglethorpe Avenue. She had a seminar in half an hour, but she didn't want to leave. She felt dissatisfied by what the man had told her. If Todd had really left that building, he would have contacted her. They hadn't known each other for long, but Iola was able to tell an honest, forthcoming person from a flake or a liar. Her mother said that sense was a gift.

She reluctantly started in the direction of her school. She glanced back at the apartment building once, and it was then she saw the tall bald man coming down the stairs. It was Thorner— the man who'd been with that woman Orchid at Bonaventure Cemetery yesterday. Neither he nor Orchid were involved in the movie Todd was in, so what was he doing here? Iola ducked behind the fence of a house and watched Thorner get into his jeep and drive past the cemetery. Iola kept her eyes on the front of the building for some minutes, but no one appeared. She decided she'd return to see who else came out of the building.

The next morning Iola's heart was pounding while she drove along I-10. She glanced around the freeway for the white Ford Focus. That blond woman couldn't have gotten too far. And Iola was positive that had been Todd who'd left the apartment building with her. He had the same mole on his right cheek, near those lips Iola had kissed two days ago. But why didn't he respond to her when she approached the woman's car, and how did he injure his neck? It looked all bruised, as if he'd had a rope around it or someone had tried to strangle him.

Iola's eyes began tearing up, and she forced herself not to cry. She wasn't going to allow herself to think about what horrible things might have happened to Allimay, or what could happen to Todd. At least the blond woman seemed different from Orchid and Thorner and that man in the Confederate uniform. The woman seemed like a well-intentioned person.

A pawn, perhaps.

Iola released a happy squeal when she saw the Focus down the freeway, one lane over from hers. She pressed her foot on the gas pedal and told herself that whatever had happened to Allimay wasn't going to happen to Todd. Iola would reason with the blond woman once they reached wherever they were going.

A beaming Iola parked her car in the lot of the Sunshine Coffee Shop in Pensacola. She glanced down at her cell phone and saw the blond woman's text again: *I'd like to meet you. Where? My name's Kim by the way.*

Iola had the feeling she really was going to get Todd back. She'd find out what that cult had done to him, and she'd share the information with the police. Maybe the information would help the police locate Allimay. Yes, Iola was only 23, but she'd always known she could accomplish anything if she was determined enough.

She remembered her mother suggesting, "Move to Colorado after you finish school. Life will be a lot easier for you. A black woman can only achieve so much if she's living in the South."

But Iola knew she was going to stay. She was going to crack this cult open. She was going to create a successful furniture design business. And maybe she and Todd could go deeper into a relationship when he emerged from his brainwash.

She locked her car and hurried across the parking lot, glancing around in search of Kim's car. She didn't see the vehicle. She looked up at the large metal sun rotating on the restaurant's roof. She'd chosen the Sunshine Coffee Shop as a meeting spot because she'd eaten here last night, after her second disappointing encounter with Kim. She'd ordered chocolate chip pancakes for dinner and piled on syrup as consolation for not being able to get Todd to recognize her. She now wondered if Kim might bring Todd with her today.

Inside the coffee shop, she headed toward the counter. The restaurant was about one-third full, and Kim wasn't among the diners. Iola ordered a sweet tea from the waiter behind the counter and kept her eyes on the entrance.

An enormous woman entered the coffee shop, and then a father with three little girls. A light-haired woman approached the door, but it wasn't Kim. The twenty-something woman was extremely pale, and right behind her was a man who could have been her brother. They both had messy sandy hair. The man wore a T-shirt with a snakeskin design on it while the woman had on a cheap-looking white dress that barely reached her upper thighs. A rainbow applique was on the front of the dress. The pair stared back at Iola with piercing blue eyes, causing her to look away.

"Here's your tea." The waiter set the drink in front of Iola, and she smiled in appreciation.

"You're not going to have time to drink that," a woman spoke. Iola looked to her right and saw the pale woman was taking the stool beside hers. The man moved to the stool on Iola's left.

"You're going to be leaving now," the woman added.

"Oh, yeah?" Iola asked, annoyed. She wasn't going to tolerate any redneck harassment. She glanced around for the waiter, but he'd disappeared into the kitchen. "And where am I going?"

"Kim's not coming," the man said.

Iola felt a chill. She realized this pair was part of the cult.

"You're not going to get away with this," she told them. "Whatever you've done to Todd. Whatever you did to Allimay Johnson. I'm going to talk to the police. I have Kim's license plate number." She added a lie: "And I have the address of where she's staying here."

The man and woman only offered her cool stares.

Iola's anger returned as she dug through her purse for a couple dollars for the sweet tea. She thought of what Allimay had told her about the cult: "They've got some wild ideas. The woman who's the leader—'Maman,' they call her—talks to the swamp entities. She's supposed to be like 120 years old."

Iola slammed the cash down on the counter and got off her stool. The man and woman swerved around in their seats to face her.

"I hope you all go to jail," Iola told them. "And I hope your old lady croaks in the swamp."

She felt a sting as the woman slapped her.

Iola slapped her back.

"Hey!" the waiter called. He stood in the doorway to the kitchen. "We'll have none of that in here."

Iola glanced around and realized the diners were staring at her. "Call the police," she told the waiter. "These people are criminals."

"Call the cops yourself," the waiter barked. "Now get out of here! All of you!"

Iola glared at the pair once more and headed out into the parking lot. She decided that when she was clear of these creeps, she'd try to text Kim.

Before backing her car out of its space, she saw the cult members getting into an old blue Buick on the other side of the parking lot. *I'll drive right to the police station if they follow me,* Iola swore to herself.

She took a left turn out of the lot, and she soon spotted the Buick in her rear view mirror. The car was speeding toward her.

She once again heard her mom's advice about getting out of the South, and the promise, "Life will be a lot easier for you."

Iola slammed her foot on the gas pedal. She was flying along a straight road with no businesses on it. On either side were steep, water-filled ditches. Iola glanced at her rearview mirror again. The Buick was right behind her. The man was driving while the woman pressed her white forehead against the windshield. The woman appeared to be smirking.

The Buick suddenly took a right onto an intersecting street, and Iola continued to speed along the road. She was looking in the rearview mirror again, wondering why the cult members had given up the chase, when she heard the horn blaring.

A battered bus was in her lane, coming right toward her. She couldn't see the driver, but she saw a quilt covering the left half of the windshield. The bus would crash into her in seconds.

She veered her car to the right, sending it down the side of the ditch. The vehicle flipped. Before losing consciousness, Iola heard the sound of splashing water and shattering glass.

9

Kim was too upset to speak to Sander or Eustace or whomever it was sitting next to her in the rental car. For the first hour of the drive to New Orleans, she remained quiet and gripped the steering wheel with white-knuckled hands. The image of Iola's crashed car kept flashing in her head. She'd spotted the vehicle while she drove out of Pensacola. A tow truck had lifted it up from a ditch onto the road, and Kim saw the bent hood and smashed windshield. She would have pulled over to ask the tow truck driver about what had happened to Iola, but the blue Buick was tailing her, making sure she followed Aunt Lizanna's instructions: "You're not going to stop until you're in New Orleans, and you're not going to give Jack and Rayna the slip. If you try anything, we try something with your friend in Seattle."

They killed Iola, Kim knew as she passed the wrecked car. She shivered when she thought of one of them tracking Malia's movements.

While Kim drove through Mobile, Alabama, she finally turned to her passenger. She couldn't believe this man's body truly housed the spirit of her dead fiancé. "So what do you want me to call you? Sander or Eustace?" Her voice cracked. She told herself she wasn't going to start crying.

"Eustace is fine for now. That's what you called me before."

"If you're really him," Kim said. She tried to think of a question only Eustace could answer. "Can you tell me where I was the night you...used the gun?"

He looked down at the urn in his lap and then touched one of his temples, as if his head ached. Finally, he spoke, "You went out to dinner with a co-worker."

That was what Kim had told Eustace. She'd never mentioned Malia's name to him. A tear rolled down her cheek. She recalled the lie she'd told Eustace before going out on her date with Malia. "And why did I tell you I wouldn't be spending the night at your place that night?"

"The next morning you were going to pick up a patient who lived in your neighborhood and take her to chemo." He reached over and squeezed her side in just the way Eustace had when he was being affectionate.

"Oh, god," Kim whispered, "it's really you." Her tears flowed, and she tried not to swerve as she drove. Questions raced through her head. Did Eustace know she'd cheated on him? Had he come back as some sort of punishment? Or was his original plan to return after his suicide? Moments later, she wiped her eyes and asked, "So what is this all about?"

Eustace gave her a questioning look. Kim noticed the grayish color had returned to his skin.

"What you did to yourself," she explained. "Who these people are." She glanced at his new beautiful yet sickly-looking face. "Who you are now."

"I'm still becoming," Eustace said. "You're helping me. My family is helping me."

"'Family,'" Kim said with disdain. "Are any of these people even related to you? I've come to doubt that."

"They're my brothers and sisters," Eustace said, looking nauseous. He stared ahead at the road, as if he were trying to focus on something. "They're your brothers and sisters, too."

"Bullshit," Kim said.

"I'm your fiancé," Eustace said, sounding wounded. "Why are you challenging me? That's not like you."

Kim acknowledged they'd never truly fought during the nearly two years they'd been together. Their communication usually remained on a comfortable, superficial plane. But she felt anger boiling up inside her now.

"You tricked me into this situation," she said, scowling.

Eustace pressed a hand against his stomach and rolled down his window. "Pull over," he said.

Kim waited for a car to pass so she could change lanes. She saw in the rearview mirror that the blue Buick was following her across the freeway. She had just maneuvered her car into the slow lane when Eustace stuck his head out of the window and vomited.

"Are you all right?" Kim asked, bringing the car to a stop next to a stretch of brown grass. Past the grass were a road and a Gulf Fuel gas station. Eustace gave Kim a frightened look. He had splotches of black vomit on his chin.

He must have seen her shocked expression, because he quickly wiped his face with the back of his hand.

"What's going on here?" a woman spoke.

Kim glanced out Eustace's window and saw the couple from the blue Buick nearing the car. In Pensacola, she'd learned their names—Jack and Rayna. Rayna was glaring at Kim, but her eyes softened when she looked at Eustace.

"Sander?" she asked with concern. She opened the passenger's side door, and Eustace vomited black fluid near her feet.

"Let's get him to a bathroom," Jack said, motioning toward the gas station in the distance.

Rayna helped Eustace out of the car. "You're coming, too," she informed Kim.

Kim hesitated, thinking she could slam her foot on the gas pedal and be free. But she doubted she'd be able to call Malia and warn her before Jack and Rayna phoned Aunt Lizanna or another cult member.

Kim picked her purse up off the backseat of the car and followed the other three through the grass, watching Eustace as he staggered along. He still clutched the urn. Whatever energy he'd gained in Pensacola was quickly depleting. Kim had the idea he was ill because he wasn't supposed to be on this earth anymore. And he was in the wrong body. In her heart was the dark wish that he'd never returned from the dead. Life was for those who'd never passed away.

Like Malia.

Kim glanced around for a payphone as they crossed the gas station's parking lot. She thought how today was Tuesday, and it was a little after 1 o'clock in Seattle. She might be able to reach Malia on her lunch break. She remembered Malia telling her about the condo her uncle owned up in the resort town of Whistler, British Columbia. That was about a four-hour drive from Seattle. Malia would be safe there.

Kim didn't see a payphone. The restrooms were in back of the gas station.

"Come on," Rayna snapped, impatiently waving for Kim to join her outside the men's room. Jack and Eustace headed into that restroom.

When Kim approached, Rayna asked, "What'd you say to him? You upset him, didn't you?"

"We were just talking," Kim said, shaking her head. "About his family. About you and your people. You're his sister, too, aren't you?" she asked with sarcasm.

"Don't get cocky," Rayna said, her hands on her hips. "We appreciate you for what you've done and what you're going to do, but you're no better than any of us. There are great powers at work, and it's important for us all to be humble before those great powers."

The term "great powers" gave Kim a chill. She asked, "What are you going to do with me?"

"Just you never mind for now."

"I need to use the toilet," Kim said. She didn't really have to go, but she wanted some time away from Rayna so she could think clearly.

"Pee fast," Rayna said. "And don't you lock that door."

There were two stalls inside the restroom, but unfortunately nobody else occupied the small space. If someone else had been in there, Kim could have asked to borrow her cell phone.

She heard Eustace throwing up past the thin wall dividing the restrooms. She thought how she'd never heard him be sick to his stomach while they were together. He'd gotten a couple colds, and she'd made him split pea soup and her comforting Irish soda bread. But today she had no desire to nurture him.

And she wanted to reach Malia.

She dug inside her purse until she found a pen. She glanced around the bathroom for something to write on. She could scrawl on the mirror with her lipstick, or she could write on the side of one of the stalls. But what if Rayna came in here after her to check for any such messages?

She snatched a piece of paper towel out of the dispenser by the sink and held it against a wall. She wrote:

> *please this is an emergency*
> *call Malia Kai 206-555-5434*
> *tell her to go to her uncle's place*
> *she's in danger*
> *Kim will meet her there*

Kim no longer heard Eustace through the wall. She hurried inside one of the stalls and lifted the toilet lid. She was going to hide the note between the lid and the tank. Someone would eventually find it there. She was bent over the toilet, positioning the piece of paper towel, when the bathroom door opened with a bang.

Kim jerked upwards and accidentally dropped the note.

It fluttered into the toilet bowl, and water made Kim's words bleed.

"Shit," she whispered.

"What's taking you so long?" Rayna asked.

"Coming," Kim said. She flushed the toilet, watching the paper towel swirl away. She gave Rayna an irritated glance before washing her hands.

"I'm riding with you two," Rayna announced, "and you're not going to talk to Sander. Lizanna wanted you two to be alone together, but this is just how it's going to have to be." She left the restroom.

Kim looked at herself in the mirror. Her cheeks were red with rage. In a low voice, she told herself, "He's not the one I want to talk to."

The sky was an apocalyptic orange when Kim exited the freeway in New Orleans. The sun was setting, and Kim felt like she'd been driving for two days straight. Rayna instructed her from the backseat on what streets to take. Kim drove past houses that looked as historical as Savannah's. The structures were lower, and many had long, shuttered windows and lovely pastel coats of paint. She wished she were visiting this city as a tourist, discovering its offerings. Instead, she was a hostage, and she dreaded what awaited her at the end of the drive. She glanced in the rear view mirror and saw Jack was still following the three of them in the blue Buick.

"Dauphine Street," Rayna said. "This is our street."

Kim soon pulled over into one of the few parking spots. Jack slowly drove past them, apparently searching for his own space. Kim turned to Eustace, who was watching her with loving eyes that had dark circles around them. He still looked gravely ill.

"Thank you for getting me here," he told her.

When they were out of the car, Rayna pointed at a pink one-story house with a sign outside reading *FOR SALE/LEASE*. "That's the one." She came over to Eustace and hooked her arm around his, helping him across the street. She held the urn with her other arm. Night was falling, and the sky had turned a bruised color.

Kim knew now was her opportunity to run and find a phone. If she didn't reach Malia, she could at least leave a message and tell her to sneak away from the hospital or wherever she was and get to Whistler as soon as possible. But Kim was concerned about locating a phone soon enough in this residential neighborhood. She gave up the idea of fleeing when Jack appeared beside her. He motioned for her to head toward the pink house.

The front door opened as they ascended the few stairs to the porch. Kim stopped on the top stair when she saw who stood inside.

"Teressa," she said. She recalled what that elderly woman had told her outside Teressa's apartment in Charleston: "White witch is up there, and I don't mean 'white' as in 'good.'"

Teressa wore a moss-green robe over a plain black dress. She was barefoot. She embraced Eustace, and as she hugged him, she looked at Kim. "Thank you so much for bringing him here." She sounded sincere. "You've been an amazing chaperone. We all knew you would be."

"'Chaperone'?" Kim asked.

Teressa ignored the question. "Come on in, y'all," she said, stepping aside so the four could enter.

Rayna placed a hand on Kim's lower back, nudging her toward the doorway.

"Don't you touch me," Kim grumbled. She headed into the house to get away from Rayna's loathsome presence.

Past the doorway was a high-ceilinged living room and, beyond that, a dining room and kitchen. No walls separated the spaces. The smell of burned meat filled the air, just like it had at

Teressa's apartment in Charleston. Kim noticed that all the living room's furniture was pushed back against the walls. Two thin men in their early twenties sat on the edge of a couch. One of them held what looked like a dead rooster. In the center of the living room was a blue tarp littered with cornhusks, beaded necklaces, and a palm frond. Kim remembered the disturbing ceremony she'd witnessed in Pensacola.

She was surprised to see Eustace stumble into the middle of the tarp and begin undressing. He unbuttoned his shirt and turned to Teressa, "Let's begin. Time isn't on our side."

"What's going on here?" Kim asked. "Why are you doing another one of these...rituals?"

"Oh, come on," Teressa said. Her former sweetness was missing from her voice. "Keep up, Kim. You came to Charleston with a container of ashes. You gave us those ashes, and now look who's standing here." She motioned toward Eustace, who dropped his shirt on the floor. His pale, muscular chest seemed to glow under the dim ceiling light.

Rayna came toward Eustace and reverently set the urn at his feet. He had a look of self-assurance—no, entitlement—on his face.

Kim was suddenly certain that Eustace's return to life had nothing to do with her. He didn't come back to punish her or be with her. He didn't care about her, and she doubted he ever really had. He was here for something much bigger than her.

"It's time for you to leave," Teressa told Kim.

"You're letting me go?" Kim asked, her eyes large with hope.

Teressa walked toward Eustace, who was struggling to unbuckle his belt. She helped him remove it. "You're going to leave while we do what we need to do here."

Eustace pulled down his jeans, watching Kim as he did so. He wore black boxer briefs. Kim couldn't even remember what kind of underwear he'd worn when they were together in Seattle.

The man she'd been with in Seattle was shorter and thinner and didn't resemble an ailing Adonis.

"And then you're coming back," Teressa said.

"So this is the same old routine," Kim said in a flat voice.

"Excuse me?" Teressa had obviously forgotten about her appreciation of Kim's chaperoning.

"You get me out of your house. You do your black magic shit. I come back so you can manipulate or force me into doing something else for you."

"Would you just leave?" Eustace barked. An angry red had replaced his ashen complexion. His hands had formed fists. "You're supposed to be helping me."

Taken aback by his raised voice, Kim retreated toward the door. Eustace had never spoken to her like that before. Kim thought this must be Eustace's true self: quick to anger, and long in deceiving her. She decided she shouldn't be surprised since he'd always been a familiar stranger to her.

"The French Quarter is near here," Teressa said in a perky voice. "Keep on Dauphine and you'll be in it as soon as you cross Esplanade. Have yourself a good ol' time seeing the town. Jack and Rayna will follow and make sure you don't get lost. Because if you do you could lose a friend in Seattle."

Kim glared at her, resenting the threat against Malia. Kim's hand was on the door handle when she remembered who was supposed to be here today. She glanced back at Teressa. "Where's Vess?"

Teressa paused before responding, as if she were considering what lie to deliver.

"Eustace's grandmother," Kim added. Eustace was shaking his head. Clearly, he'd never expected Kim to be so headstrong.

"There is no Vess," Teressa said. This sounded like the truth. She glanced at Eustace, as if she were checking whether she could continue speaking.

He nodded.

"Maman is Vess," Teressa said. "She couldn't come because she's been very ill, very weak. She's incredibly pleased you're here, though. She thought you'd make it."

"Maman?" Kim asked, confused. "But you said she was born in the 1890s."

"She was."

Kim looked from Teressa to Eustace, who was now smiling smugly. "But that would mean she's over 120 years old."

Wandering through the French Quarter with a pair of cult members trailing her, Kim felt like she was in a nightmare. The buildings were charming enough with their ironwork galleries and balconies, their hanging ferns, and their flickering gas lamps, but Kim kept sensing the ominous. What lurked behind all those shuttered windows? Why were most of the passersby on this street drunk on a Tuesday night in April? How come so many of the stores sold merchandise related to voodoo and the occult?

Kim was outside one such shop when she turned back, waiting for Jack and Rayna to catch up with her. They'd remained about a half a block behind her for the last 45 minutes. Kim had passed a couple policemen, but she figured they'd want an explanation before allowing her to telephone Malia. Jack and Rayna would be able to make a phone call before she could.

She now pointed at one of the store's windows, which was filled with skeleton dolls, brightly dressed figurines, potion bottles, and half-melted candles. "Is this what your rituals are all about?" she asked the pair in an accusing voice.

Rayna offered a slanted grin. "We've got different gods," she said, "and you can't make deals with any of them."

The shop door opened with the jingle of a bell and a tall, wide man with a face painted like a skull stepped outside. A corncob pipe protruded from his lips. He wore a black cape and a top hat with a jeweled cross and red feathers attached to it. He took Kim by the arm and led her along the gallery, away from Jack and Rayna.

"Why so glum, child?" he asked. He sounded like he was from the Caribbean. "You look like a lady of light."

Kim didn't know how to respond. She glanced behind her and saw that Jack and Rayna continued to follow her. They allowed her some space, but she could tell they were suspicious of this man with the painted face. Kim wasn't afraid of him at all.

The man led her around the corner. "You need to get back to your light," he said, squeezing her arm.

Kim thought of Malia. "Please," she said, "I want to sneak away from those two people behind me and find a telephone. I can't let them see me sneak away. Would you be willing to distract them for me?"

The man gave a knowing nod. "Bien sûr, for the lady of light." He told her, "Up ahead on the left is St. Louis Cathedral. There's an alley next to the church. You run through that alley and head past Jackson Square toward the river. You'll find a pay phone down there."

"Thank you," Kim said.

The man tipped his top hat. "De rien." He released her arm and spun around to face Jack and Rayna. He raised his cape, blocking the pair's view of her. "You creep behind me, do you?" he asked in a booming, accusing voice.

Kim didn't wait to hear what else he said. She sprinted along the street until she saw a white cathedral and a sign for *Pirates Alley*.

Kim was running beside the shadowy park that was Jackson Square when she realized she didn't even have any money to make a call. Rayna had instructed her to leave her purse in the pink house. Kim saw a crowd of people who looked like tourists. They ate powder-sugared beignets out of bags, and they laughed loudly as they took pictures of each other on a gas lamp-lit gallery that paralleled the park. Hanging above the gallery was a small sign reading *Haunted Apartment For Rent.* Kim considered asking the tourists for change or one of their phones so she could make a call, but she questioned whether she even had the time to talk to them. She thought she spotted Jack and Rayna in the distance. She pushed past the crowd, took a sharp right, and hurried through a store's open door.

She was in an antiques shop. Old paintings adorned the walls, showing a steamboat on the Mississippi, a packed 19th-century ballroom, solemn-faced women in colorful headdresses, a sunlit version of the cathedral Kim had just rushed past. Elaborate quilts were between the paintings and glimmering crystal chandeliers hung from the ceiling. There were cases displaying jewelry, crockery, cutlery. A smartly dressed white-haired woman was showing a young couple a set of leather suitcases. She smiled at Kim. "Evening. Be right with you."

"Oh, I'm just browsing," Kim said, not wanting the woman to bother her. She pretended to admire an ebony sculpture of a horse, and then she moved toward the back of the store, out of sight of the white-haired woman and whoever might peek inside the entrance.

She spotted a back office and, inside that space, a desk with a push-button telephone on top of it. She checked again to make sure no one was watching her, and then she ducked inside the office and quietly closed the door.

She picked up the handset and dialed Malia's number. She was amazed she still remembered the digits.

"Hello?"

Kim was stunned Malia had picked up. "Malia, it's me. We don't have much time to talk."

"Kim! I've been thinking so much about you over the past two days."

Kim couldn't believe only a couple days had passed since their conversation outside the Waffle House. It felt more like a couple months.

"Listen, Malia, I need you to go to your uncle's condo in Whistler right away."

The office door opened, and the white-haired woman stepped inside the room. "What are you doing here? This is a private office."

"This is an emergency," Kim snapped. "I'll explain in just a minute."

"An emergency?" Malia asked. "Kim, what's going on?"

"There are people watching you, people who could hurt you."

"What?" Malia asked. "You're scaring me."

"There's a reason to be scared. Eustace was in a cult, and they want me to help them do bad things. They know who you are, and say they'll kill you if I don't cooperate. I can't help myself until I know you're safe. Please go to Whistler now, and don't let anyone see you leave. I'll meet you there as soon as I can. I'll explain when I see you. I need to go now."

"But-"

"Goodbye, Malia. Leave now. Be careful."

"I miss you, Kim."

"I miss you, too."

Kim hung up the phone. She saw her reflection in a gilded mirror on the wall. She looked 45 instead of 29. Strands of her dirty blond hair stuck to her sweaty face. Her tears had smeared her mascara. She was as colorless as Jack and Rayna.

"You can get out of my office now," the white-haired woman said, her arms folded over her chest. She probably thought an insane person had invaded her store.

"Not yet." Kim picked up the phone to dial 911.

The woman turned toward the front of the store, as if she'd heard someone enter.

Kim was relieved to hear the operator answer.

"911. What's your emergency?"

Loud footsteps sounded outside the office. Jack appeared in the doorway. He rushed toward Kim.

"I've been abducted by a cult," Kim spoke into the handset in a panicked voice. "I'm in a store near-"

Jack reached the phone and ripped the cord out of the wall. Kim still held the handset with a shaking hand.

She dropped it when she saw who else stood in the office, watching her with a grin on his face.

"Hello, Kim," Eustace said. He now looked revitalized, like he had after the ceremony in Pensacola. His cheeks were a healthy shade of red, and Kim could even see a vein bulging slightly on one of his temples.

The white-haired woman's face was a mask of outrage. "What's going on here? Who are you people?"

Jack approached the woman. In one quick motion, he snapped her head to the side. She collapsed on the wood floor.

"Oh, god," Kim whimpered, cupping a hand over her mouth. Jack exited the office.

"Was that Malia you called before?" Eustace asked her in a calm voice. "You two have become quite close. You were already too close when I passed."

Kim's lips parted, but she failed to speak. She kept staring at the lifeless body in the room. She finally whispered, "So you know about Malia and me."

"I know so much about everything now that the fourth ceremony is complete," he said. "I know who Malia is. I knew where to find you. I know there's a bird singing outside the window of the room where you and I are going to spend the night tonight."

Kim was speechless. Tears filled her eyes. She forced herself to look away from the corpse.

Eustace came near her and reached for her hand. She recoiled from his touch, but he took her hand anyway. His own hand was surprisingly warm. Still shocked by the murder of the woman, she allowed him to lead her out of the office.

She regained some clarity in the main room of the store, however. She saw Jack and Rayna waiting for them by the entrance. She thought that maybe the police had traced her call and would arrive here soon. She pulled away from Eustace, but his grip tightened.

"Let me go," she said, now thrashing. She backed up against a bookshelf, and a few ancient-looking tomes fell to the floor. She glanced down and saw the title of one of the books: *Nights with Uncle Remus.*

Eustace grabbed her. His strength surprised her.

"It's getting late," he told her. "We've got a long drive ahead of us."

Kim shook her head. "I'm not driving anywhere else."

"No, you're not going to drive," Eustace said, guiding her outside the store. "You're going to be a passenger."

He and Jack led her past Jackson Square in the direction of the river, each holding one of her arms. Rayna followed them. Kim recognized the group of tourists she'd seen earlier. They were climbing into a cream-colored, horse-drawn carriage with four bench-like seats. They all held cups that must have contained alcohol.

"Help me!" she shouted.

Some of the tourists gave Kim bewildered looks.

Jack placed a hand over Kim's lips. Rayna hurried in front of the trio and gave the tourists a thumbs-up. "It's okay," she called to them. "This girl's gone through too many hurricanes tonight." The tourists smiled and offered understanding nods.

Parked not far behind the carriage was a dilapidated bus with a painting of a vulture on its side. It was the same bus Kim had seen near Aunt Lizanna and Guthrie's house in Pensacola.

Eustace and Jack pulled her toward the vehicle. She tried to jerk away from them, but they held her too tightly.

"I don't want to go!" she screamed, causing some pedestrians' heads to turn. But before she could attract more attention, the doors to the bus opened. Two sets of tattooed arms reached out and pulled her inside.

10

You can't pussy out again, Harlon told himself. Dressed in Confederate uniform, he lay on the bed across from Todd's. Thoughts zoomed through his mind while his guest slept. What if Bird hadn't been able to find Todd earlier in the evening, and Todd had never returned to the apartment building? Then Harlon wouldn't have to kill him. Harlon closed his eyes and repeated in his head, *Help me be strong, Maman. Grandpappy, let me be brave. May I remember that we don't kill for our own needs, but for what is greater than ourselves.*

Still anxious, he looked to the portrait of Grandpappy he'd set against the closed bedroom door. He wished he could see the details of Grandpappy's face. Viewing that painting always gave him some confidence for the colossal task Maman had assigned him. Grandpappy had sacrificed his own teenage son in the swamp, so why should Harlon be nervous about killing a man who was practically a stranger to him? And why hadn't he been able to take care of that woman Allimay in New Orleans last spring?

In May, a group of Family members had checked out a house in the Garden District. Lizanna was there, of course, being the senior minister, along with a few newer recruits. Only Harlon and Lizanna knew they were viewing the house as a possible location for the New Orleans ceremony. They'd already found the apartment in Charleston where Teressa would stay and greet the chaperone, and, of course, the Family owned the apartment building in Savannah. All Family members were aware that Maman was expecting a successor, but they didn't know the successor was living in Seattle and preparing for his journey back to the South.

"This place is too big, isn't it?" Harlon asked as he entered the master bedroom on the second floor. "Too conspicuous. The chaperone might wonder why 'Grandma Vess' lives in a mansion."

Lizanna stood by a window, peering out at the backyard. She smiled and watched him with those violet eyes that were able to conceal any emotion. When Harlon had been a new recruit nine years ago, another Family member told him, "Lizanna's learned how to have gator eyes over the decades."

"You're exactly right, as usual," Lizanna said. "We don't need a living room with 25-foot ceilings. A boy we found at LSU is the one who owns this house. He inherited it from an uncle. He told us the place is very private."

Harlon joined her at the window and looked outside. Surrounded by a high, white brick wall, the massive yard included a bean-shaped pool and a cabana. The quiet crew cut guy from Missouri was crouching by the pool, puffing on a cigarette, while that woman Allimay sat in the shade of the cabana, looking uncomfortable. Harlon had only seen her at a couple teachings in Savannah, and he didn't like the skeptical questions she asked during the sessions. He knew she still lived in her own condo somewhere near the French Quarter.

"She doesn't fit, does she?" Lizanna asked.

"Not really."

Lizanna turned those violet eyes on him again. "We want you to disconnect her."

Harlon's brow furrowed. "You mean....?"

Lizanna nodded.

"What about the swamp?"

"She's a nonbeliever and a loose tongue. That's not the kind of offering we give to the swamp. That's someone we dispose of."

Harlon felt beads of sweat on his forehead. He stepped back from the window.

"You do want to be a leader for the Family, don't you?" Lizanna asked. "I know how much faith Maman has in you."

Harlon stopped holding his breath. "I do."

Lizanna smiled again. "There's a shower in the basement bathroom and a piece of pipe lying on the counter. Show her the shower."

"I can do that," Harlon said, trying to sound confident. He sounded just the opposite.

Lizanna opened the window. "Allimay!" she called. "Come inside. Harlon's going to meet you in the kitchen."

Harlon felt a tightening in his stomach as he watched Allimay approach the house.

"Keep your eyes on her," Lizanna instructed. "I think she's a slippery one."

Harlon now watched Todd roll over in his sleep. Todd's handsome face had a slight frown on it. Harlon thought how in a few hours, that face would have the mask of death on it. And that mask would never lift if the Savannah ceremony didn't work. Harlon wished he could do the killing this instant, when the man's eyes were closed. It would be so much easier if Todd weren't looking at him.

Allimay's eyes had betrayed her suspicion and fear. She glanced back at him while they descended the staircase to the basement. "What is it you need me to help carry upstairs?" she asked.

"Remember what Lizanna said about asking too many questions," Harlon chastised her. He wasn't able to keep eye contact with her for long. He didn't want her to sense his nervousness.

The basement was dimly lit from the slit window that spanned the top of one wall. Thin, red carpeting covered the cement floor. Harlon spotted the bathroom at the end of a hallway. He pointed toward the room. "It's in there."

Allimay glanced back at him once more before entering the bathroom. She flipped on the light switch and looked around the space. "There's nothing in here."

Harlon saw a blue tarp in the bathtub. He pointed at it. "There it is," he said.

Allimay cautiously ventured toward the tub. "The tarp?" she asked, giving Harlon a confused look.

Harlon's palms were wet with perspiration. He reached for the piece of pipe that was beside the sink. "Get in the tub," he told her.

Allimay's eyes became round with terror when she looked at the pipe in Harlon's hand. "What are you going to do to me? Please just let me go. I won't say anything bad about the Family, brother. I'll keep my mouth shut."

"The shower, sister," Harlon said, his voice not forceful enough.

"Please." Allimay's eyes were now tearing. "What do you want? My family has a lot of money."

"Most of our families have a lot of money."

Harlon thought she was stepping toward the tub. He felt like the pipe was going to slip right out of his sweaty hand. He guessed he'd have to hit her in the head. How many blows would it take?

He was about to lift the pipe when she ran past him, pushing him against the bathroom counter. The back of his head knocked against the mirror above the sink. Allimay was almost through the bathroom door when Lizanna stepped into the doorway with a knife in her hand. She plunged that knife into Allimay's stomach. Allimay moaned loudly and doubled over, her hands cupping the wound. She stumbled out of the bathroom and crashed against the wall of the hallway. She braced herself against the wall with one bloody hand.

Harlon was horrified, but he felt a thrill, too. He'd been equally excited when the Family visited his parents' estate outside of Memphis.

Lizanna trained her steely gaze on him. "Are you going to disconnect her?"

Harlon nodded and approached Allimay. He raised the pipe above his head, but his arm became paralyzed when he heard her whimpering.

She looked up at him and whispered, "Please."

"That's enough," Lizanna said. She stepped toward Harlon and grabbed the pipe out of his slick hand. She brought the weapon down on Allimay as many times as it took.

Todd stared across the bedroom at Harlon.

"How you doing, brother?" Harlon asked, hoping his trepidation wasn't apparent. He assured himself he was going to be able to do this. But he also knew there was much more he needed to accomplish than killing Todd. "Just go back to sleep," he said. "Our pivotal scene's in the morning."

When Harlon finally let go of Todd's neck, he realized the man was staring up at him with blank, bulging eyes. Harlon shrank back from the corpse floating in the courtyard fountain, yet his revulsion soon gave way to elation.

He did it. He killed Todd. He helped make room for he who comes.

"Let's bring him upstairs for the ceremony," he told Thorner and Bird.

The gargantuan-sized Thorner delicately lifted the white snake out of the water and draped it over Orchid's shoulders. She was beaming at Harlon.

"Maman's going to be so proud of you," she told him.

"We're not done yet," he said, watching Thorner and Bird pick up the dripping corpse.

Harlon reached out and squeezed Todd's dangling hand. He'd never touched his parents' or his sister's dead bodies, and he wanted to touch this man's. If all went as it was supposed to, that body would be moving again—with Sander's spirit inside.

Harlon had once thought—once hoped—it would be his spirit that entered the vessel. But Maman had dispelled his fantasy.

"Sander's the successor," she'd told him in a raspy voice two years ago. They were on the Family farm in Mississippi. This was the last time Maman had left the Swamp House and the only time Harlon had seen her up close. Of course, he couldn't really see her because she was wearing a gray cloak with a veil over her face. The only ones allowed to see Maman were the ministers. He could tell her body was petite and frail, but between her concealing clothing and the blinds being drawn in the room they shared, that was about all he could tell. They sat on two wooden chairs, facing each other.

Harlon bowed his head upon hearing the news about the successor. The bow was partly out of respect, but Harlon was also trying to hide the disappointment on his face. He should have known Maman would know exactly how he was feeling.

She reached out and placed a small, gloved hand on his knee. Her fingernails were long and sharp, and one had pierced the silk of her glove. "You question my decision," she said. "I've always known Sander's the one. The swamp showed me where to find him, just like it showed me where to find so many of you."

Harlon knew better than to challenge his teacher. He nodded and placed a hand over hers. He thought maybe the ceremonies wouldn't work. Maybe Sander's spirit would fail to enter its vessel, and the Family would have to decide on another successor. Harlon could be a candidate. He was young, and healthy, and loyal, and-

"You have the potential to be a minister," Maman said, squeezing his knee.

Harlon raised his head. He was grinning widely. The Family only had three ministers—Lizanna, Guthrie, Teressa. They were the members over the age of 30.

"You're going to make me a minister?" he asked.

"Why do you think we came for you?"

Harlon remembered looking out his bedroom window when he was 18 and seeing three people climbing the fence of his parents' estate. All three had worn fish head masks.

"I knew you were special," Maman continued. "But in order to prove you're special, you must do something special."

"Anything," Harlon immediately said.

Maman stopped touching his leg and folded her hands in her lap. "You're going to have to kill, and I'm not talking about an animal."

Harlon hesitated before saying, "As you like."

"And you're going to have to deliver Sander's spirit into that dead man's body, and you're going to have to make that body breathe again."

Harlon was too stunned to speak. Of course, he knew this process was how Maman had come to be Grandpappy's successor. Through ceremony, she went from being ashes to being the head of the Family—a woman who could communicate with those in the swamp, and know so much more than any average human could know, and live past 120 years. But how could Harlon possibly be capable of performing the ceremony that would ensure the Family had a successor to Maman?

"You don't know Grandpappy well enough yet, do you?" Maman asked, as if she were reading his insecurity.

Harlon certainly knew of Grandpappy. The same portrait of the stately man hung in every living room in the Family's Savannah apartment building. As part of their earliest teachings, Family members learned of Grandpappy's transformation from plantation owner to founder of the Family. They heard about Grandpappy coming for Maman in 1917. He executed her parents and delivered the troubled young woman out of their mansion in New Orleans and onto the path of her power. He sent her on her mission to New York in 1919, and he died at the age of 121 a couple years later—just after Maman became the successor.

But Harlon viewed Grandpappy as more of a legend than a spiritual teacher, even though so many Family members said they felt his presence, and a few claimed to have seen him walking through the swamp.

In response to Maman's question, Harlon said, "I suppose I don't know him that well. But I'd like to."

"You will," she said. "I want you to pray for the swamp to send him to you. And I want you to listen and watch for him. He's the one who's going to help you complete this special task."

"Yes, ma'am."

Maman turned away from him in her chair, and he sensed she was done speaking. He rose from his seat and started for the door.

"Harlon?" Maman asked. She still faced one of the covered windows.

"Yes, Maman?"

"If you fail, you won't become a minister. And I'm not sure the swamp will have you."

Harlon now scowled when he saw Thorner and Bird hauling away Todd's corpse. One of the dead man's feet bumped against a potted plant in the courtyard.

"Careful!" Harlon said. "We can't make any mistakes." He opened the door for the two men to carry Todd up the stairs to the lobby. He passed them to get the door at the top of the stairs. He realized he was sweating profusely in his Confederate uniform.

His eyes went wide after he opened the door.

A pretty, light-skinned black woman was standing in the lobby, looking slightly afraid.

Harlon turned back toward the shadowy figures of Thorner and Bird on the staircase. "Wait! Stay there."

He wasn't going to fuck this up.

The woman stepped toward him. Harlon's self-assurance withered when she said, "I'm looking for my friend—Todd Regan. He came to this building yesterday for a rehearsal for a movie." The woman eyed Harlon's Confederate uniform. "Are you one of the actors?"

Harlon's confidence returned, and he suddenly felt a burning rage toward this woman. He knew that if she challenged him, he could kill her, too. "Todd's no longer in the movie," he said. "We decided he wasn't right for the role. He left here last night. I don't know where he went."

"Put the body there," Harlon told Thorner and Bird. He pointed at the bed where Todd had slept the night before. While the men lay the corpse on the mattress, he pulled the window curtains shut. He wanted to block the mid-day sunlight blasting into the room. He glanced down at Todd's graying face and the bruise marks on his neck. What if he'd squeezed the neck so hard that Todd's body would be uninhabitable for Sander? He frowned and glanced around the bedroom, hoping for some sign of Grandpappy.

He saw none.

"What's wrong?" Orchid asked. She stood barefoot in the doorway, holding the plate filled with Louisiana swamp soil and two helping hands. "You should be thrilled. You got that girl out of the building quick enough."

He replied in anger, "You were supposed to scare her away when you followed her and Todd to the cemetery."

Orchid momentarily looked ashamed.

"We'll keep him on the bed for the ceremony," Harlon told her. "Put the soil around him-"

"And the hands over the eyes," Orchid chirped. "I know how to do it. Teressa told me."

Harlon gritted his teeth and tried to let his annoyance pass. He reminded himself the chaperone would be here sometime this afternoon, and he'd need to pretend he was Orchid's loving husband. What irked him most was Orchid's aggressive optimism. Why didn't she ever doubt like he did? Didn't she know that if they failed to summon Grandpappy, then they'd botch the Savannah ceremony? But then again, she wasn't responsible for the ceremony. He was.

Todd sensed Grandpappy at the plantation, Harlon reminded himself, *and here in the apartment last night. You will, too.*

He heard his phone ringing in the kitchen, and he motioned for Bird to go take the call. While he waited for the man's return, he watched Orchid sprinkle soil around Todd's head. He wanted to see a green glow surrounding that head, but he only saw a dead man's face.

"Jack and Rayna phoned," Bird said. He entered the room and closed the door behind him. "The chaperone's on the road. She's eating breakfast at a Waffle House off of Route 17."

"Then let's get started," Harlon said. "This could take a while."

He took his position, sitting on the bed beside the corpse. Orchid finished spreading the soil and began massaging Todd's bare feet. Thorner stood by the window while Bird remained by the door.

"Make room," Bird and Thorner chanted. "Make room."

Harlon glanced at the portrait of Grandpappy, which was on the other bed, propped against the wall. Harlon detected a look of displeasure on the founder's face. He closed his eyes and waited, and listened.

"Make room. Make room. Make room."

Harlon remembered being 19 and feeling Lizanna's pointy boot poking him in the ribs in the middle of the night. He'd emerged from his sleep and realized he was still in his sleeping bag on the floor of the bus. He'd slept in that vehicle beside the Family's recruits during the past two weeks of orientation. The bus was parked down the road from the Swamp House. While he was attending one of the teachings in the front yard, he'd glanced up at a second-story window and seen an ancient-looking woman peering out at him.

Lizanna crouched by his sleeping bag and whispered, "It's time for you to enter the swamp."

Harlon was in the rear of the line of recruits that filed out of the bus and into the muggy blackness of the night. There was a smell of decaying vegetation in the air. The other recruits were all about the same age as Harlon. Most were teenagers, but some were in their early twenties. They followed Lizanna, who led them down a road in the opposite direction of the Swamp House.

She pointed a flashlight at the trees that bordered the cracked pavement, illuminating snaking branches and ghostly Spanish moss. "Walk into the trees until you see the green light," she said. "But be careful you don't fall into the water."

Harlon only ventured past a few trees before he pressed his back against a wide cypress trunk. *I'm not going to go stepping on no gator or water moccasin,* he told himself.

"I see it!" cried the blond girl from Tampa. Then the others joined in the affirmations. Harlon glanced around the edge of the swamp, but he didn't see green light—or any light for that matter. How could he expect to remain in the Family if he witnessed nothing?

"I see it, too!" he called out. He hurried back in the direction of Lizanna's flashlight, and he soon noticed the look of disappointment on her face.

She recognized your falsehood, Harlon told himself as he sat beside Todd on the bed. *And now Grandpappy's punishing you for that falsehood by not showing you any sign. You've never seen the green light, and you'll never become a minister.* Harlon kept his eyes clamped shut, afraid to open them and look at Todd's grim death mask once again.

"Did you see that?" Orchid asked.

Harlon cracked open his eyes and looked down at Todd's corpse. He didn't notice any change from before.

"He blinked," Orchid said.

Harlon spotted a fluttering of eyelashes between the fingers of one of the helping hands. He immediately lifted the hands off of Todd's face and set them on the mattress.

Todd blinked a few times, and then his eyes remained open. His pupils were dots of green light.

"Thank you, Grandpappy!" Harlon shouted.

And then the eyes shut again.

"Wait!" Harlon said. He used a thumb to lift one of the eyelids. There was no longer any light in the eye. Only death.

"Does this mean the ceremony worked?" Orchid asked. She gawked at Todd's corpse.

Harlon shook his head. He felt like crying. "I don't know."

As soon as Orchid led Kim out of the apartment, Harlon removed the urn from the tote bag. He admired the steel container for some seconds, so thankful to be holding these ashes that had come so far. He then brought the urn down the hall toward the closed bedroom door. "We got him," he announced.

The door immediately opened. Thorner and Bird stood inside the space. Todd's corpse was still sprawled on the bed beyond them. Both men stared down at the urn with reverence.

"You did it," Bird whispered, nodding enthusiastically.

Harlon shook his head. "I ain't done nothing yet." He heard his father's voice: "What are you going to do with your life, boy? Sit around on the couch like white trash and watch cartoon characters that swear at each other? 'Cause that's about all you do in our house. I should have done that instead of get a law degree. You want the school to hold you back another year?"

Harlon jerked his head to shake off the memory of his father. "It's time to finish the work," he told Thorner and Bird. He motioned for them to leave the room.

"You sure we can't help?" Bird asked.

"I've got to do this part of the ceremony on my own," Harlon said. "That's what Maman asked of me." He hoped his last words didn't betray his anxiousness. Once the door closed, he looked at Todd's body, which appeared to be turning a darker shade of gray. But maybe it was just the evening light. Harlon went to the window and opened the curtains. He peered down at the fountain in the courtyard and remembered his hands wrapped so tightly—so confidently—around Todd's neck.

You did that, and you can do this.

He set the urn beside the corpse, and then he lit the thick green candle and shards of dried mangrove root Bird had placed on a plate in the center of the floor. The scent of the candle and the smoking root momentarily calmed Harlon. He saw Grandpappy's portrait was still propped up on the bed that was opposite Todd's. He stared into Grandpappy's eyes, hoping again for some sign.

Now he heard what his mother had once told him: "Would you please stop zoning out like that? It makes you look stupid—and weird. I heard other mothers talking about you at the Brennons' party the other night. They referred to you as 'the space case who started the dumpster fire at the high school.' Can you imagine my embarrassment?"

"Shut up," Harlon said aloud in the bedroom. He blinked his eyes rapidly to get rid of that image of his mother's sour expression. He saw his family's bodies littering the white carpet of the living room, someone in a fish head mask standing over each of the three corpses. After the killings, Harlon sat on the plush sofa chair where only his father had been allowed to sit.

Harlon watched the glowing green candle as he prayed to those in the swamp. *May I open the door so that he who comes is he who has returned. Please guide me. Please empower me. May Grandpappy and Maman lend me their wisdom.*

Harlon moved onto the bed where Todd lay and opened the urn. He poured a cupful of ashes into the palm of his hand and sprinkled them along the body—in Todd's eyes, on his lips, down his torso, across his toes.

He had the thought that if the ashes didn't bring Sander back to life, he'd have to kill Kim when she came back to the apartment. The Savannah ceremony would have failed. And the Family would have to punish Harlon. He recalled Maman's words again: "If you fail, you won't become a minister. And I'm not sure the swamp will have you."

As instructed, Harlon began smacking the ashes into the body with an open hand. He started with the feet and moved up the legs. The smacking became more forceful when he reached Todd's chest.

He felt his sister hitting his own chest on the day of the killings. Darla had beat her fists against him when he dragged her away from the front door and into the living room, toward their parents' crumpled and bleeding bodies. She was crying and screaming hysterically. "Who are these people, Harlon? Were they with you at the detention center?"

"They're my friends," Harlon responded with some pride. "They understand me."

Harlon hadn't cried when the Family stabbed his parents, but the tears came when Lizanna pulled his 16-year-old sister away from him and pushed her toward the man with the machete.

Harlon smacked Todd's body harder and cried in a desperate voice, "Come into him, Sander! Come into him!"

He knew that if the swamp wouldn't have him, he'd end up going where everyone else went when they died. He needed to go to the swamp, like the honorable sacrifices and the ministers. The swamp was a place of green fire, of pure power. The spirits of the dead flowed with that power through the countless trees, along the surface of the murky water, down into the deepest and darkest gator holes. The place where everyone else went was where his parents and sister had gone. Where they could be waiting for him. Where they'd confirm what they'd always implied: He wasn't good enough.

Harlon was smacking Todd's bruised throat when he heard the noise.

A gasp!

He stared down at the corpse. The mouth was open, and the eyelids were fluttering again. The chest rose and fell with breath.

Harlon patted one of the cheeks and asked, "Sander? Sander, are you here?" He'd told Orchid to tell Kim that "cousin" Sander had an "intellectual disability" and was out of it. But what if the resurrected Sander was just a vegetable?

"Sander, nod if you can hear me." The room was becoming dim with evening, and the single candle wasn't providing enough light. Harlon thought he saw the chin move, but he was uncertain.

"Sander, can you speak?"

A groan sounded in the throat, but no words came out of the mouth.

Harlon placed his hand against the cheek, which felt like it was warming. "Sander, if you're here and I've done my job, please say 'Yes.' Just a simple 'yes.'"

The chin appeared to move again, and there was a second groan.

Harlon's eyes teared up when he heard Sander speak. "Yeeesss."

11

The young men with the tattooed arms dragged Kim up the stairs of the bus, and then they released her. Kilby sat in the driver's seat. He offered Kim a goofy grin.

"Now you know what I do for work," he said.

Kim rushed into the second row of seats and pulled up a quilt that concealed the windows. She banged her fist against one window. "Help!" she screamed. "I'm being kidnapped!"

None of the passersby looked up at her. A pack of college-age girls in feathered party hats roamed past Jackson Square, their squeals nearly as loud as Kim's shriek.

The bus pulled away from the curb, and Eustace came behind Kim and grabbed her wrist. "The windows are soundproof," he said. "Nobody can hear you." His grip was painful, and it only tightened when she tried to pull her arm away from him. "Come to the back of the bus."

"Let me go!" Kim howled. Her heart hammered against her chest. Were they going to kill her like they had that white-haired woman in the antiques shop? She thought of that poor woman's bent, lifeless body and began to cry.

"I'm not going to hurt you," Eustace said. "Come along."

Kim wiped her tears away with the back of her hand. She knew she needed to calm down so she could figure out her escape. Eustace tugged on her arm again, and she went with him, balancing herself by touching the tops of seats.

After four rows, the aisle opened into what looked like living quarters. Despite the darkness of night and the quilts that covered some of the windows, Kim could see a card table and two chairs that were fastened to the floor. Suspended from one wall were mesh bags containing canned and boxed foods. Sleeping bags and a cluster of duffel bags lined the opposite wall. Aunt Lizanna sat between Teressa and Guthrie on a row of seats at the very back of the bus. Her eyes closed, Aunt Lizanna looked like she was in the middle of meditating or praying. Teressa and Guthrie stared at Kim with dazed expressions, and Teressa signaled silence by placing an index finger over her lips.

Kim glanced over her shoulder and saw that Jack and Rayna sat across the aisle from the young men at the front of the bus, probably guarding the doors in case she tried to flee.

"You don't seem to be happy in our home," Aunt Lizanna said.

Kim looked at the rear of the bus again. Aunt Lizanna was staring at her.

"We're actually very pleased to have you here," Aunt Lizanna said with a smile. "It's not exactly spacious, but it's where we live. The Family saves its houses for teachings, ceremonies, and the spirits. Buses are our homes because we don't have many attachments in this world. I can see you still have your attachments on your mind."

Kim thought of Malia. She hoped Malia had listened to her and would immediately get to Whistler even though it would soon be night on the West Coast.

Eustace motioned for Kim to sit at the table. She begrudgingly lowered herself onto one of the chairs. Eustace took the seat opposite of hers.

"Why don't you just let me go?" she asked Aunt Lizanna. "You've got Eustace—I mean Sander—back." She glimpsed disappointment in Eustace's eyes.

"You've got him back, too," Aunt Lizanna said. "Your fiancé."

"But he's not the man I thought he was." Kim avoided eye contact with her resurrected fiancé. She thought what a fool she'd been to believe Eustace offered her security, respectability, and a means of not turning out like her mother. He'd always been a gleaming trap waiting to snap shut.

"He's so much more than the man you agreed to marry," Aunt Lizanna said. "You should be grateful he's willing to have you."

Kim ignored the woman's crazy words. She glanced out the window and saw the bus was now speeding along the freeway. Even if she could push past the people near the doors, she wouldn't be able to jump from the moving vehicle. A full and yellow moon glowed above the rooftops of New Orleans.

"Where are we going?" she asked, her voice cracking.

Aunt Lizanna grinned widely. "Where else? The swamp."

Kim sat in terrified silence for most of the hour-long journey that took them from city to countryside. She didn't know how she'd ever be able to get out of this situation. She was in a state where she didn't know a single person, and now she was heading toward Louisiana's backwoods—or back bayous—where there would be even fewer people who could possibly help her. Seattle and Malia seemed like they were a galaxy away.

The bus took a right onto a narrow road, and Kim peered out the window at the dark foliage. She kept thinking if only she could exit this bus, she could quickly disappear among those dense trees. She spotted a sign reading *FLEUR NOIRE PLANTA-TION*. She had trouble breathing as she wondered what they'd do with her at a plantation house. Was this the cult's home base? Or was this just the place where they'd finally dispose of her?

The bus veered left onto a dirt road and soon approached a well-lit white wooden house. The compact structure was two stories tall and raised above the grassy ground on brick stilts. Thin columns lined the front gallery and supported the sloping red roof. Kim guessed the house couldn't contain more than two or three bedrooms.

"Welcome to the Swamp House," Eustace told her. He used a respectful tone of voice when naming the destination. "It's your home now."

Kim shook her head. Before she could protest Aunt Lizanna sang, "Welcome indeed. It was a lot of work getting you here, Kim. You did a lot of work yourself, and we thank you for it."

"I'd rather be anywhere else than your goddamn plantation house," Kim muttered.

"I told you it's the Swamp House," Eustace corrected her. As the bus slowed to a stop, he took hold of her wrist again and pulled her up from the table. Aunt Lizanna, Teressa, and Guthrie also stood.

"The plantation house and the slave cabins burned down in the Civil War," Aunt Lizanna told Kim. "All that was left was the overseer's house, and that's been perfect for Maman. She's lived there for nearly a century."

"Maman?" Kim asked. She wondered if she'd actually meet the ancient woman. She tried to picture what a 120-year-old woman would look like. She couldn't imagine how someone born at the turn of the 20th century could have kept her sanity after experiencing so many decades of life. But Kim knew the Family was far from normal—or natural. "Maman is the mother of this cult, isn't she?"

"Don't use that word," Eustace scolded her. He wheezed when he spoke. "It's such a small word." He let go of her wrist.

"Sander, honey," Aunt Lizanna said, "preserve your strength." She came over to him and slipped her arm around his side. Kim noticed how much he'd deteriorated during the drive. Dark lines curved beneath his eyes, and his skin seemed to have lost its previous glow. Maybe the ceremonies hadn't worked that well after all.

"I'll be fine," Eustace said, frowning at Kim as if he'd heard her thoughts.

"You will," Aunt Lizanna told him. "You'll be complete after the final ceremony tomorrow." She turned to Kim. "Maman will be passing over soon, and Sander is her successor—and your fiancé. I ask that you pay him the respect he deserves."

Kim looked into Eustace's eyes for some sign of the person she'd known and cared about. He turned away from her and said, "I want to go inside and be apart from Kim for a while. It's okay now that we've completed the New Orleans ceremony."

"Of course," Aunt Lizanna said in a consoling voice. "You two will be together again tonight." She walked with him toward the front of the bus.

Guthrie placed his hand on Kim's lower back. "Go on and follow them, girl." As Kim walked behind Eustace and Aunt Lizanna, she felt a rage rising within her. Eustace didn't deserve any more respect from her. She'd lugged his ashes from Southern city to Southern city out of misguided respect, but mostly out of guilt. And she didn't feel that guilt anymore. Eustace's treachery had erased it. She was going to see Malia again, and the Family could only stop her by killing her.

As they crossed the grass toward the house, Kim considered trying to sprint away. But in what direction? Teressa, Guthrie, Jack, and Rayna trailed behind her, and beyond them was the bus with Kilby and the two young men inside. Just down the road were a couple other battered buses, most likely also housing Family members. The only direction she could run in was toward the wall of trees that was about a hundred yards past the rear of the house. She guessed those trees marked the start of the swamp.

Kim was staring at the trees when she heard a scream come from their shadows.

Aunt Lizanna turned toward Eustace and smiled. "Sounds like your helping hands are almost ready." She glanced back at

Guthrie. "Go show Kim what real respect looks like. Teressa and I will take Sander inside."

Guthrie caught up with Kim and pointed toward the trees. "Come on with me, girl. Walk with heavy steps when we're in the tall grass. We can't have a snake biting the chaperone."

"I'm not a fucking chaperone," Kim said. "I'm someone you duped into coming here." She checked over her shoulder and saw that Jack and Rayna were just behind her.

Guthrie shook his head and walked ahead of her across the grass. He smiled at her. "You don't even know how important you are, do you?"

Kim was about to give a sarcastic reply when she heard a woman's moan.

"We're here, baby," Guthrie called out. "And it sounds like you did it. Maman's going to be so happy with her baby girl."

A hulking bald man stepped from the darkness of the trees into the moonlight. Kim could make out the Confederate flag on his T-shirt. She could also see he held a machete. The blade gleamed, and Kim guessed it was wet. A knot of fear formed in her stomach.

The bald man used the blade to motion for them to approach.

Rayna placed a hand on Kim's back and nudged her forward. "Go on."

"No!" Kim tried to dart back in the direction of the road, but Guthrie grabbed her by the wrist.

"Calm it, girl," he said. "That blade's not for you."

Kim understood there was nowhere she could run to right now. She walked with wobbly legs in the direction of the man with the machete.

When they were close to the trees, a yellow light brightened. The bald man held a portable lantern. Below him was a large tree stump, and two people sat leaning against the stump.

Their features were hazy because of the dim, but Kim could see the man on the left side of the stump had a tattooed face and appeared to be dozing. One of his arms was tucked beneath his armpit. The woman on the right side seemed to be watching Kim. When the bald man set the lantern on the stump, Kim gasped.

The woman was Orchid.

"Hi, y'all," Orchid spoke. Her voice wasn't much more than a whisper. "These pills work real good. Bird got lucky and passed out." She smiled at Kim. "Heya, chaperone."

Kim was too shocked to speak. She gawked at the bandage at the end of Orchid's left arm. The man with the tattooed face also had a bandage. His was on the arm he held beneath his armpit. Next, Kim saw the two bloodied, dismembered hands on the tree stump.

Her entire body began shaking.

"Aw, Kim," Orchid said in a consoling voice. "Don't be afraid." She glanced at the gruesome hands with sleepy eyes. "You should consider those wedding presents."

"I'm not so sure she appreciates them," Guthrie said. He pulled Kim toward the tree stump.

"Please, no," Kim whispered. She tried to resist, but Guthrie yanked her by the wrist violently.

"I told you he's not going to cut you," he said. "I just want to show you how everything goes to good use round here."

As they neared the mutilated pair, Kim spotted the chain-link fence past the tree line. The bald man set his machete on the ground and picked up the lantern and one of the hands from the tree stump. It was the smaller, more feminine hand—Orchid's hand. He went to the fence, and Guthrie and Kim followed him.

Kim glanced at Orchid, but the woman's eyes were now closed. Orchid looked like she'd lost consciousness.

Beyond the fence was a circular pit filled with muddy water as dark as coffee grounds. The bald man made a surprisingly high-pitched yapping sound, like a small dog, and Kim watched in terror as an alligator's massive head rose above the murky water. Its slightly parted jaws made it look like it was grinning.

Kim recalled her dream of the huge alligator floating above her, and she tried to step back from the fence. Guthrie gripped her tightly.

"Feeding time, girl," he said.

The bald man flung Orchid's hand above the gator, and the huge, dark gray creature rose out of the muck and slammed its jaws shut on the piece of human meat.

After swallowing, it sank partway beneath the water. But its eyes remained above the surface, in the glow of the lantern. Kim sensed those eyes were watching her.

Kim felt woozy as Guthrie led her toward the Swamp House. Guthrie had his arm hooked around hers, and Jack and Rayna followed them. She kept thinking about the alligator feeding and how Orchid and she had clasped hands while they danced together in Savannah. Kim tried to focus on the grass before her, but the scary thoughts kept coming. If they'd mutilated their own members, what were they going to do to her? And what would happen to Malia if they caught her sneaking away to Canada?

The thought of Malia helped Kim center herself. She needed to be focused if she was going to get off this property and back to Seattle. She inhaled and exhaled deeply a few times, and she felt like she was fully inside her skin by the time she ascended the steps to the Swamp House's front gallery.

She looked behind her. Jack and Rayna remained on the grass, the moonlight making their pale faces look ghoulish.

"Only the ministers can enter Maman's house," Guthrie said to Kim. He touched her shoulder. "And special guests like yourself, of course."

Kim was relieved to be free of Jack and Rayna for at least a while. Guthrie moved past her and opened the house's screen door. The door creaked loudly.

"Après vous, mam'selle," he said.

Kim stepped into a small entrance hall. Apparently, the house had no air conditioning. She immediately began sweating.

"Cooks in here," Guthrie said, "but extreme temperatures don't bother Maman. She's upstairs resting, by the way. So's Eustace, I'd imagine."

Kim glanced up a narrow staircase that ended in darkness. She then looked around the hall. The walls were covered in light blue-green paint that was cracked and peeling. Kim peered above her head at one of the worst patches.

"Before Maman moved in, there was a fellow from South Carolina who lived here. Supposedly, he was having trouble with some ghosts—maybe the overseer's, maybe a slave's. He painted the walls haint blue."

Kim gave him a puzzled look.

"A haint's a ghost or a spirit," Guthrie explained. "Haint blue is supposed to keep them away because spirits can't cross water. But as you can see, the spirits have chipped away at that paint over the years."

Kim had the thought that the Family wouldn't be feeding her all this information if they were going to kill her tonight. She sensed she was still important to them, which meant she had more time to plan how to get away.

"Guthrie," a woman spoke.

Kim looked to her left and saw Teressa's wide body in a doorway to what looked like a dining room.

"Come on in, Kimmy," Teressa said.

Kim winced at the sound of that nickname she hated, and she pictured her drunk stepfather sneering at her.

She decided to follow these people's directions for now. While feigning obedience, she'd find her means of escape. She entered the dining room, which was connected to a small kitchen. She glanced out one of the open windows offering a view of the front yard. She didn't see anyone standing on the moonlit grass. There was a glow in the distant bus with the vulture painted on its side. She wondered if the bald man had taken Orchid and Bird there.

"Can you hear the swamp?" Teressa asked.

Kim listened and heard the incessant, high-pitched chorus of what must have been insects and frogs.

"An owl was hooting earlier," Teressa said. "Sometimes we can hear the hiss of a gator—either our gator or the many other ones out there in the water. It's good to be home again."

"Sure is," Guthrie said. He stood behind Kim. "Looks like the table's all set for tomorrow's feast."

Kim glanced down at the dining table, which had five chairs around it. A tablecloth with a palm frond pattern covered the table. Lying atop each of the five dark green placemats were a fork and a large carving knife. A red candle flickered on either end of the table.

"I just got the coconut oil ready," Aunt Lizanna said. She entered the kitchen from a hallway near the rear of the house. She had a manic look in her violet eyes. "I think we're all set," she told Teressa and Guthrie. "You two want to bring her in?"

Kim's voice trembled when she asked, "Are we about to be in another ceremony?"

"'We?'" Aunt Lizanna grinned and shook her head. "I don't think you've been in any of the ceremonies so far, Miss Seattle. But tomorrow you will be. The final—and the biggest—ceremony of them all."

Sweat now soaked Kim's blouse. She considered reaching for one of the carving knives, but Teressa blocked her way to the table. Kim glanced around the kitchen for something that might serve as a weapon. The counters and shelves were bare. Hanging on the walls were bundles of bulbous roots and a little black doll with a red dress and long white feathers sticking out of its head. The doll was hanging upside down above the stove.

"Don't you love her?" Aunt Lizanna asked, grinning at the doll. "Sander gave her to Maman as a present when he was just a teenager."

Kim didn't answer. Recognizing there was nothing in this kitchen to help her, she said, "Let's get on with it. I'm ready."

Aunt Lizanna led her into the hallway behind the kitchen. The hallway stretched back to the entrance hall. Across the way from the kitchen was a small room containing a single bed. On top of the mattress lay what looked like some kind of weird armor made of alligator skin. Kim saw a breastplate and long gloves with claws at their ends. She also noticed a door leading out to the house's back gallery.

"That's none of your business in there," Teressa said. She placed her hands on Kim's shoulders, guiding her along the hallway. Kim stepped forward to avoid her touch. Aunt Lizanna took a left through the next doorway down, and Kim realized there was no longer anyone to block her path. She could dash into the entrance hall and head for the front door.

When she was outside the room Aunt Lizanna had entered—a bathroom—Kim rushed down the hallway. "Guthrie!" Teressa shouted.

Kim heard pounding footsteps as he came out of the dining room toward the front door. She knew she'd run right into Guthrie if she tried to get out the way they'd come in. She saw another door in the entrance hall. If the door led to a rear chamber that was like the corner bedroom, she might have a way out to the back gallery. She flung the door open and then slammed it behind her.

Kim felt a lock below the doorknob. She turned the lock.

This room was nearly pitch-dark and even hotter than the rest of the house. Kim didn't see a door to the gallery, but she did see two wide-open windows. Of course, they'd have screens on them, like the windows in the dining room, but Kim could get those off somehow. As Teressa or Guthrie fiddled with the doorknob, Kim started toward the windows. She could hear Teressa cursing on the other side of the door.

Something brushed against her leg.

She froze. She wasn't able to see exactly what had touched her, but as her eyes adjusted to the dark, she realized there were four people sitting on the floor. She stood in the center of them.

"Leave her be," Aunt Lizanna commanded through the closed door. "She won't be ready until tomorrow."

"I don't want trouble," Kim whispered for whoever was in the room with her.

Someone lit a match, and Kim saw a young man's scowling face near the flame. The skinny fellow couldn't have been much older than Kilby. He was bare-chested and wore tattered shorts. He brought the match to a candle near Kim's feet, and the light grew stronger.

Kim realized all the seated figures were young men, and they were dressed alike. They looked equally undernourished.

And all were missing body parts.

Kim's mouth dropped open, but she was too stunned to scream.

She saw the one who'd lit the candle had legs that ended in stumps. Two were missing their right hands. The fourth one—the one that leered at Kim—appeared to be without a nose or lips.

Kim ran to one of the windows. She tried to punch out the screen, but the door slammed open and heavy footsteps sounded behind her.

"Come on now, girl," Guthrie said, hooking his arm around her middle.

"No!" Kim shrieked. The screen finally gave way, and she held on to the window's ledge. She tried to crawl out onto the gallery, but Guthrie pulled her back through the window.

"Help me!" Kim screamed in the direction of the swamp. "Someone please help me!"

She was about to cry out again when something hard hit the back of her head.

Kim awoke to someone dragging her by the legs across floorboards. Her arms were stretched out behind her body. She opened her eyes and saw Guthrie holding her ankles. He grinned down at her as he pulled her back through the hallway leading to the kitchen.

"Now that was stupid of you, wasn't it?" he asked.

Kim lifted her arms to try and grab a hold of something, but she realized someone had tied her wrists with rope. She attempted to kick her legs and get free of Guthrie. She had little strength. The top of her head ached from whatever had collided with her skull before.

Teressa walked in front of Guthrie. The bitch wielded a large metal candlestick holder.

Guthrie stopped outside the doorway to the bathroom Aunt Lizanna had entered earlier. Teressa tread carefully past Kim's prone body. She set the candlestick holder on the floor and grabbed Kim's outstretched arms. She stared down at her.

"Kimmy, we need you to behave now. You were such a good fiancée up until the time you got to Pensacola. I think you owe it to your Eustace to-"

"I owe him nothing!" Kim said, seething. "Not anymore."

Teressa glared at Kim. "One more outburst and I swing that candlestick holder again. You hear me?"

Kim knew she needed to preserve her strength. She nodded.

Guthrie and Teressa carried her into the bathroom, which was surprisingly large. Bundles of sweet-smelling flowers hung from a hook and a towel rack on the green-tiled wall. Kim heard the squeaky turn of a faucet and then water pouring into a bathtub. She looked to her left and saw Aunt Lizanna sitting on the edge of the tub.

"You calmed down now?" Aunt Lizanna asked. "If not, you will be soon."

Kim didn't answer. She watched Aunt Lizanna dip her hand into the partially full tub, as if testing the temperature of the water. Aunt Lizanna rose and came over to her.

"Let's get her clothes off."

"No!" Kim said, squirming.

Teressa dropped Kim's upper body, and her head knocked against the bathmat. She howled in pain. She wished she could rub the back of her head, but the rope around her wrists prevented her from doing so. Exhausted, she lay still on the floor, staring up at the twirling ceiling fan.

She squirmed again as Teressa leaned over her and began unbuttoning her blouse. Guthrie lowered Kim's legs and pulled off her pumps. Aunt Lizanna kneeled to unzip her jeans.

"We're not going to hurt you," Aunt Lizanna said in a soothing voice. She pulled off Kim's pants. "Will you get into the bath on your own, or are we going to have to carry you and hold you down?"

Kim decided not to resist anymore. She would go back to playing along with them until she had a better option. "I'll get in the tub," she said.

Aunt Lizanna nodded approvingly. Teressa untied the rope and motioned for Kim to sit up. Teressa then removed Kim's blouse all the way. They left on her bra and underwear.

Kim stood and walked over to the bath. She slowly lowered her toes, and she found that the water was refreshingly cool but just warm enough to keep her from feeling chilled.

When she sat in the tub, she noticed the painting that rested on top of the faucet. It was a portrait of a narrow-faced, balding man with a pointed chin—the same man Kim had seen in that painting at Aunt Lizanna's house in Pensacola. He wore a red vest, a black shirt, and a thin red necktie. There was something sinister about his narrowed eyes. With paint cracking in places, the portrait looked ancient.

"We call him Grandpappy," Aunt Lizanna said. She returned to her perch on the side of the tub and turned off the water. "Does he look like anyone you know?"

Kim stared at the portrait. She shook her head.

Aunt Lizanna shrugged. "Paintings never do justice to flesh and blood." She pointed at the sink and told Teressa, "Bring the jars."

While Teressa went to the sink, Guthrie fetched a cardboard box that lay in one corner of the room. When he brought it over to the tub, Kim saw it was filled with flower petals.

Guthrie sprinkled the petals in the water. Pink and red, they stuck to Kim's wet thighs and forearms. Teressa set two large jars on the side of the tub.

"Honey and coconut oil," Aunt Lizanna said. "I'll let you choose which one to put on first."

Kim removed the lid of the jar of coconut oil. She looked at Aunt Lizanna while she applied the oil to one shoulder with trembling fingers. "What is this all about?" she asked.

Aunt Lizanna smirked. "We're getting you all cleaned up—and smelling as sweet as a sugar bear."

"No," Kim said. "I mean all of this—the bath, the men in that room, the chopped-off hands."

Aunt Lizanna gave her a knowing nod. "This is about devotion, about sacrifice."

Kim watched her in silence. Despite the warm water and the house's heat, she shivered.

"You know a little about sacrifice," Aunt Lizanna said. "You left the comfort of your apartment and brought your beloved fiancé's ashes to the deep and dirty South even though Eustace was dead and couldn't make you go. Well, the Family knows a whole lot about sacrifice. We don't just give up our comfort or our time. We give our bodies and we give our lives."

"You're still alive," Kim said in an accusing voice.

"Maman wanted me to stay. She made me a minister, and a minister's got a responsibility to stay. Finish up with the coconut oil."

Kim poured some of the oil on her knees and quickly spread it down her shins. Aunt Lizanna took the jar from her and handed her the honey.

"Few Family members stay around past 30," she said. "The swamp usually wants them by then."

"For what?"

"The swamp needs to be fed, just like us all. And this feeding is a fair exchange for what the swamp gives us: knowledge, a connection with something much greater than ourselves, power…. The swamp has allowed our leaders to live very long lives. Grandpappy was on this earth for 121years, and Maman has lasted for even longer than that. And Sander—your Eustace—will outlive both of them."

Kim folded her arms over her chest in a protective embrace. Frowning, she asked, "So you're going to feed me to the swamp?"

Aunt Lizanna turned to Guthrie and said, "Towel." She then smiled at Kim. "Sugar bear, what we're going to do with you is rinse you off and put you to bed for the night."

Before they left the bathroom, Teressa held up a beige rayon slip in front of Kim. "You don't want to sleep in your wet underwear, do you? Now are you going to put this on or do we need to do it for you?"

Guthrie faced a wall while Teressa removed Kim's damp bra and panties. Kim stepped into the slip. Even though she felt a little cold in the bathtub, she was now sweating again from the heat of the house.

"We're going to take you upstairs," Aunt Lizanna said while Teressa retied the rope around Kim's wrists. "Don't try any more foolishness."

Kim followed Aunt Lizanna out into the entrance hall and up the narrow staircase. On the second floor, she glanced out one of the windows and saw a distant figure on the lawn. Whoever it was ducked behind a tree.

A long table on the second floor landing held a row of burning candles. Between the candles were what looked like animal skulls. One had a thick, curving beak and another possessed stubby horns. On either side of the table was a closed door.

Aunt Lizanna led Kim past one of the doors. Kim thought she heard raspy breathing coming from beyond the door.

"Maman's chamber," Aunt Lizanna said, sounding reverent. "She's breathing like that because she's going to pass any day now." She nodded toward the second door. "And this is your and your fiancé's room."

Kim's body became tense once more. She remembered Eustace referring to the bedroom when they'd been in New Orleans. She glanced behind her, thinking she might try fleeing down the stairs, but Guthrie and Teressa blocked the stairway.

"Don't look so anxious," Aunt Lizanna said. "You two have shared a bed before." She opened the door and motioned for Kim to enter.

After a moment of hesitation, Kim walked into the candlelit chamber. Flower petals covered the carpet. Across the room from her was a queen-sized bed with Eustace sprawled on top of it. He had on the alligator skin breastplate and sharp-fingered gloves she'd seen downstairs. Atop his head was a small crown made out of what looked like animal bones. He wore nothing else except for a pair of black boxer briefs. He stared at her, looking both sickly and smug. He then patted the mattress beside him with one of the clawed gloves.

"Come on in, sweetheart," he said.

Kim backed up toward the doorway until she knocked into someone. She reeled around and saw Guthrie standing there.

"You heard him, girl," he said.

Kim tried to bolt past Guthrie, but he took hold of her upper arms and dragged her toward the bed. He shoved her on the mattress and held her down. Kim wasn't strong enough to free herself. Teressa went to the night table on Kim's side of the bed. On the table were a burning red candle and a few coils of rope.

Teressa and Guthrie tied Kim's arms and legs to two bedposts—one at the top of the bedframe, and one at the bottom. This room was just as hot as the dark one downstairs, and Kim's perspiration soon soaked the sheet beneath her.

Guthrie and Teressa exited the bedroom, and Aunt Lizanna momentarily remained in the doorway. She told Kim, "Enjoy your last night with your Eustace," and then she shut the door.

Kim turned to Eustace, who was smiling at her.

"Try to get some sleep," he said.

She saw no sign of his previous disappointment or irritation with her. He reached over and rested one of the gloves on her stomach. She whimpered when she felt the claw's sharp points through the material of her slip. But what scared her more were Eustace's next words.

"Tomorrow's our wedding day."

12

On the day he was to shoot himself in the head, Sander walked along a snaking road that connected Seattle's Capitol Hill and Eastlake neighborhoods. This was one of the few barely populated streets in the city. Paralleling the I-5 freeway, the tree-lined road bordered a densely forested hill that led up to the rear of a large church.

Sander sensed that someone was following him. He turned his head and glimpsed a young man with unkempt hair and soiled clothes. This one was stockier than most of the street punks Sander saw in the city. They were all over downtown, asking for a dollar on corners or crashed outside markets with their friends and pit bulls. Sander guessed this fellow was interested in him because he was wearing one of the suits he put on every weekday morning for the law firm job he'd fabricated. The street punk most likely figured Sander could have a wallet or a smartphone for the stealing.

Sander didn't mind this street punk trailing him. The only one who absolutely couldn't see where he was going this morning was Kim—and she was at work at the University of Washington Medical Center.

Increasing his pace, Sander walked around a bend in the road and then started up a faint trail that cut through ivy and rose into the forest. He glanced behind him to make sure the young man was still following. When he saw his pursuer, he grinned to himself and kept walking briskly. After all, he had a lot to do before he killed himself this evening.

Sander passed through a scattering of potato chip bags, chocolate bar wrappers, cigarette butts, and dirty paper towels. Nearby was a collapsed tent with burn marks on it. Someone had spray painted the image of a lizard—or an alligator—on the side of the tent.

Sander knew he was close. "J'aime ma mère," he called out. *I love my mother.*

"J'aime ma famille," someone responded from farther up on the hill. *I love my family.*

Sander saw Brandon and the other four recruits emerge from behind a cluster of tree trunks in the distance. All in their early twenties and all hollow-cheeked, the men descended the hillside with beaming faces, looking pleased to see Sander. As well they should be, considering he'd been their teacher for nearly a year.

Sander had met Brandon during the May Day protests. Brandon was one of a group of black-clad anarchists with shoulder-length hair who were smashing windows in Seattle's retail core. Maman had advised Sander to seek those who were furious with both their parents and society, and Brandon turned out to be one of these—as did the other four, whom Brandon invited up from their anarchist enclave in Olympia. Brandon had informed them at the first teaching, "This guy's got connections to actual spirits and shit that are on our side. He's told me stuff about myself that no one else knows, and he's promised that if we help him, he'll teach us some of his magic."

Sander now pointed at the ruined tent. "You been messing with the homeless folks again?" he asked.

Brandon gave a lopsided grin. "We got bored." He nodded toward the street punk down the hill. "Who's that fool?"

Sander turned toward his pursuer. "Hey!" he called. "Get on up here if you want to make some extra cash." The street punk looked hesitant, but then he continued the climb. Sander figured he recognized his own kind standing among the trees.

Sander motioned for the recruits to sit on the littered stretch of hillside before him. They'd met on this hillside before. Sometimes the teachings had taken place in empty parks or condemned homes or warehouses. "You sit, too," Sander told the street punk. The young man shot a cautious glance at the others, and then he squatted over a patch of dirt to the left of them.

"Today's the last day I stand before you like this," Sander informed the group.

"Already?" Brandon asked, scowling.

"Maman has decided that today I must come home." He looked past the trees behind him. Beyond the freeway were Seattle's skyscrapers and the Space Needle. Ash-gray clouds drifted over the cityscape. "And, as you know, I'll be leaving my body here."

The street punk look puzzled.

"But what if it doesn't work?" Brandon asked. "What if you just…die like everyone else does?"

"This is horseshit," the street punk interjected. He rose from the ground and started down the hill. He sneered at Sander as he passed him.

"You're so sure of that?" Sander asked.

"I'm sure you're a fucking wacko. I've met enough to know."

Sander followed him a few steps down the path. He would have blurted out something about the street punk that nobody was supposed to know, but he didn't actually have the power to do that yet. Orchid and a couple other Family members had quickly developed psychic abilities, and they were the ones that called him with messages the swamp had given them about his Northwest followers. But Sander would gain that power when he succeeded Maman, just like he would gain so many powers.

He had other abilities, though, and they always got him the attention he wanted.

"So you think you know me?" he asked the young man.

The street punk paused in his descent and glared at Sander. He looked like he might start back up the hill and swing a fist at him.

"Look again," Sander said. He pinched the skin of his chin and pulled it upwards so the street punk would see what Sander wanted him to see: the peeling of skin and the partial revealing of a skull with muscles and tendons still intact.

"Holy shit." The street punk was gaping at him.

"Get up here or I'll show you a lot worse," Sander said. He brought the skin back into place. He remembered when Maman had taught him that trick. "Boo hag vision," she'd called it. "You can use it to make yourself look good, too. You'll use it for your bride-to-be."

The street punk hesitated, as if he were considering running, and then he returned to the group of followers. The young men watched their teacher with glimmers of admiration in their eyes.

"As I was saying," Sander told them, "today is the day."

Brandon nodded.

"But it's not the last time you'll see me."

"Will you come back up here?" Brandon asked.

Sander shook his head. "I belong in the South, near the swamp. I'm going to be the heart of the Family. Like Maman is, and like Grandpappy was before her. But you'll come down to the swamp when there's no more need for you here." He looked at Jason, the thinnest one in the bunch. "Did you find the bus like I asked you to?"

"It's waiting for us in Puyallup," Jason said. "I've just got to hand over the cash."

Sander nodded approvingly. "You'll drive that bus to Louisiana when we give you the word. That bus will be your new home."

Brandon suddenly looked upset. "But how will we know everything worked and you're...all right?"

"The Family will tell you. But before that, you'll see me in your dreams. There'll be a green light around me. What are the words I taught you?"

Everyone in the group except for the street punk recited: "Steadfast in hurricane, destroyers of both slave and master. Watch for their green lights."

"That's right," Sander said, smiling. He felt a couple raindrops land on his head. He decided now was the time to leave. He didn't want his suit to get muddy and cause Kim to wonder where he'd been today. She'd have enough to wonder about tonight. He approached the group and embraced his recruits briefly, speaking a few words into each one's ear. He didn't hug the street punk, who stood apart from the others, appearing nervous.

When Sander reached Brandon, he whispered, "You'll become a minister. I'll see to that." Brandon lit up with excitement.

Sander started down the hill, and he stopped when he was beside the ransacked tent.

"You need to do whatever we ask of you," he told the recruits. "If we want you to watch someone, you'll watch. And if we want you to do more, you'll do it. You've all told me you're worthy of the tattoos we're going to give you."

The recruits gave affirming nods.

Sander grinned when he remembered how Maman had asked him over a decade ago to bring that baby goat to the water. Sander had only been living on the Swamp House property for about a year, and he'd immediately become fond of the animal after Guthrie delivered it to the house. "You're going to take the goat to the place where we've seen the most gators," Maman had said, "and you're going to push it into the water. If it climbs up on the bank, you're going to kill it yourself with this machete and toss its bits to the reptiles."

Sander had felt a moment of guilt as he walked back to the Swamp House with blood splatter on his shirt and a red machete, but the bone-tingling embrace Maman gave him made him know what he'd done was exactly what he should have done.

"I'm asking you to do something for me now," Sander told his recruits. He pointed at the street punk. "You see this skeptic here?"

The street punk gave Sander a startled look.

"We can't trust this one," Sander continued. "Don't let him leave the forest alive."

"What the hell?" the street punk asked. He shot up from his seated position and ran in the direction of the church.

"Go now!" Sander told his recruits, and he was relieved to see them quickly pursue the young man, a couple of them pulling knives from their pockets. Brandon was in the lead. He raised his knife high as he caught up to the quarry.

Sander descended the hill, whistling as he walked. When he reached the street again, he was glad to see no sign of mud or dirt on his suit.

Downtown once again, Sander passed a shop with a display of Easter chocolates in its front window. He eyed the chocolate eggs and bunnies wrapped in brightly colored foil and considered buying something for Kim—a last present for his fiancée. But he guessed she'd have no appetite once she found his remains in the kitchen.

And what exactly would he look like after he did it? Aunt Lizanna had told him he'd need to put the gun in his mouth and aim upwards, toward his brain. He guessed his face would still be intact. He wouldn't have minded if Aunt Lizanna had instructed him to point the gun between his eyes. He'd always disliked his face because he looked so much like his father. But what mattered was that his body would be ash within days—ash that his chaperone would deliver down South if all went as the Family had planned.

Sander entered his apartment building and headed toward the elevator bank. He tried to look as despondent as possible for the lobby camera that would be recording his movement. The police might eventually watch that recording.

When he reached the 23rd floor, he was relieved to see the hallway was empty. Betty—that nosy, redheaded hag who lived next door to him—always managed to open her door and step outside just when he was returning to his apartment. He didn't feel like putting on a sad face for the old lady today. Of course, she'd be welcome to enter his home after he shot himself. He'd leave the door unlocked.

He glanced around his orderly apartment. He'd cleaned the place last night, prepping it for Kim and any detective that might poke around his home. The urn was on the kitchen counter, and the gun lay on the dining room table. Before meeting the recruits this morning, he'd gathered his ceremonial tools—the ancient slave rattle, the candles, the snakeskin, the possum teeth, the handkerchief that had once belonged to Grandpappy's wife— and deposited them inside a cloth bag with a couple heavy stones. He dropped the bundle off the end of a rotting pier that jutted into Elliott Bay. As for the two decaying helping hands, he tossed those onto the flat rooftop of a nightclub that was located on an industrial stretch of Eastlake Avenue. The city crows would probably devour the hands, bones and all.

Sander went to the table next to his reading chair and picked up the framed photo of Maman in her old flesh. She'd given him the nearly 100-year-old picture a little over two years ago, on the last day he'd seen her or spoken to her. In the photo, she sat on a bench in New York's Central Park, holding a parasol. Her dark, pretty eyes had a mischievous look, and there was the slightest grin on her heart-shaped lips. Maman had told Sander she'd jumped off a building to her death the day after posing for that shot.

"My chaperone and I should never have married," she told him one night at the Swamp House. "That was the mistake Grandpappy made, letting us get so far in our relationship. My husband didn't want to take my ashes to the South, like I'd asked him to in my letter. He wanted to trap me in a Long Island cemetery where he could join me when he eventually died. Luckily, the Family had a couple ministers who convinced him that I'd never be able to rest in the North. Of course, I didn't rest at all once I was in my new flesh, and when my husband realized I'd come back, he tried to convince me to get on a train out of New Orleans. As if he could explain to his Manhattan friends how his wife was the same old Gracie even though she had a different skin!"

Maman's laughter soon turned into a phlegmy cough. She pressed her claw-like hand against her chest, and then continued.

"But Grandpappy knew my husband would ultimately be a good fit. Henry had the blood, even though he wouldn't recognize Grandpappy from Adam. I can sense that your chaperone's a better fit, though. She's got the blood, and she won't have the attachment to you that Henry had to me."

Sander smiled at the photo of Maman. "You're always right," he whispered. "Kim doesn't have that attachment."

Even when he'd first approached Kim at that fundraising art auction at the Fred Hutchinson Cancer Research Center, Sander detected a distance he'd never be able to span. The distance became just a bit smaller after he took her on a date to the Palace Kitchen. The pair grew closer the first time they had sex (on Sander's couch, with their shirts still on), the freezing spring weekend they shared a beach cottage on the Oregon coast, the Fourth of July when she apologized for her "coldness" and told him about her stepfather's verbal abusiveness and drinking. But over the past couple years—even on New Year's Eve, after he'd proposed to her—Kim maintained a protective layer around her. Sometimes it was an arm's length, and other times it was as thin as the condoms Sander used when he was inside her. But it was always there. And even though Sander had never really fallen in love with her, he admired her—and respected her—more and more each day.

She was going to be his chaperone, after all. And, if she completed her journey, he was going to finally make her his wife. He wanted that bonding ceremony between him and Grandpappy's descendant.

As he took Maman's photo out of the frame, he realized the distance between him and Kim was best not only because it would help her stay sane when he was dead, but because it would help her go through what he and the Family ultimately had to do to her. No matter how close they became, Sander would never be able to prepare Kim for what must be her fate, even if he explained the everlasting power of the swamp, or Grandpappy's rise from lost plantation owner to someone supernatural, or the bloodline that connected Kim to Grandpappy .

Sander's cell phone rang in his pocket. Pulling it out, he saw Teressa's number on the screen.

"Sister," he said into the phone.

"Brother." She hesitated, and then she asked, "How you holding up?"

"I've been ready for this day for nearly two years."

"That's good." He could hear the worry in her voice. He guessed he and Maman were the only Family members who were certain he would be coming back.

"His name's Todd Regan," Teressa said. "Guthrie found him in Miami. Everything's ready. I'm texting you a picture so you can see what he looks like."

"You get ready, too, sister," Sander said.

"Sander?" she asked. She sounded as if she were going to try and dissuade him from killing himself. After a pause, she said, "Never mind. I'll see you in your new flesh in New Orleans."

"Count on it, sister." Sander hung up the phone and stared down at its screen until he saw the text message with the attachment. He tapped on the attachment and watched an image fill his phone's screen.

A handsome man with gelled, curling brown hair stared back at him. The tanned, muscular fellow only wore black-and-white striped briefs, and he sat on top of a cage with wheels on it, his legs and bare feet dangling over the bars. Emerging from the open door at the side of the cage was an enormous albino tiger. Below the image were the words:

Sit Tight
Skin Tight
SIN TIGHT
underwear for the uncaged

Sander grinned at the advertisement and studied the model's face. He'd need to remember it.

He turned off the phone and went to open one of the windows that looked out on Seattle skyscrapers. Below that side of the building was a fenced-off parking lot that was going to be torn apart for the construction of a new condo tower. Sander threw his phone and Maman's photo in the direction of the parking lot, and he waited until he saw the phone shatter on the pavement before shutting the window.

He undressed and hung up his suit in his bedroom closet. All he had on now were a white T-shirt and white briefs.

Lying on his bed were the suicide note and the envelope with Kim's name and phone number written on it. He picked up the note and read two of the sentences: *Death is not an end. We will see each other again.*

He felt a flicker of fear, and then he reminded himself there was no reason to doubt. Maman had chosen him to be her successor because she knew he was the only one who could be.

Sander folded the note and tucked it inside the envelope. He went to his front door and checked outside to make sure no one was in the hallway. He then crept outside and set the note in front of the hag's door.

Here's something to gossip about, old bitch.

Back inside his apartment, he looked around once again to make sure he hadn't forgotten anything. All was ready for his passing.

He sat at the table and picked up the gun. He spent a moment feeling its weight and the coolness of its metal. He remembered Maman crouching by that 80-year-old gator with its mouth tied shut. "Touch its scales," she'd told the 18-year-old Sander. "Feel its danger."

Sander stared into the black barrel of the gun. He closed his eyes and spoke aloud, "Deliver them the young and the strong so they may feed. They wait for you in the darkest shadows. Watch for their green lights."

He opened his mouth and slipped the gun inside until it touched the roof of his mouth.

The sound of an explosion, yet Sander somehow knew it was actually the sound of an implosion. Without pain, he sensed that all the cells of his body had burst at once, and now they were collapsing inwards. He felt like he was falling.

Blackness surrounded him, and then he was gradually able to see thanks to a faint red light. His pale arms and hands. He used them to discover that the top of his head was still intact. His legs and bare feet. Rock walls—no, cave walls. How Maman said it was going to be.

"You'll find yourself in a cavern. Don't go toward any light or any person who's beckoning you. Seek your new host out, and then get his spirit out of your way. Listen for our voices."

Sander heard a woman's voice coming through one of the cave walls. He placed his ear against the cold, rocky wall and listened for her. She wasn't speaking. She was whimpering.

His mother's whimpering.

"You let them in the bedroom, didn't you?" his father asked through the wall. As always, the man's voice was disappointed, accusing. "Did we really deserve that, son?"

Sander immediately stepped back, shaking his head. "I'm done with you," he said. He'd tried not to think about his parents since Maman had taken him out of their house on Tybee Island so many years ago.

"We still love you," his father called, but Sander placed his palms over his ears.

He hurried away from the part of the cave where he'd heard his parents. He wasn't able to move quickly enough. The rough floor scraped the soles of his feet, and he felt a force trying to suck him upwards, toward the black, tarry-looking ceiling of the cave. He pressed on in a zigzag path, keeping his body on the ground by holding on to protruding rocks. Ahead of him, the passageway branched into two paths.

"Brother?"

Sander saw three shadowy figures blocking one of the paths. The closer they came, the more the mysterious red light illuminated their features. On the left was the skinny young recruit Sander had driven from the Swamp House to Gulf Shores. Sander had strangled him on the beach and then dragged his body into the water. Maman had said he was the worst in a "bad batch" of recruits. "He's just a Christian who's mad at his church, and he's going to tell his preacher all about us if we don't get rid of him." The young man—Bradley had been his name—now had damp, rotting skin and no lower jaw. He stared at Sander with the hollow eyes of a skull.

Next to him were the twin sisters from Brownsville, Tennessee. They weren't much older than teenagers. They'd transformed from shoplifting meth heads to a couple of the Family's most knowledgeable and valuable recruits, but when they heard they each needed to sacrifice an ear for ceremonial purposes, they protested in shrieking voices and fled into the swamp. They stabbed a minister to death when he caught up with them, so Sander shot them after he found them crouching beneath a wooden bridge. He dumped their bodies in St. Louis Cemetery

#1 in New Orleans because Maman informed him, "Those disrespect-
ful bitches won't have resting places anywhere near here."

Sander couldn't remember the name of either one, but their
hateful gazes showed they knew who he was, and they both fin-
gered the bloody bullet holes in the fronts of their tattered dresses.

"How could you have called us Family when you did this to
us?" one of the girls asked him.

"You thought you'd get your high and mighty place in the
swamp," Bradley told Sander, shaking his head, "but now here
you are stuck with us."

Despite the chill in the cave, Sander began to sweat. Was
this going to be his afterlife? Wandering through a red-lit cavern,
bumping into all those he'd turned into corpses?

"COME INTO ME, BROTHER!"

The voice came from somewhere down the other path. Sander didn't recognize the voice, but the words seemed to be the ones
he was waiting for. He moved in the direction of whoever had spoken them, and when he checked over his shoulder, he was relieved
to see the murdered recruits weren't following him.

The path became a pitch-black tunnel, and then Sander saw
the red light again. It now illuminated a tall, broad-shouldered
man who seemed to be trying to climb up to an opening in the
cave wall. As Sander neared, he saw the man wore a Confederate
uniform. He had dark brown curls—the same hair as the model in
the advertisement, but shorter.

"Todd Regan," Sander spoke, grateful that he remembered
the name.

Todd glanced at Sander. There was terror in his eyes and
perspiration on his forehead. He didn't say anything to Sander. He
continued upwards to the opening. His filthy bare feet dangled a
few feet above the ground.

Sander noticed there was no longer a force pulling him upwards. Now gravity had become overbearing, pressing him to-

ward the floor of the cave. Beneath him was that same black muck that had been on the ceiling, and his feet stuck to it. Despite the adhesion, he continued toward Todd.

"Come down from there," he said, grabbing the back of the man's uniform.

Todd swatted at him without looking at him. Clearly, he was much more concerned about what was beyond that opening.

Sander jumped up and held on to the lower lip of the opening. He noticed that lip was slick and vibrating, as if it were in the process of closing. He managed to pull his body up until he was shoulder-to-shoulder with Todd and peering down a long, steep shaft.

Harlon was at the end of that shaft. He held Todd's head beneath the sunlit water of a fountain, his hand around Todd's throat.

Sander grinned at the sight, and his grin widened when he saw that Orchid, Thorner, and Bird stood around the fountain. As planned, the Family was making a way for Sander's passage into his new body.

Sander turned to the Todd that shared the cavern with him. "Just let go. It's over."

Todd shook his head. Tears were in his eyes. "My mother," he said.

"You can't go back. Your time is up." Sander reached over, grabbed Todd by the shoulder, and pulled him down toward the cavern floor. Their bodies hit the ground with a wet sound. As they wrestled, the black goo stuck to their skin and clothing. Sander could feel the suck of the floor. It was as if the cave were trying to consume them.

Todd punched Sander in the face, making Sander lose his grip. Todd rose and stumbled back toward the opening, which appeared to be shrinking. Sander grabbed Todd's legs and yanked him away from the wall. Todd fell face first onto the ground.

"This is your fate!" Sander shouted. "Can't you understand?" He threw himself down on Todd's back, forcing him into the muck. Todd managed to wriggle out from beneath Sander.

While Todd rose to his knees, Sander summoned the energy to pounce on him. Sander put his hand on the crown of Todd's head and pressed his face into the floor. Todd tried to raise himself again but failed. Sander heard a gurgling, and, after some convulsions, Todd's entire body went still.

Sander glanced up at the opening. He was worried it would become too small for him to fit through.

"Come into him, Sander!"

That was Harlon's voice.

Sander scrambled up the wall to the opening again. Peering into the chute, he now saw Todd's body lying on a bed in a candlelit room. Harlon was leaning over that body, smacking it with his hand.

"Come into him!"

"I will, brother!" Sander called, and then he pulled himself into the chute.

Blackness surrounded him again, and he wasn't able to breathe. He felt as if he were no longer within a body. He was in a dark box. Whatever he was now—a soul, a spirit, a ghost— banged against the sides of that container until the blackness gave way to a dim green light.

Sander gasped. The oxygen was refreshing—as if this were his first breath.

"Sander, can you speak?" Harlon asked. "Sander, if you're here and I've done my job, please say 'Yes.' Just a simple 'yes.'"

Sander felt he had a tongue once again. It was a dryer, bigger tongue than he was used to. He said, "Yeeesss."

And then he opened his eyes.

13

"I'm not going to marry you," Kim told Eustace as they lay in bed. "You and your people can tie me up in your Swamp House, but you can't force me to be your wife."

Eustace was on his side. He had no sheet over him—most likely because of the insufferable heat. His head rested on a pillow, and his bone crown tilted toward the back of his skull. He had dark pouches beneath his eyes. He looked as if he were going to slip into sleep—or possibly death.

"I suppose you think you don't need me since you have Malia," he said.

Kim frowned. "How do you know about her?"

"I know so much now that I'm in my new flesh, Kim. And I'll be able to do so much after tomorrow—after our wedding."

Kim shook her head. "I don't love you. All I know about you is that you're a liar and a manipulator." She worried about exactly what Eustace knew. Could he actually read her thoughts? Was he aware that Malia might be driving to Whistler right now?

"And I suppose you love her," Eustace said with a sneer.

Kim glanced up nervously at the ceiling, and then she faced Eustace. "I could love Malia," she said. She noticed a flicker of pain in his eyes.

"Tell me, Eustace," she continued. "Why'd you and your people pick me for this? Or was it just chance that got me here?"

Eustace smiled weakly, looking even more exhausted than before. "Nothing is ever chance, Kim. Each of us has a fate."

Kim squirmed in the bed, hoping she could loosen the ropes. They felt just as tight after she stopped moving. Perspiration covered her body. "And my fate is to be your prisoner wife and live miserably ever after?" she asked.

"We need to sleep now," Eustace said. "Tomorrow's a big day for us." He reached toward her and brushed one of her cheeks with his clawed glove.

Kim winced at his touch. "No!" she said. "I want to know what's going to happen to me."

Eustace took off his crown and set it on the night table next to his side of the bed. He lay with his back to Kim. His breathing quieted, and Kim sensed he was actually falling asleep.

"Tell me!" Kim said. "Are you going to keep me in this house?"

"Just until tomorrow evening," Eustace said in a faint voice.

"And then what?"

"Then I'm going to eat you, Kim. We're all going to eat you."

While Kim wept, Eustace remained on his side. His breathing had become a deep and steady wheeze. Apparently, his talk of cannibalism didn't hinder his sleep. Kim knew Eustace had been telling the truth when he said what he and this cult would do to her. She'd seen the carving knives on the table downstairs, and she recalled Guthrie's words: "Looks like the table's all set for tomorrow's feast." She felt nauseous at the memory of the honey and coconut oil bath. She was struggling with her bonds again when a face appeared in the bedroom window.

It was Iola.

Kim's mouth fell open. She'd thought Iola was dead. "Thank god," she whispered.

Iola pried off the window screen and stuck her head inside the room. Kim realized Iola was the person she'd spotted outside on the lawn when Aunt Lizanna brought her upstairs. Iola pointed at Eustace's body and gave Kim a questioning look. She placed her hands together and rested her cheek on them, inquiring if he was asleep.

Kim nodded.

Iola climbed through the window and neared Kim's side of the bed.

"I'm so happy to see you," Kim said in a quiet voice, her tears returning.

Iola gave a cautious glance at Eustace's sleeping figure. Kim was worried Iola was going to try and wake him so she could rescue her friend "Todd." But Iola stayed on Kim's side of the bed and removed a folding knife from her pants pocket. She began cutting through the part of rope that stretched from Kim's wrists to the upper bedpost.

Eustace moaned, and Kim's muscles tightened. She watched him with frightened eyes. He didn't move.

After freeing Kim's arms, Iola freed her legs.

"We need to get out of here now," Kim whispered, carefully sliding her body off of the bed. She started toward the open window.

"We can climb down the tree I came up," Iola said. "But first I need to check for my friend Allimay."

"No," Kim said, shaking her head. "They'll catch you. Your friend isn't here."

"You've looked in all the upstairs rooms?"

Kim didn't bother to respond. She checked to make sure Eustace hadn't overheard them, and then she nodded in the direction of the window. She had one leg over the windowsill when she glanced back and saw Iola heading toward the bedroom door.

"Shit," Kim said with an impatient sigh.

She hurried back into the room to fetch Iola, but by the time she reached the doorway, Iola was standing outside Maman's chamber, her hand on the doorknob. To the right of the door was the table holding the animal skulls and flickering candles.

Kim waved her arms until she caught Iola's attention. Kim shook her head in protest. Iola gave an apologetic look. She cracked open the door and peeked inside the room. Then she entered.

Kim left Eustace's room and moved toward Maman's chamber as quickly and quietly as possible. She recalled Aunt Lizanna's comment that the woman was going to pass any day now. She hoped Maman would be comatose, like Eustace. Reaching the table, she picked up the skull with the horns, thinking she could use it as a weapon.

She grimaced as a floorboard creaked beneath her weight. She waited for the sound of someone coming up the stairs to investigate, but she didn't hear any movement.

Tiptoeing past the table, she peered down the staircase. Guthrie sat on the bottom step, his eyes closed and his back against the wall. He looked like he was dozing. A machete lay on the step above him.

Kim's heart was slamming against her chest. She stood in the doorway. Maman's chamber was pitch-dark and by far the hottest room in the house. Kim didn't hear the raspy breathing she'd heard before. As her eyes adjusted to the dark, she spotted Iola standing in the middle of the room. She could only see Iola's back, but she noticed the woman had a tense posture. Iola was clutching her knife. With her free hand, Kim reached back toward the table in the hallway and picked up one of the lit candles. She held it before her as she crept inside the room.

At first, she only saw what looked like food scraps on the floor: a rotten three quarters of an apple, some half-eaten chicken drumsticks, a piece of pie smashed into the carpet. Then the candlelight revealed the narrow bed that Iola faced, and, on its dirt-covered mattress, a prone, curled figure. Whoever it was looked brown, small, withered. Perhaps even deceased.

Iola glanced back at Kim with an alarmed expression.

Kim moved closer to the bed. She smelled decay. Blinds covered the windows that were just past the mattress. "Is it Allimay?" she asked Iola. But when the figure slowly uncurled, Kim realized how wrong her guess had been. The person didn't have brown skin. She had strips of alligator skin sewn onto her pale body. Her claws were like Eustace's, but they weren't just gloves. They were stitched to her wrists.

The woman rolled over to face Kim and Iola, and that's when Kim saw her dark eyes, the wisps of white hair that protruded from her nearly bald head, the teeth that someone had filed until they'd become sharp points. The woman hissed, her little, cat-like tongue showing in the center of her mouth. Horrified, Kim tried not to scream. She stepped back and slipped on some slimy piece of food. She went down on her rear, and the skull and candle she'd held tumbled in the direction of the bed.

A flame danced upwards from the carpet, and Kim noticed the tipped-over bottle of whiskey lying beside it. The fire spread quickly, and the woman's—Maman's—hissing grew louder and louder. The ancient woman sat up on her knees, her limp breasts sagging over her hard alligator-skin belly. She swiped at the growing flames with her claws.

"Come on!" Iola said, pulling Kim up from the floor.

They fled from the room, and the hissing behind them became a scream.

"Maman!" Guthrie shouted.

He came bounding up the staircase. Kim dragged the table to the top of the stairs and shoved it down toward him. The furniture and its contents crashed into Guthrie, and the fallen candles created more bursts of fire. As she and Iola ran back toward Eustace's room, Kim saw the flames flickering outside the doorway of Maman's chamber.

Kim flung open the door of Eustace's room. Eustace still lay on his side. Maman's screaming became louder. Kim turned to

Iola and frantically motioned toward the open window through which Iola had entered.

Iola glanced at Eustace's sleeping figure. "What about him?"

Kim rushed toward the window. "His Family will have to save him."

When the women were out on the sloping stretch of roof that sheltered the back gallery, Kim felt a blast of heat come from behind her. Flames now climbed the walls of Eustace's bedroom. Kim realized with revulsion that her fiancé would be burning within minutes.

As soon as she had the thought, the roof collapsed beneath her.

She and Iola hit the back lawn with a thud. Something tore in Kim's ankle. She moaned in pain, and then she remembered she needed to be quiet. She glanced at the back gallery. Thankfully, it was empty. She saw the two windows of the room that had held the people with the missing body parts. She wondered if those people were peering out the window at her and Iola now.

Voices sounded in the front of the house, and then another shriek came from upstairs—from Eustace's bedroom.

"Where are we going to go?" Kim asked.

Iola helped her stand. "They'll catch us if we try to make it to my car. We only have one choice—the swamp."

As they ran toward the dark trees, Kim glanced back at the second floor of the house. A burning figure passed before the window of Eustace's room, his arms waving wildly.

Kim followed Iola through thickly treed forest. Iola barely lit the way ahead of them with a weak flashlight attached to her keychain. Kim could see a moonlit bayou through the trees to their left. She had goose bumps along her arms from the dangling Spanish moss that kept brushing against their heads. She glanced down at her soiled beige slip. She couldn't believe she was limping through swampland barefoot and only dressed in underwear.

The grass beneath her was tall and wet and occasionally gave way to muddy puddles. Kim shuddered when she pictured leeches clinging to her ankles and feet. But she had to go forward. There was only death in the direction of the Swamp House.

"Damn," Iola said.

"What is it?" Kim asked.

"My cell won't turn on. I must have landed on it when we fell off the roof."

Kim looked ahead of them into the darkness of the trees. They seemed to be wandering deeper and deeper into never-ending swampland. "We don't even know where the hell we're going."

"There's a nature preserve near here with a boardwalk trail running through it," Iola said. "I used to go there with my mom when we both lived in New Orleans. We just need to find the trail, and that should lead us to a road."

"How did you get down here?" Kim asked. "I saw your car all smashed up in a ditch."

"One of their buses ran me off the road. I managed to get out before anyone could reach me. I rented a car and drove back to that neighborhood where you and I talked when you first got to Pensacola. On my way, I spotted the bus. I followed it down here."

"Thank you for coming," Kim said.

Iola turned her head and smiled in the moonlight. It was a sad smile. "I'd hoped to find Todd and Allimay. You were right about that man not being Todd. While I was hiding outside and watching the house, I saw him come out and stand on the back gallery. He faced the swamp and said some weird prayer. That wasn't Todd praying."

Kim nodded and continued trudging through the swamp. She was thankful the grass seemed to be getting drier. The trees thinned out a bit, and when Kim looked at the bayou again, she saw the moon was larger and more yellow and almost radiating. There was something hypnotic about it. The moon illuminated a few enormous, wide-trunked cypress trees in the middle of the water. Surrounding the trunks were spiky roots protruding from the bayou.

Kim checked to make sure she had no leeches on her feet. Her skin felt clear of anything except mud. When she looked up again, she didn't see Iola.

"Iola?" she asked.

She only heard the chirping of insects and frogs. She hurried in the direction they'd been walking, hoping to catch up to Iola. The trees became denser again, and it was harder for Kim to see the moon or water. The Spanish moss was hanging lower and lower, oftentimes sticking to her now sweating face. She swung at the moss in annoyance and called Iola's name again—this time more loudly.

She realized she shouldn't be so noisy since the Family could be searching for them. She was relieved to hear footsteps to the right of her. She glanced in that direction, expecting to see Iola coming toward her through the trees. Instead, she saw a man.

He was about twenty feet away, walking parallel to her. He was bone-thin and wore a wide-brimmed panama hat that covered his face. Kim couldn't discern his clothing in the dark. It appeared to be white, like his hat.

Kim stopped, her heart hammering away again. The man paused in a patch of moonlight and turned toward her, his hat still concealing his face. Kim could see he wore a skinny necktie. He brought a hand up and slowly lifted the hat from his head.

It was the man from the paintings—Grandpappy. He had the same balding head with patches of gray hair on either side of it, the same beaklike nose and pointed chin. But his face was more skeletal, more malevolent than the faces in the portraits. He glared at Kim and said, "Disobedient bitch."

Kim was trembling. She could see through the man's body to the cypress trunk just beyond him. "No," she whispered, "you can't be real."

Terrified, she fled through the forest. The farther she ran, the more her feet sank into the mud. She felt like the swamp was trying to swallow her. She whimpered as she struggled to make headway. During her next step, her foot and calf completely disappeared in the muck. She grasped at the ferns ahead of her, hoping she could hang on to them as she pulled her leg free. She was grateful as her arms wrapped around something solid in the greenery. It felt like a large, rubbery trunk. When she got out of the mud, she saw what she actually held.

It was the bent leg of a corpse that lay on the ground.

Kim shrieked and let go of the rotten flesh. The swollen extremity belonged to a bloated and naked man. Beyond him was a long row of unclothed and stinking corpses, the first ones black and the distant ones white.

Kim screamed and couldn't make herself stop.

"Hush! Kim, hush, or they'll hear you." Iola spoke the words, and she cupped a hand over Kim's mouth.

"Don't you see them?" Kim asked. She wiped the tears from her eyes before pointing ahead of her.

But the bodies had vanished. She glanced over her shoulder, looking for Grandpappy.

No one was behind her.

"There was a man," Kim told Iola. "I swear. And dead people's bodies." She checked the forest floor once again, but she only saw an expanse of ferns and purple irises that stood higher than the greenery. There was something sinister about the flowers. "Where were you?" she asked.

"I thought I heard someone walking with me," Iola said. "I assumed it was you, but when I turned around, you weren't there, and I came back."

"Let's not get separated again," Kim said.

"We won't." Iola took Kim's hand and led her through the ferns. "I'm sure we're getting closer to the preserve. I thought I spotted a fence up ahead."

Kim was grateful for Iola's presence and the gentle touch of her hand. She remembered Guthrie dragging her by the ankles through the Swamp House. Moving through the trees, she kept looking around for Grandpappy.

"There it is!" Iola pointed ahead of them, where the trees thinned and gave way to a narrow stretch of moonlit water. "Do you see it across the water?"

Kim spotted a low wooden fence past a willow tree.

"If I'm right the boardwalk trail is just beyond that fence. Come on!" Iola squeezed Kim's hand and increased her pace.

After leaving the trees, they descended a grassy slope to the water. Kim noticed how bright and full the moon was. The yellow orb was weirdly mesmerizing. She had to force herself to stop looking at it and concentrate on the water ahead of them. It wouldn't be difficult to swim across, but Kim didn't like the idea.

"Aren't there alligators in there?" she asked, recalling the huge, charcoal-gray reptile that had swallowed Orchid's dismembered hand.

"They're more scared of us than we are of them," Iola said. "If we swim fast we'll be fine. Try not to splash. If there are gators around here, you don't want them thinking you're an injured animal."

"But isn't that what we are?" Kim joked. Neither woman laughed.

"I'll go first," Iola said, releasing Kim's hand. "Why don't you wait here until I see what's on the other side of that fence? This could be a dead end." She went down to the water and removed her shoes. Kim followed.

Iola slipped into the water soundlessly, holding her sneakers above her head as she swam. Kim saw the other bank was much steeper, and bushes grew thickly around the base of the willow tree. Iola put her shoes back on and scrambled up the slope. She made it to the willow tree's trunk and peered over the fence. She turned toward Kim. "The boardwalk's right here! Come on across! It's easy enough!"

Kim stepped into the water, which was surprisingly warm. Her bare foot sank into slime, and she was about to let her body fall into the water when someone grabbed her by the arm.

She glanced back to see Grandpappy holding on to her. He was leering at her. His eyes glowed green beneath the brim of his panama hat.

"Let go!" Kim screamed. She yanked her arm free of his grasp and fell into the dark water with a loud splash. She quickly swam on her back across the waterway, watching the terrifying man to make sure he didn't follow. His eyes continued to burn green even as his figure faded like mist. Finally, the eyes disappeared, too, and Kim turned over onto her stomach to finish her swim.

"You made it!" Iola said.

"Did you see him?" Kim asked when she reached the other bank. She was panting.

"See who?"

Kim checked once more to make sure Grandpappy wasn't behind her. She didn't see anyone, but she wanted to get beside Iola as soon as possible. Her feet kept slipping in the mud beneath the water, and she wasn't able to stand. She reached for the black branches of a small, dead-looking tree that was right by the water.

The branch she grabbed broke off, and she fell back into the water. She swallowed a mouthful and gagged.

"Let me get you some light," Iola called. She sidestepped partway down the steep slope and shined the light toward where Kim was reaching.

Kim could better see the branch she grasped, but she could also see another, more distant branch that appeared to be moving. There was a burst of white beyond her forearm, and her entire body froze. The white was the inside of a snake's mouth. Kim could see the reptile's two long fangs as it hissed at her.

"What do I do?" she whimpered.

"Stay still," Iola said. "Move away slowly when it closes its mouth. That's a cottonmouth."

"That's what you deserve," a man whispered into Kim's ear.

Kim shrieked. She pulled her hand away from the branch to defend herself against Grandpappy. The snake struck and bit Kim's wrist.

She cried out as the cottonmouth fell to the ground and wriggled away into the grass. Holding her wounded wrist, she turned toward the water, expecting to find Grandpappy.

No one was behind her.

Iola clambered down the hill and helped Kim up onto the bank. "Am I going to die?" Kim asked. She was sweating again. She forced back her tears while she held her burning wrist.

"We've just got to get you to a hospital soon," Iola said. "But you can't walk too quickly. We don't want the poison to reach your heart."

Kim couldn't tell how long they'd been following the boardwalk when she started having the chills. She felt disoriented, and the moon had changed from yellow to a pale shade of green. Occasionally, she turned her head to make sure Grandpappy wasn't behind them. Iola said she hadn't seen him once when they were back at the water. Kim looked down at her aching right wrist and saw that it and her hand had become puffy. She kept it by her side, thinking that would prevent the venom from spreading up her arm too quickly.

Iola glanced back at her. "You're going to be all right. We'll get you antivenom."

Kim nodded, not believing she'd receive treatment in time. "There's a woman who's on her way to meet me in Canada," she told Iola. "She'll be in Whistler, British Columbia. Her name's Malia Kai. K-A-I. If I don't make it out of here and you do, would you try to reach her? Tell her I wish I'd stayed in Seattle with her."

"You can tell her yourself," Iola said.

"I don't know if-"

"I do. Look!" Iola pointed ahead of them at a lit parking lot. The parking lot was empty, but beyond it was a road. Kim saw a car drive past the lot.

"Come on," Iola said. She held Kim's hand as she led her toward the road.

Kim soon heard the sound of an approaching car. Headlights appeared from around a bend. Iola ran into the center of the road and waved for the driver to stop. Kim dreaded that one of the Family members could be driving. But the vehicle wasn't a bus—it was a red Volvo.

The car stopped in front of Iola, and an elderly man popped his head out of the driver's side window. "You girls all right?" He gaped at Kim's filthy slip.

"Please," Iola said, "we need a ride to an emergency room." She pointed at Kim. "A snake bit her."

"Did you call 9-1-1?" the man asked, obviously skeptical.

"My phone doesn't work," Iola said, "and she doesn't have one. Please."

Kim heard a woman say, "Let them in, Hank. Look at that poor girl's arm. It's all puffed up."

"Hop in," the man said.

Kim sighed from relief. She hobbled toward the car, and Iola helped her into one of the back seats. The man and woman in front looked like they were in their early seventies. The car started up, and the woman clicked on the overhead light, illuminating a beautiful blue and yellow scarf wrapped around her head. She stared at Kim with wide, empathetic eyes.

"I'm Clarice," she said, "and this is Old Hank. Step on it, Old Hank."

Kim forced a smile. "I'm Kim. Thank you."

"My name's Iola. Thank you so much." Iola's hand was resting on the leg of her damp, muddy jeans. Kim could see it was shaking.

"Child," Clarice asked Kim, "where'd you get bit?"

Kim raised her arm just enough to show her the two red marks on her wrist.

Clarice nodded, and then she asked, "And what happened up there?" She looked at Kim's upper arm.

Kim glanced down at her exposed skin and saw dark purple bruise marks around her bicep. That was where Grandpappy had grabbed her. She let the feeling of fear pass, and then she responded, "Do you have a cell phone I can borrow? There's someone I need to call."

Three Days Later

"I didn't think this evening could get any better," Kim said. She watched Malia return to the rumpled bed where they'd just made love. Malia wore a white fluffy robe and carried a small porcelain bowl filled with chocolate eggs.

"Don't eat too many," Malia said, sitting on the edge of the bed. "Remember I ordered us Chinese for dinner."

Kim sat up and plucked one of the eggs from the bowl. She couldn't believe she was staring into those lovely hazel eyes again. She stroked Malia's long, curling hair. She had the sense of finally being home. "Thank you for driving all the way up here. I know it seemed like a crazy request."

Malia turned away from her and gazed out the bedroom window with sorrowful eyes. "I just hate that you had to go through all that."

Kim popped the chocolate egg in her mouth. Snow was falling outside the window, and lights were blinking on in the streets as evening descended. The glow, charm, and cheer of the Canadian ski town made Kim feel like she was in some Christmas village. She couldn't believe it was April and she'd been wading through a Louisiana swamp only a few nights ago. She tried to focus on the taste of the melting chocolate and not the memory of Grandpappy's eyes burning in the night.

"Why don't you go to bed after dinner?" Malia suggested. "You must be exhausted from all the traveling."

Kim nodded and came out of her daze. "A decent night's sleep would do me good—especially if you're right next to me."

Kim had stayed in a New Orleans hospital for two nights. The doctor that treated her snakebite wanted to monitor her health for at least 24 hours. Iola kindly picked her up yesterday morning, and they spent last night at Iola's father's house in a suburb of the city. Nightmares kept Kim from sleeping much during her last days in Louisiana. The police detective didn't ease her worries when he told her the so-called Swamp House had been abandoned for years.

"Derelicts set up camp in that house all the time," he said. "We found the place was burnt to the ground. We didn't see evidence of a cult living there other than the fenced-off pit with the gator in it. We'll keep looking into this and give you updates. At least we located your rental car in the Ninth Ward."

Kim also described the locations of the "homes" she'd been to in Charleston, Savannah, and Pensacola, but she doubted the police would find much in those places either. Of course, she didn't mention that her dead fiancé had taken over another man's body.

"I'm going to go set the table for us," Malia said, standing from the bed. "You stay here and rest."

Kim gave an appreciative nod. She picked up the bowl of chocolate eggs to hand it to Malia. She felt a burst of pain in her arm and dropped the bowl. The eggs spilled across the carpet.

"Is it the snake bite?" Malia asked. She lowered herself onto her hands and knees to gather the chocolate.

"The doctor said the venom will affect my right hand for a couple weeks," Kim told her. "But then my grip should return to normal and I'll actually be able to make a fist. I could have been a lot worse off."

"I'll bet you'll recover soon," Malia said. "You're a strong one."

Kim recognized the old, familiar tenderness in Malia's eyes. Despite Kim's coldness and her attempt to end what she and Malia had together, Malia never stopped caring for her. With an ache in her chest, Kim said, "I won't leave you again, Malia. I promise."

Malia rose and kissed her on the forehead. "I believe you."

After Malia left the bedroom, Kim put her jeans and T-shirt back on. She spotted her reflection in a mirror on one wall. She looked so much older than she did a week ago—and somehow more lost.

She'd noticed a similar look on Iola's face when Iola had driven her to the airport in New Orleans. Kim had asked Iola what her plans were.

"Go back to Savannah and finish school, I guess," Iola said. "And then I need to decide whether I want to stay in the South. My mom's been trying to get me to join her in Colorado. I didn't want to before, but now I'm thinking the mountains sound real safe."

Kim heard a knock on the condo's front door. She peeked out of the bedroom and saw Malia moving from the dining table to the door.

Malia glanced at Kim. "It must be the food. It's weird they didn't just buzz me from outside. Someone must have let them in."

Kim felt a tingling rise through her spine. Why would a delivery person come inside the building without buzzing?

"Wait!" she said.

She was too late. Malia had already unlocked the door and was pulling it open.

A pale twenty-something man with dark, shoulder-length hair stood in the hallway. He wore a red jacket with a lapel that said *General Tso Good*, and he held a large bag of what must have been Chinese food.

Kim sighed, and she almost laughed at herself for being so frightened. She came toward the door and stood behind Malia.

"You had the barbecue pork chow mein, the lemon chicken, and the potstickers?" the man asked.

"That's it," Malia said, reaching for the bag of food. And that's when Kim gasped at the familiar tattoo on his wrist, peeking out of his jacket sleeve: an alligator chasing its tail.

"Shut the door!" Kim shouted at Malia. "He's one of them!"

The man looked at Kim with surprise, and then what was obviously anger. Thankfully, Malia acted quickly and pushed on the door.

But the man stuck his arm into the space, preventing the door from closing.

"Don't let him in!" Kim hurried into the nearby kitchen. She yanked open drawers until she found a large carving knife. She moved toward Malia, who was leaning against the door while the man's hand grasped at air. His tattoo was now even more apparent.

"No more!" Kim screamed. She slashed at the exposed wrist, making the man yowl. Blood dripped on the carpet. He retracted his arm.

Malia shut the door all the way, and Kim turned the lock. Standing with her back to the door, she told Malia, "Call the police!"

While Malia fetched her phone, Kim heard the man speaking to someone outside. He wasn't alone. Kim glanced down at the bloody knife in her right hand. She was afraid, but her adrenaline overpowered both her fear and the pain that coursed through her arm. She and Malia wouldn't be the Family's victims. Her grip on the knife tightened.

Acknowledgements

I'm grateful to Montag Press and publisher Charlie Franco for gladly taking on my second novel. I appreciate your desire to publish works that both blend and defy literary and genre fiction. Kate Sargeant, thank you for your astute edits and your enthusiasm for character building. My writers group members provided essential criticism, encouragement, and pizza. Thank you, John Flick, Colin McArthur, Kevin O'Brien, and Garth Stein. Stacey Glenewinkel and Josh Rogin deserve thanks for reading the manuscript in its entirety and offering crucial feedback. Cheers to Jamison Oishi for serving as my crime scene consultant, and thank you to my consultants on Southern living: Eric Minchew, Joe Simpson, and my pa, William Massengill. Stafford Lombard, I'm grateful for your unflagging faith and support. And thank you to my family for appreciating my books even at their most terrifying moments. Finally, some love to the gorgeous and mysterious cities of New Orleans and Savannah. Thank you for spooking me in such a good way.

David Massengill is a Bay Area native who has lived in Seattle for two decades. His father hails from Tennessee, where there are many Massengills. David is also the author of the novel *Red Swarm* (Montag Press), about lethal insects invading the Pacific Northwest, and the short story collection *Fragments of a Journal Salvaged from a Charred House in Germany, 1816* (Hammer and Anvil Books). His short works of horror and literary fiction have appeared in numerous literary journals, including *Eclectica Magazine*, *Pulp Metal Magazine*, *Word Riot*, *The Literary Hatchet*, *The Raven Chronicles*, and *Yellow Mama*, among others. Visit his website at www.davidmassengillfiction.com.